Maggie Craig

It was terrible, the doctor told his wife that evening, terrible seeing that young girl, pink-cheeked and dry-eyed, calmly telling him that she would manage.

'Talking about having Irish navvies living in, and her no more than seventeen and as bonny as a morning in spring. I remember her mother as a bonny woman, but young Maggie Craig is a real beauty, and as innocent as a new-born babe. I'd stake my life on that.'

His wife shook her grey head. 'It's to be hoped she doesn't take up with the wrong one now that she is entirely alone. That girl has got to find love and affection from somewhere, it stands to reason.'

Bates fingered his watch-chain.

'There was a whisper about a boy at the mill, but I don't think there can be anything in it. Maggie's only a child.'

MARIE JOSEPH

Maggie Craig

ARROW BOOKS

For
Marilyn and Kate

Arrow Books Limited
17-21 Conway Street, London W1P 6JD

An imprint of the Hutchinson Publishing Group

London Melbourne Sydney Auckland
Johannesburg and agencies throughout
the world

First published by Hutchinson 1979
Arrow edition 1981
Reprinted 1981, 1982 (twice), 1983, 1984 and 1985

Printed and bound in Great Britain by
Anchor Brendon Limited, Tiptree, Essex

ISBN 0 09 925390 9

Maggie Craig

I

Maggie Craig was just six years old when she took on Miss Hepinstall, Infant teacher at her father's village school. She challenged that strict disciplinarian with such fury that the children, sitting upright in their scarred desks, felt their mouths drop open, and their eyes stand out like chapel hat-pegs.

Teddy, the youngest of Maggie's three brothers, an incurable chatter-box, had been told to stop talking twice. Twice when once should have been quite enough, and when Miss Hepinstall caught him bobbing his brown head towards a boy across the narrow aisle, her beetle brows drew together, and her mouth set into a tight, thin, angry line.

So angry was she at having her authority flouted that it seemed to her startled class that the little top-knot skewered to the top of her head quivered as if it had a life of its own.

'Come out to me, Teddy Craig!' she shouted. 'I warned you, and I will not warn you again. Out here! This very minute!'

The children shuffled their feet, holding their respective breaths, some with fear, and some with a kind of shamed excitement, because once Miss had drawn blood. Last year, which was even better, Millie Hargreaves had fainted dead away, only coming to when her face had been fanned with the register. And the next day her mother had come to the school and had shaken her fist at Miss and threatened to report her to the School Board, but nothing had come of it.

On the not infrequent occasions when Miss wielded the thin and flexible cane, it swished down through the air with a terrifying sound then landed with a thwack that felt its echo in the palms of the watchers, causing the more sensitive amongst them to close their eyes. Some were actually in tears at the remembrance of the stinging agony.

Thomas Craig, Maggie's father, in charge of the older children on the other side of the sliding doors dividing the two classrooms, also possessed a cane, but his was laid harmlessly across his desk next to the Bible. No one could ever remember it being used.

'A good man, but too soft by half,' Miss Hepinstall often told her mother, a hopeless cripple, gradually seizing up with the arthritis; an old woman with a tongue on her that would make a whiplash seem like a whisper of silk.

'Me daughter makes a good teacher because she's frustrated at never having had a man. It has to come out somewhere, even if it's only on the childer's hands at school,' she had told the embarrassed minister from the Mission Hall one day. 'It's not natural for a woman not to have a man to boss her about, tha knows, Vicar.'

In her daughter's class the children sat at their desks as straight as if they'd been born with pokers for backbones, sometimes for half an hour at a time, with their hands on top of their heads. Miss's word was law, and the fact that the eight-year-old boy approaching her desk now with dragging feet was the son of the schoolmaster, mattered less than nothing to Miss Hepinstall.

Disobedience would not be tolerated, and must be punished with something far more telling than a reprimand.

'Hold out your hand, Teddy Craig!' she ordered. 'Your *hand*, if you please!'

Her arm was actually upraised to administer the first of the three strokes, when Maggie shot out from her desk in the front row with the force of a stone shot from a catapult.

Pink cheeks reddened to fury, long hair flying free from its restraining ribbon, feet in boots too big for them,

8

tripping over a crack in the floorboards, Maggie went into action.

Throwing herself dramatically in front of her brother, she spread her arms wide, and glared into the face of the astonished teacher.

'Don't you *dare* hit our Teddy! He's got a gathering on his thumb he has. Yes he has! It would have a bandage on it if me mother hadn't said it had to have the air get to it. Don't you dare hit him! Don't you dare!'

The shocked surprise on Miss's face was so immense that it was comical to see. The fact that anyone so small would dare to question her methods stunned her into immobility at the child's undoubted courage. For a moment she actually did not know what to do.

'You will sit down at your desk, Maggie Craig,' she said quietly, 'and you will hold out your *other* hand, Teddy Craig,' she said, even more quietly.

But although the cane was raised three times, to swish down with venomous power on the boy's left hand, Miss Hepinstall knew, and the class knew, that Maggie was the winner of that particular battle.

'I told Miss she couldn't hit our Teddy on his sore hand. I told her good and proper,' Maggie announced to her mother after school was over for the day.

She was sitting round the big scrubbed table in the living-room of the School House, eating her second slice of bread, still warm from the fire-oven and spread thinly with rum butter as a special treat.

Hannah Craig looked at her four children eating stolidly; Teddy signalling to Maggie to keep quiet, with Benjamin and Jonathan, unidentical ten year-old-twins, nodding at their little sister with approval.

Maggie's brown eyes, the left one flecked with green, shone and sparkled with the triumph of the afternoon as she basked in the attention she was getting from her brothers.

'As good as a boy any old day,' they often said.

'Trust our Maggie to stand up to old Miss,' Jonathan said, and Maggie glowed.

Hannah tried hard not to smile as she watched her little daughter showing off as she played to the appreciative audience. How bonny and sturdy she was, smiling round the table through a milk moustache, glorying in their obvious adulation.

'She's going to be the strongest lad in the family,' Doctor Bates had said when she was born.

'And the cheekiest,' Thomas, her father, had said with an indulgent smile.

But enough was enough.

'Stop that, and get on with your tea,' Hannah said, as carried away with her success, Maggie was brandishing a knife to give a near perfect imitation of Miss Hepinstall's grim expression as she wielded the cane.

'You *naughty* boy, Teddy Craig!' Maggie said, and able to keep her face straight no longer, Hannah joined in the laughter.

As the mother of three rough sons, boys with permanently scarred knees, black finger-nails, and hair that grew straight up no matter how hard she tried to smooth it down, Hannah had been overjoyed when Maggie was born.

Here at last was the girl child she had prayed for, the dainty little mite who would follow her around the house, lisping prettily in spotless white pinafores, sitting on a footstool at her mother's knee, learning to knit and to sew.

Instead of that Maggie preferred to be out with her brothers in the long summer evenings, fishing with a piece of string in the stream, climbing the low stone walls, working the pump at the well for the pails of clear cool water for the next day's washing, cooking and cleaning.

Only the summer before when Maggie was just five years old and the well was not full enough to keep the pump going, Hannah had caught her lying flat on the ground with her bloomers showing, dangling a bucket on a rope down into the murky depths, the great iron lid moved to one side.

Maggie it was who collected the yard-sticks for the fire-oven, and Maggie who had been caught peering through the filthy window of the derelict cottage at the end of the village, trying to catch a glimpse of the two hermit bachelors who lived there in squalor. One of them had come out to chase her, brandishing an old violin above his head.

'I'll scalp thee alive if I catches thee again tha little varmint,' he'd shouted, and Maggie had run home, skirts flying, tam-o'-shanter falling from her head, not to throw herself in her mother's arms as she sobbed out her fright, but to ask exactly what a varmint happened to be.

There was something *fierce* about her only daughter, Hannah often thought. Then she would think what a funny word fierce was to use in describing a little girl as pretty as Maggie. It was just that she was so protective of everyone, afraid of nothing, certainly not of Miss Hepinstall who in the weeks following the caning episode, picked on her un-mercifully.

'Every time I go through into the other classroom our Maggie seems to be standing in a corner facing the wall,' Thomas told his wife. 'There's not much I can do about it either without being accused of favouritism.' He rubbed the left side of his nose with his forefinger, the way he always did when worried. 'It's a tricky business having my own children in my own school.'

Hannah smiled on him with love. 'It'll do our Maggie good to have some of the spots rubbed off her. She's spoilt enough at home without being kowtowed to at school.'

And you would not relish having to stand up to Miss Hepinstall, Hannah told herself, but silently, shaking her head at her husband as he stood before her, dark eyes anxious, neat well-formed head on one side as he waited to see what she thought about it all.

She smiled on him with such love, this man of hers, this scholarly gentle man who had met and married her when she was in service, keeping house for three middle-aged unmarried sisters over at Todmorden.

He had been on a walking trip, carrying his belongings around in a parcel looped over his shoulder with string, sleeping in barns, and meeting her one bright summer's day as she carried a pail of warm frothy milk down the lane from the farm to the house where she worked.

The ten years' difference in their ages hadn't seemed to matter at all, nor the fact that at seventeen she could barely read.

'I will teach you,' he said, and so he had, sitting with her in the downstairs living-room of the School House, holding her hand, and running her fingers over the words: kissing her when she stumbled over a long word.

The village he taught in was spread over the outskirts of a cotton mill town, a part of the Pennines flanked to the east by the Yorkshire wool towns, and by the Lancashire cotton towns to the west.

It was a straggling stark place, with grey stone houses set against sombre skies in winter, which even in summer still retained their greyness as if not even the sun could warm their stones to light. Originally a hamlet, the village was built across a tributary of a river, a river whose valleys were filled with factories, mills and sloping streets, the terraced houses packed close together, sometimes back to back and interlocking into each other.

Thomas Craig did not visit the towns unless he had to, and even then he hurried back to his village as quickly as he could. He loved his village, and the moors behind it. With more money to spare for his education, he would have been a botanist, but as an amateur he walked for miles, bringing weeds home in his pockets and laying them on the kitchen table. Then he would search in his books of reference to find the names, and point out his treasure to Maggie.

She was the child of his heart, and he would take her to a hill he knew, and they would lie in a hollow until the silence was broken by the song of a lark, or the call of a grouse. He would show her the shifting peat bogs, formless and menacing, and he would point out a hunk of tree-knot, and explain that once, many thousands of years ago, there had been a forest growing there.

Thomas Craig was a small man, no more than five feet six inches tall, but the way he held himself gave the impression of height. It was from her father that Maggie inherited her direct glance, and her way of walking with her head held high. But it was from her mother she got her thick brown hair, and her practical way of assessing a problem, making a quick decision, then getting on with it.

An ardent and practising Methodist was Thomas Craig, but although the doctrine of THOU SHALT NOT had been instilled in him from his childhood, Thomas wanted no truck with a being who could condemn any of his congregation to eternal damnation. When the paid minister was sent away from the Mission House for lack of funds, it was Thomas who led the prayers and read to the dwindling congregation of the gentle love of Jesus.

When someone died in the village, it was Thomas who prayed over them, and Hannah who helped with the laying-out, washing them for the last time, and crossing pale hands over nice clean chests.

She was called to help with a laying-out very early one morning, just a month after Maggie had stood up to Miss Hepinstall. . . .

Little Amos Smith, a sickly child, the youngest in a family of eleven, had died of inflammation of the throat the night before, choking to death on a membrane his mother said was like a piece of tight muslin across the back of his throat.

'It was the quinsies, Mrs Craig,' she sobbed. 'No matter how many vinegar poultices I put on him I could not bring the fever down.' She lifted her apron and wiped her eyes. 'Every spring regular as clockwork he got the quinsies. It was pitiful to see him, but this time he didn't seem to have the strength to fight.'

'For a shilling a week paid regular she could have brought Doctor Bates to that child,' Hannah fretted to Thomas when she got back to the house. 'Moses Smith works in the Quarries, so it's not as if there's no money coming in.'

She unpinned her hat from her shining hair. 'For one shilling a week the whole family could have benefited, with free medicine as well. Some folks don't seem to have the sense they were born with.'

Thomas hovered about, trying to help with the rushed breakfast, but doing no more than getting in the way.

'That's all right, love,' he reminded her gently, 'but a shilling a week is a shilling a week when there are eleven mouths to feed. It's a fortune to Maria Smith, remember.'

'Misplaced thriftiness,' Hannah fumed, bustling round the room, long skirts swishing as she moved from fire to table, then from table to fire. 'There's some as never get their priorities right,' she grumbled, setting a pan of milk to warm.

The three boys, boot-laces trailing, shirts hanging out of their trousers, hair standing on end, got on with the important task of spreading honey as thickly as they dared on great wedges of bread. Maggie sat with knife poised, more interested in what was being said.

'Who's dead then?' she asked, in a light conversational tone.

Hannah snatched the pan of milk from the fire, just catching it in time.

'Little Amos Smith has gone to live with Jesus,' she said.

'Will he like it then? Living with Jesus? Amos Smith always had a candle coming down his nose. Will he not have one now that he's gone to . . . ?'

Hannah's voice, more stern than Maggie had heard it for a long time, stopped her saying what she had intended to say.

'Maggie Craig! If you don't get down from that table and come here this minute, you'll be late, and then what will Miss Hepinstall say?'

'Late again, Maggie Craig!'

Her little daughter's pursed-up mouth was so like her teacher's that Hannah smiled for the first time since coming into the house.

'Come here then and have your rag pinned on,' she said, and tweaked at the wings of the white pinafore in a vain effort to stop them slipping down the sleeves of Maggie's dark green dress.

The ritual of nose blowing insisted on by Miss Hepinstall before morning prayers meant that a clean rag had to be found every day, plus another for wiping the children's slates.

'That rag smells awful when I've been spitting on it all day,' Maggie grumbled as she twitched away from her mother.

'Then stop sniffing at it,' Hannah said, standing at the door and waving as the four of them walked down the short lane to the school, waiting as usual until she had seen them turn into the playground: Maggie, first as always, tammy slipping to the side of her head, the thick weight of her hair already coming loose from its ribbon fastening, calling over her shoulder to her brothers, telling them to hurry up. Benjamin walking pigeon-toed and tripping over his own feet; Jonathan whistling and trailing a hand along the low stone wall, and Teddy bending down to pick up a stone and hurl it hopefully at a bird rising suddenly out of the hedge.

Four of them, and each one as different as chalk from cheese, Hannah thought as she went inside. Then putting the memory of the small dead face she had washed so carefully not an hour before, out of her mind, Hannah built up the fire with sticks, turning the room into a furnace. Wednesday was baking day, just as Monday was washing day even if the moors were awash with rain.

Little Amos Smith was buried in the churchyard a few days later with all the village in attendance. Mr Jarvis, the undertaker, could always be relied upon to give a dignified performance, and the sight of his long thin face set into lines of professional suffering, held Maggie spellbound. Funerals fascinated her, and she often wondered who would bury Mr Jarvis when *his* turn came to die? Who would arrange for six men of equal height to carry the coffins, sometimes for miles, over rough unmade roads, over moorland and across streams, to the little churchyard? It never occurred to her that Mr Jarvis was merely doing a job; to Maggie he was the sole instrument of God, the middle-man between this world and the next.

Hannah saw nothing wrong in having her four children lined up at the edge of the newly dug grave, heads suitably bowed, bunches of wild flowers in their hands. Thomas was not quite so sure, but his wife told him firmly that death was a part of living.

'No good pretending it doesn't happen. That's what makes folks grow up frightened of it.'

Thomas was to remember her words, when just two weeks later Hannah died of the undiagnosed diphtheria that had killed little Amos Smith.

Hannah *was* afraid of dying. It showed in her eyes, and it showed in the desperate way she clung to his hands, and in the rasp of her tortured throat as she made him promise to keep the family together.

'I promise,' Thomas said, but he had no idea what it was she had asked him to promise. He was stunned. He was numbed. He could not and would not believe that his Hannah would leave him.

She was his joy and his strength; he had the intelligence to realize that. He might be the one with the book-learning, but she was the one with the commonsense, the one with her feet on the ground. Without her he was nothing, nothing at all.

Doctor Bates had been angry and amazed, when called

to the School House. He had found Hannah already too far gone for him to do much more than demand to know why he had not been called out before?

A choleric gentleman, with a nose that looked as if it might burst like a ripe plum at any minute, he shook his big head sadly when Thomas told how his wife had gone on working in the house, keeping to her rigid day-to-day timetable, even pretending to eat with them at table.

'She swore she was just coming on with a cold, then when she was forced to take to her bed, I found a hunk of bread crumbled in her apron pocket. She must have dropped it in there so we would not notice. . . . Oh, God! What am I going to do?'

'Why should God want to punish us like this?' he cried, when Teddy followed his mother to the grave a week later, choked with his own spittle.

'You've still got me, Dada,' Maggie said, standing by his chair, solemn-eyed with the awfulness of it all.

'And us,' the twins added in unison.

Thomas looked at them as if he did not know them; almost as if he had never seen them in his life before.

For the rest of that summer, into the mists of autumn, on into the freezing winds of winter, Thomas Craig turned his back on life, teaching with automatic practice during the day, and leaving his three children to the kindly but intermittent care of the village women.

The nights he read away, refusing to go up to the room he had shared with Hannah; dozing in his chair by the fire.

At times Maggie would be awakened by the sound of wood being thrown on to the fire, and creeping downstairs, a matronly little figure in her long nightgown, she would find her father asleep, his arm trailing to the floor where a book had slipped from a listless hand. At seven years old, she accepted the fact that she would never see her mother again; an acceptance that Thomas, it seemed, would never acknowledge.

The house grew dirty, with a layer of kitchen grease adhering to the pans that were seldom used; the children climbed in and out of unmade beds, and when one day Miss Hepinstall held her tongue from telling Maggie that potatoes could be grown in the tidemark round her neck, she decided the time had come to act.

Leaving her mother settled down for the night, as comfortable as the old woman's aching joints would ever let her be, she rammed her hat down over the black bun on top of her small head, skewered it into place with a pearl-handled hat-pin, buttoned her coat over her one-piece bosom, and heedless of the biting wind, set off for the School House.

The door was on the latch, and after two brisk raps with the knocker, and getting no reply, she marched inside. From his customary seat by the fire, Thomas raised his head from his book and glared at her.

Expecting the look and ignoring it, Miss Hepinstall wrinkled her nose at the smell of neglect, averted her spinsterly eyes from a pile of intimate washing spilling out from a tub in the corner, and sat herself down. Because she had come on an errand of mercy, she did so without wiping the seat of her chair first with her handkerchief. It would never do, she decided, to antagonize Thomas before she had even opened her mouth.

He closed his eyes rudely, and willed her to go away. Since Hannah's death he had as little to do with women as possible, hating them because they were alive and his wife was not. Besides, Miss Hepinstall was sitting in Hannah's chair, as angular, dark and hard, as Hannah had been curved, brown of hair, and soft. Even the mask of kindness sat on the teacher's face like a grimace. She leaned forward, resting gloved hands on her tall umbrella.

'What I've come to say won't take a minute, Mr Craig, but it's got to be said; there's nothing more certain than that.'

The lift of Thomas's eyebrows was an insult that a lesser woman would have flinched from, but used to her mother's black looks and bitter tongue, Miss Hepinstall said in her loud penetrating voice:

'How long are you going to sit there feeling sorry for yourself, Mr Craig? Your wife is not coming back, you know.'

The words, as sudden as they were unexpected, hit Thomas like a blast of hot air from the carelessly opened door of a furnace. He actually rose from his seat, and for a moment Miss Hepinstall thought he was going to step forward and strike her. Then, with his fingers gripping the arms of his chair, he sank back again.

The long umbrella was pointed directly at his face, as she went on with the saying of her piece:

'If you carry on like this, the children will be taken from you, and you will end up in the Union Poorhouse. I've held my tongue for long enough, Mr Craig, and what I'm saying is only for your own good. I've never been one to mince my words, you know that.' She took a necessary breath. 'I've seen you standing up in front of your class with half your dinner spilt down your front, and I don't mean just one day's dinner neither. The discipline in the school has gone to pot, and your Maggie's neck is that mucky I've a job to tell whether she's taken her scarf off or not. Why, when your wife was alive, that child's hair shone like the sun on a copper warming-pan. I would not be surprised to find that it's alive with nits.'

It was, it must have been, the mention of Maggie's hair that did it. Shining like the sun on a copper warming-pan . . . like Hannah's own hair, thick, long, clean-smelling hair, washed every week without fail with green soft soap.

Thomas opened his mouth as if gasping for air. How often had she sat on the floor between his knees whilst he dried it for her? Hair that cascaded over his hands when he sometimes took the pins out for her at night, a tender prelude to their love-making. Upswept hair, with tiny curling tendrils wisping down into the soft hollow at the back of her neck. . . .

Miss Hepinstall watched his mouth working with a kind of detached sympathy, already forming in her mind the wording of the suggestions of practical help she had in mind. She was totally unprepared for what happened next, and embarrassed to the point of panic when it did.

With a great shout of anguish, an animal howl of grief, Thomas abandoned himself to the agony of loss multiplying silently inside him. With mouth wide open, and tears streaming down his face, he sobbed his torment, quite oblivious to the fact that Miss Hepinstall had crept away.

Shocked and dismayed she walked back down the lane in the rain, the umbrella held over her head but unopened and unfurled.

And although neither of them made any reference to the visit, from that day onwards, things began to improve a little. Thomas took on a woman from the village, a forty-year-old widow, with faded hair drawn back so tightly that her expression was one of perpetual surprise.

He would not have her about the house when he was there, so the minute he came in from school in the afternoon, she knew that was her signal to go. With no more than a nod in Thomas's direction, she would fold up her print apron, lift the kettle from the fire and fill the teapot already warming in the hearth.

'There's your teas ready,' she'd say, and Maggie would sit in Hannah's old place at the table, pouring the tea into blue-edged cups. With two cushions on the chair to raise her up, she would slice a loaf into man-sized wedges for the boys, her pink tongue protruding from the corner of her mouth.

'She'll cut her fingers off one of these fine days,' Jonathan said.

'Why does she have to do everything so fast?' Benjamin wondered.

'Because I'll never get through if I don't,' said Maggie, crimson with importance.

Thomas noticed nothing, and at the end of another drifting year, with only a token resistance from their father, the boys started work at the Quarries.

They walked the five miles there and back, working mornings one week, and afternoons the next. Their job was to wheel the drilled-out stony rubbish away on four-wheeled bogies to the tip.

'Hannah Craig would come back and haunt that husband of hers if she knew them two lads had gone as muck-chuckers,' the village women said. 'You'd have thought their father would have wanted something better for them.'

But Jonathan and Benjamin grew tall and strong. They sang as they walked up the fell together, happy to be released for half a day from the tedium of book learning, and the closed-in boredom of their father's classroom.

In the mid-nineties, when Maggie was twelve years old, and there was talk of the Quarry being shut down, the two boys walked off together to the nearest recruiting centre and joined the army.

They were jubilant from the moment of entering the Barracks, excited at the prospect of what promised to be a life of adventure, weaned completely and at once from the travesty of what had been a happy home.

At the end of their first year of soldiery, with merely a handful of letters to remind Thomas that once he had two sons, the still heart-broken man had a stroke.

Barely aware that anything had happened, he tried to talk to Maggie when she came downstairs, but the words he spoke were a meaningless jumble.

Maggie was petrified.

'Sit there, Dada,' she said, trying to smile. 'You're poorly. Sit there and I'll go and tell Doctor Bates.' Fear made her heart flutter in her breast, and running helter-skelter down the lane she stopped first at Miss Hepinstall's cottage.

'Me father can't talk,' she said. 'And his face looks funny.'

'Daisy?' Miss Hepinstall's mother's voice spiralled downstairs, and even in the middle of her bewildering anxiety, Maggie felt a twinge of surprise. Whoever would have thought that anyone as unflower-like as Miss could possibly be called Daisy?

There was a short cut to the doctor's house, and Maggie knew she would have to take it, in spite of the bull that had a nasty habit of running down the hill with its tail stuck up in the air, trying to jump the wall when anyone passed by in the lane; in spite of the fact that the lane itself was supposed to be haunted by a coach driven by a headless driver, she knew she had to go that way.

She was solely responsible for her father now, just as Miss was responsible for her awful mother, and bulls with their tails stuck up in the air, and headless drivers of ghostly coaches were as nothing compared to the importance of that.

With her face set into a determined mask, Maggie ran on, praying that God would save her if anything untoward happened.

Thomas Craig never taught again after that day. Believing that he might find a mundane job in a factory, Doctor Bates somehow made the time to find them a terraced house to let in a cobbled street in the nearby cotton town, and another teacher and his family moved into the School House.

The mill was no more than a stone's throw from the back door of the little house at the bottom end of Foundry Street, and on the day after they moved in Maggie walked across the bridge over the canal to see the overlooker.

He was a man with small eyes as hard as moorland stones, and he took Maggie on as a doffer. She started work at six o'clock in the morning, and spent her day running round the weaving shed with the bobbins. Her task was to fill the big basket skips, then, standing on a piece of wood because she was too small to reach the looms, she would put the bobbins on the machines, climb down, wheel the skip along the damp floor, and start all over again.

Working without a break she ran home at dinner-time to make sure her father had a bite to eat, and if she was late back the overlooker would swear at her.

'The old skinflint's docked me money again,' she would tell Thomas, and he would look at her as if it was her own fault.

In the evenings there was the food for the following day to be seen to. There was the washing, the baking, the ironing, everything done to a set routine, just the way her mother had done it.

Thomas, shrivelled into a tiny gnome of a man, followed her around, mumbling in the strange language that had got only minimally better since his stroke. 'To think we should come to this,' was what he was trying to say. 'Oh why should the good Lord punish us like this?' he would ask, but Maggie was usually too busy to listen.

Because she was young and strong, the work got done somehow, but she was only twelve and a half years old, and after a long day in the mill, followed by an evening spent cleaning and cooking, she would fall into bed and feel as if she was dropping sheer away, down through the feather mattress into a sleep so deep it was a kind of dying.

Her father's face seemed to alter in bone structure as he complained in his hesitant speech of one cause of discontent after another. His eyes and cheeks sank into hollows, and he developed a nervous habit of rubbing his thumb and forefinger together, as if he were rolling a piece of bread into crumbs.

At the end of a sultry July afternoon, Maggie came home from the mill with her cotton blouse sticking to her back with sweat. It ran uncomfortably down her sides, and stood out in glistening beads on her rounded forehead.

There was nowhere to wash at the mill, and as she stood at the slopstone and splashed cold water over her face and arms, Thomas sat with his back decently turned, grumbling in his stuttering monotone:

'I left the back door open today to catch what bit of air I could. I swear the noise of the looms shivered the ornaments on the mantelpiece. How you stick it I don't know. Your mother would turn in her grave if she knew that you'd gone in the mill. You know she was set on you being a teacher, don't you?'

'Now how could I have gone to be a teacher and left you? Perhaps when you're better and I'm older,' Maggie said vaguely, soothing him, as she wiped herself dry on the coarse roller towel hanging behind the back door.

The soap she had washed herself with was the same mottled soap she used for scrubbing the floor and the washing, but her skin was as petal soft as the wild roses in the hedges bisecting the fields of her country home. Smoothing her hair down with still damp hands she went to stand in front of Thomas, challenging him to meet her eyes.

But her father never looked anyone straight in the face nowadays.

'Look at me, Father!' Maggie ordered. 'Come on! I'm going to give you a bit of a telling off.'

Thomas's eyes slid away, indicating that he was not interested in anything she might have to say, but Maggie persevered.

'There's nothing to stop you walking up to the park now, is there? I know you walk slow, but you've all day to get there and back. I'll make you a bite to take with you if you like.' Exasperated, she put both hands on her hips.

'Father! Listen to me! It's not doing you any good just sitting here in the house. You're going to start *growing* into that chair if you're not careful.'

Thomas's eyes were dreamy. 'How like your mother you are when you get your paddy up. You grow more like her every day.'

'The *park*,' Maggie repeated.

Thomas nodded, as if the meaning of the word had just become clear to him.

'Oh, yes, the park.' His words became jumbled as he

went on. 'Well, I admit I did like going there once or twice, when we came here at first.' He sighed heavily. 'Just to see a glimpse of green, but it's not the green we used to know, Maggie. That green is mucky green. The grime in the air has filtered down and coated the grass with a film of soot. It has, Maggie.' He held both hands idle on his lap and began to roll the fingers and thumbs together. 'I picked a blade and pulled it through my fingers, and do you know what? They were coated with filth. No, I'm better off staying in.'

'But you can't stay in for the rest of your life!'

Maggie pulled a clean blouse over her head. 'You can turn round now, Father.'

But he had said his say, and was gone from her again, staring at nothing, wishing back a life that would never be again.

At the end of that year, he walked no further than the row of shops at the top of the street, making his laborious way, shuffling his feet, his eyes downcast, like an old man searching for his last halfpenny.

'I can't seem to cheer him up at all,' Maggie wrote to her brothers, posting it off to their regimental address with the feeling that she might as well be posting it into a tree.

Doctor Bates surprised her one Saturday afternoon, riding out from the village in a hill farmer's high trap which was delivering eggs to the market stalls.

'I've to be back there to meet him in under the hour,' he said. 'Is your father upstairs, Maggie?'

She was down on her knees polishing the fire-brasses when he came down again, wrapping them in an old sheet to keep them clean and shining for Sunday, the way her mother had always done. But as soon as she saw the doctor she stood up and stared at him, anxiety creasing her forehead like a roll of corrugated cardboard.

'He's no worse, is he, Doctor?'

Doctor Bates fiddled with his watch-chain. She was very bonny, this girl, this *child* standing before him. She had the bold solid look he'd noticed in so many East Lancashire girls. Soft in colouring, but with a fierce determination about her. Aye, fierce. That was the word to describe young Maggie Craig. With her childhood gone before she had savoured it, solemn-eyed, hands folded in front of her over the sacking pinny covering her flowered cotton overall. Brown hair looped back from a centre parting and pinned high at the back of her head in a tight bun.

How much simpler things would have been if the good Lord had issued a double ticket when Hannah Craig had died of the diphtheria. One for her and the other for her husband.

The twins were as self-centred as their father, and they could have got on with their soldiering, and this little lass could have come to live with him and his wife in their three-storeyed house set into the hill.

Maggie was bright and pretty, and would have filled their declining years with joy. He touched the end of his violet nose with his finger, and Maggie looked quickly away.

The doctor was going to tell her something serious; she could tell that by his expression. She was worried sick about her father, but that nose! Jonathan had once said that if you set a match to it there would be an explosion.

'The doctor would disappear in a cloud of blue smoke. Pouff!' he'd said.

Maggie gulped the giggle back in her throat, a little girl again with her brothers teasing her straight face away, then raising their eyes in mock despair as her laughter bubbled out.

Just for a moment she could hear Miss Hepinstall's piercing voice:

'Out here at once, Maggie Craig! You'll be laughing the other side of your face before the day's out. Hold out your hand!'

Miss *Daisy* Hepinstall. 'Oh, flippin' heck,' as the girls at the mill were always saying. 'Maggie Craig thinks sum-mat's funny again.'

'Your father,' the doctor was saying carefully, 'has some-thing wrong with him. A sort of nervous complaint which is making him grow old – senile – before his time has come to grow old.'

He fingered the nose again, but for Maggie the urge to giggle had gone, and her face flushed red with a terrible anxiety.

'That's it,' she agreed. 'He does look like an old man. His hair is turning proper white, and he won't walk anywhere if he can help it. But there's no pain because I keep asking him, and anyway I'd know. My father is not a very good sufferer.'

Doctor Bates permitted himself a fleeting smile, but oh, dear God, it was all wrong that this lovely child should have full responsibility for the failing man upstairs. He tapped the nose, then his head. 'There's a *fault* in your father's brain, and this fault is preventing the messages getting through to his limbs – telling them to move. Do you see? That is why he shuffles instead of lifting his feet up when he tries to take a step, and that is why he spends so long in his chair, and lying on his bed. His reactions are those of some-one much older.'

'Is he going to die, then?'

Maggie's voice was low and pleading, but her eyes demanded that she be told the truth, no matter what.

'No, he's not going to die, love. He could live for a very long time, but he's never going to do a day's work again. Certainly not teaching. There might be something in the mill. . . .'

'Never!' Maggie's tilted chin emphasized her defiance. 'Me father's not going in the mill, not sweeping or some-thing like that, and that's what it would be because his fingers aren't quick enough for him to be a weaver.'

She spoke with quiet determination. 'Me father was a teacher, Doctor, and he wouldn't be like he is if me mother were still alive. It's his heart what's stopped those messages getting through to his legs, isn't it? It nearly killed him when me mother died.'

Doctor Bates took his watch out of his pocket, and raised bushy eyebrows as he saw the time.

Out of the mouths of babes, right enough. But he did not go the whole way with that theory. No, Thomas Craig was a sick man, but a weak man also, and more than a bit of a coward come to that. He should have pulled himself together, smartened himself up a bit, and looked around for a woman to marry.

Not to put in his wife's place, or even in his bed for that matter, but a woman who would have taken the burden from this little lass's shoulders.

He walked towards the curtain that separated the living-room from the front parlour, and parted its folds with an impatient gesture. He had come to help, and what had he achieved? Nothing.

'Heard from the boys?' he asked as he stepped out on to the pavement.

'No, not for a long time, but they're not much at writing letters. They'll just turn up one day, the both of them brazen as brass.'

Doctor Bates hesitated before walking away up the street. There was something in the way Maggie held her head . . . by the gum, but she was going to be a bonny woman. She was smiling at him as graciously as if she was showing him out of a grand house, and she wasn't a child at all. The blue stuff of her cotton blouse atop the awful sacking pinny was pulling in creases underneath her arms, and the buttons down the front looked ready to pop at any minute. He tried to work out exactly how old she was, and wondered vaguely if there was someone, another woman, to explain certain things.

As if she had been conjured up out of his thoughts, a short stout woman came out of the house next door, a cup held in an outstretched hand.

'Have you such a thing as a cup of sugar, love? I've got me scones half mixed and I'm that much short.'

Then she saw the doctor, and whipped the cup out of sight beneath her pinafore. 'Ee, I didn't know you'd got company, love. I'll come back when it's more convenient like.'

The doctor raised his hat, his mind registering the twinkle in Maggie's eyes. Either the borrowing was a regular occurrence, or the neighbour had seen him through her front window and come to see what was going on. And Maggie knew it. She'd all her chairs at home had young Maggie Craig.

He continued on his way, his mind more at ease. Yes, that neighbour looked like the salt of the earth type. She would keep a motherly eye on Maggie, and her father, he felt sure of that. Closer than Siamese twins the folks in some of these little streets. In and out of each other's houses with basins of nourishing broth, and running for the doctor if one of them looked like dying. Yes, he'd done his duty by the Craig family, more than his duty come to that. His own widespread practice was as much as he could manage, and he wasn't getting any younger. His wife was always reminding him of that.

Stepping out briskly, his mind at ease, Doctor Bates turned into the main street leading to the market square, and mentally crossed the Craig family from his list of worries.

'Who was that, then?' Clara Preston asked the question without preamble. If she wanted to ask anything she asked it straight out, and why not? If folks did not want to tell they could always keep their mouths shut. She would not take offence. She'd find out in her own good time, anyroad.

'He'd got a right conk on him, and no mistake. Bet you wouldn't have to tell *him* what to do with a bottle of beer.'

Maggie smiled, busy at the dresser filling the cup with

sugar. She knew that Clara had timed her appearance deliberately, wanting to know who the visitor was, and why she had not been told of his coming.

She had weighed Clara up from the first week in Foundry Street. Keep your own counsel and Clara would find out somehow. Tell her everything and she would be your friend for life.

And this wasn't the time to turn your nose up at a friend, even one as unlikely as Clara Preston, with the glide in one eye, and a mother next door who kept her as close as if she had never left the womb.

'You don't want to speak to *her*,' Clara would say of a neighbour. 'She's no better than what she should be, me mother says.'

'I wouldn't get your meat from that butcher's. They say he's got another woman,' Clara would say.

Maggie hesitated, but not for long. The urge to talk about her father was overwhelming.

'He's not really ill in his body, Clara. It's just his mind forgetting to tell his body what to do. That's why he never wants to walk far.'

Clara's left eye glided into the corner.

'He didn't say your dad would have to go in the looney-bin, did he?' She sat down obviously relishing the prospect.

'Of course not. It's just that he never really picked up after me mother died. It was the shock brought this on, you see.'

Clara brightened up. 'Aye, shock's a terrible thing. I once knew a girl who set stiff as a board when a man showed her his johnwilly down by the canal. They had to carry her home like a plank.'

Maggie's laughter rang out, then she glanced towards the foot of the stairs and clamped a hand over her mouth.

'You are a one, Clara Preston. Sometimes you say worse things than the girls at the mill. Me Grandma Butterworth would have made you wash your mouth out with soap and water if she had heard you say that.'

She picked up the poker from its stand, and moved the kettle-grid over the fire.

'Let's have a cup of tea, eh?'

'Thought you was never going to ask,' Clara said with a fat smile that almost disappeared into the folds of her neck.

'Aye, you're right, love. Compared to you I'm as common as muck, and don't deny it, for it's the gospel truth. When you first moved in and I heard the way you speak I told Arnie, I said: "Them next door is out of a higher drawer than what we are".' She set the rocking chair into motion with a movement of her foot. 'Not that it bothers me. Folks is folks, and if you do what's right, me mother says, you won't go far wrong.'

Maggie sat down in the chair opposite to Clara, and listened to her talk with amused affection. It was hard to believe that Clara was only twenty-four, a married woman for only three years. There was a middle-aged look about her flat features, and a matronly shelving of her drooping bust. There was nothing *glad* about Clara's mournful pudding of a face, but it was a kindly face just the same. She would have been surprised if she could have overheard Clara reporting to her mother:

'She knows nowt that little Maggie Craig doesn't. She might read poetry books and newspapers, but she needs telling a few things, she does that 'n all.'

So Clara had explained to Maggie what she could expect to happen now that her chest had started 'sprouting', leaving her feeling that her whole body had suddenly become dirty, with one place in particular singled out for unbelievable nastiness.

'And that's only the beginning of what women have to put up with,' Clara said, fat jowls wobbling earnestly. 'If men had to put up with what women do they wouldn't go around looking so chuffed with themselves. It's nothing to get upset about, love. Just remember never to put your hands in cold water when you're like that, and as for the other thing, well you don't need to know owt about that for

31

years yet. Just never allow a boy any liberties, that's all. All men have a nasty side to them. It's best to remember that.'

'*What* liberties?' Maggie had wanted to know, but Clara, her duty done, had pretended not to hear.

Maggie handed a cup of tea to Clara, then passed over the sugar basin.

'My father used to be able to recognize the call of birds, and he used to take me for walks and go so far that he had to carry me back on his shoulders. You wouldn't have known him in those days, Clara. I can only just remember him when he was different, but I know he was a lovely man.'

Maggie unhooked the wool-stitched holder from its nail on the wall, and bending down to the hearth, filled up the tea-pot. When she straightened up her face was flushed from the heat of the fire, and silky brown wisps of hair curled down her neck from the tight bun on top of her head.

Suddenly Clara felt inexplicable anger rise up sour in her throat, and without knowing why she was cross, said in a loud voice:

'If you'd rub your hands on the soap, then smooth them down over your hair, you'd find it wouldn't come down like that. And you need a new blouse, Maggie Craig. You're all busting out of that one, and it doesn't look nice.'

Then, as Maggie clutched at the offending button-trim of her blue blouse, Clara relented.

'If you like I'll show you how to make a tuck across your bust-bodices, so that your front won't show as *two*. It's showing two what makes it disgusting.' She patted her own bolster-shaped one-piece bosom.

'If you bring me one of your bodices down and find me a bit of thread and a needle, I'll do it now while your dad is out of the way.'

Maggie nodded. 'It is good of you, Clara.'

'I shall pass through this world but once,' said Clara surprisingly as her face creased into its squashed and joyless smile.

'Fancy Clara knowing that,' Maggie thought as she ran

32

quickly up the steep dark stairs, then she peeped into her father's room and saw that he was lying on his bed facing the wall.

In her own room she sat down on her bed for a moment and worried about him, then she worried about her shape. She wished she wasn't growing into such a rude shape. But *why* was it rude?

Of one thing she was certain. She could never ask Clara to explain some of the things the girls talked about at the mill. Not with Clara's father being the Sunday School Superintendent at the Chapel, and with her mother having wanted to be a missionary before she got married.

She took a clean white bust-bodice from the top drawer, and stared at it, then lifting her eyes, she saw her reflection in the swing mirror, and the way she was indeed busting out of her blouse.

Suddenly, without warning, she felt an almost paralysing wave of longing for her mother. For Hannah, the mother she vaguely remembered swishing her round the School House kitchen, skirts billowing out as she moved with quick decisive movements from fire to table, then table to fire.

'Feeling sorry for yourself will get you nowhere fast, Maggie Craig!' she said, putting her tongue out at her reflection. Then she ran downstairs to find that Clara was pouring herself yet another cup of tea.

2

'Oh for a man . . . oh for a man . . . oh for a mansion in the sky,' Maggie sang at the top of her clear tuneful voice.

It was the week before her seventeenth birthday, and although her father had deteriorated over the past three years, he was still alive. And the sun was shining outside the mill, even if its rays were filtered down through a maze of tall mill chimneys. Maggie had three looms to tend now, and well, if her father wasn't any better, she told herself that he could certainly have been a lot worse.

'Being happy is a state of mind, not a matter of circumstance,' she had explained seriously to one of the loom sweepers only that morning as they waited in line to brew up their breakfast mug of tea.

Then they had both burst out laughing, the nineteen-year-old boy, and the girl who was giving him what he called her 'bossy teacher's lecture'.

Joe Barton reckoned he was the only person in the tall grey cotton mill who could tumble Maggie Craig down off her high horse. Joe thought she was the most beautiful girl he had ever seen, and in the six months since he had come to know her, she had brought a colour and a gaiety into his life he had never known before.

They weren't courting, heaven's sakes not that, as Maggie said herself, but she did concede that they were a little bit more than friends. She caught Joe's eye as he walked past her looms, and when he winked at her she winked back. There was no trace of shyness in the cheeky wink. Being brought up with three older brothers had

34

knocked that sort of daftness out of her early on, and privately she thought the other girl weavers were stupid the way they blushed and giggled if a boy as much as spoke to them.

But oh no, she certainly wasn't courting. Keeping company with a boy meant you were thinking of getting married, then either living with his family or yours till you could find a house with a rent you could afford, and enough furniture to start you off. Then it was him coming home for his tea, then off to the pub every night with his mates, and you stopping at home and having babies one after the other. It was him going to the football match every Saturday afternoon, and continual arguments about money and the lack of it. An' all the fun in your life finished before you'd had any.

Maggie's fingers moved busily as she sang at the top of her voice. She was enjoying the freedom of singing her heart out against the deafening clatter of the machinery in the weaving shed. Although the stone floor ran damp beneath her feet she could sing and she could work and let her thoughts run free. As free as the birds her father used to love to watch. But by the gum it was hot! She ran a finger round the band at the throat of her striped blouse, then undid the top two buttons.

Life was strange. Look at the packet she'd had for the past three years. Solely responsible for a man aged into near senility by self-pity, no time for girl friends her own age, because let's face it, they were still having their hair-ribbons tied on by their mothers when she was chief cook and bottle-washer.

Maggie started on another rousing chorus: Oh aye, life was strange all right, and until she had met Joe Barton and walked in the park with him of a summer and laughed at nowt with him as they snuggled close together in a doorway of a dark night, there hadn't been much to laugh at really. But then you accepted what happened day by day if you had any gumption. She'd tried to tell Joe Barton that when he'd grumbled about the way the overlooker kept constant tabs on them.

'If you argue with the likes of him, you only come the worst off.'

Joe had grinned and put up his fists in a mock fight.

'If he docks any more of me money off I'll knock his block off,' he'd said. 'His *bloody* block off,' he had added, just to show Maggie that she hadn't bossed him out of swearing, not quite.

Maggie shook her head. No, Joe was wrong. You accepted what happened day by day because you knew, you were *certain* that something good was bound to happen. If not the next day then the day after. You just kept on in the meantime. You ran home at dinner-time to give your father his dinner, then you ran back, and when the hooter went at half past five, you ran home again to cook tea for a man so shelled in his own solitude that there were times she imagined he was looking at her and wondering who she could be.

And at that very moment, Joe Barton, father unknown, mostly of no fixed abode, was asking himself the very same question:

Just who the hell did he think he was? For over six months now he'd told his lies to Maggie Craig, making her believe his father was dead, letting her think he lived like she did, in a decent house in a decent street.

Foundry Street? God Almighty, compared to the two rooms he was sharing at the moment with his mother and his sister Belle, Foundry Street was bloody West End Road, up by the park where all the town's toffs lived. It hadn't mattered up to now because Maggie was nobbut a young lass, and their friendship had not been the kind where a young couple sat together on the sofa holding hands. What had there been apart from long conversations as they sat on the grass in the park together, a Sunday School ramble into the Ribble valley? But now Maggie was hinting that she

36

would like to take him to her house to meet her invalid father.

'Perhaps if you see him, Joe, you'll understand why I can't get out all that often.' She'd blushed and dimpled. 'I'm not being forward. I'm not forcing you into *declaring* yourself or nothing like that. You won't have to state your intentions and swear that you can keep me in the manner to which I have become accustomed.'

'Maggie Craig!' Joe had pinched her cheek, laughing into her eyes. 'How is it you can say the things other people only think and get away with it?' They had ended up running down the long grass slope from the Conservatory in the park, with Maggie tripping over a trailing bootlace and falling, and Joe throwing himself down beside her.

'Joe!' she'd screamed as he tickled her. 'If any of the Chapel folk come by and see us I'll be condemned to hell-fire, and you with me. Stop it! Stop it, Joe!'

Working steadily when he felt the overlooker's hard eyes on his back, Joe made up his mind. He was going to do what he should have done a long time ago. 'Come out for a bit after tea,' he told Maggie as they joined the stream of weavers thronging the street outside the mill after the hooter had gone. 'I want to take you to meet my mother.' His dark eyes were bleak. 'I think you should meet her before I meet your father.'

'Why? She got two heads or something?'

'Half past six. At the top of your street, when you've had your tea,' Joe said, then walked away.

Montague Court was only ten minutes' walk away from Foundry Street, but Maggie had never been round that way before. She'd heard about it of course, and Clara had said it was what she called the red light district.

'Red lights above the doors,' she'd said, her left eye gliding into its corner. 'There's a woman lives down there what has no nose.'

37

Now Joe was telling her that *he* lived there, that when he'd said vaguely that he lived round Queen Street way, he had not been telling exactly the truth.

'Montague Court. The bottom half of number fourteen,' he said as they walked along the canal bank. He swaggered and whistled, telling Maggie that he was upset about something. 'Two rooms with an outside tap and a lavvy we share with three other families. Dirty buggers too,' he stressed.

There was a jauntiness in his step and his voice that almost broke Maggie's heart. She knew he was poor, but then most folks seemed to be poor, and poverty was no disgrace. She knew he was doing this *before* she took him to her own home to give her a chance to change her mind.

In his own way he was saying: 'See, this is how I live, Maggie Craig. Now do you still want to be my friend and introduce me to your father who was once a schoolmaster?'

He was walking so quickly that she had to do a little skip now and again to keep up with him, and though she wanted to put out a hand and touch his arm to show that she understood, and it didn't make no difference, there was something about the expression on his face that stilled her hand. Grim was the word for it, and scared. Yes, scared to death.

'Not far now,' he said, and turned sharply left away from a main road so that they climbed upwards into a maze of streets with houses not much different from Maggie's own.

True the semi-circle of flagged pavements were mostly unmopped, and the window bottoms were without a neat line of yellow stone marking out their edges, but they were not that much different.

'Just like Foundry Street,' she said kindly, but Joe made no sign that he had even heard.

'Down here. And never let me catch you coming down here on your own, especially after dark. Ever! Do you hear me?'

Maggie felt a strange ripple of fear in her stomach as they turned abruptly into a narrow street, with the houses

38

clustered so close together that it seemed as if one minute they were in the soft yellow light of an early summer evening, and the next in the murky gloom of a February winter's night.

There were no pavements, just an extension of the cobble-stones right up to the front doors. A bare-bottomed child crawled at the feet of a woman who was sitting out on her front step, suckling a baby from a breast as heavy and pendulous as a bladder of lard. Maggie averted her eyes, and lifted her skirts away from the greasy and slimy cobbles.

Number fourteen had a front door so scarred that it gave the impression of having been kicked in more than it had been opened. A strange sweet stench met them as they stepped inside, and Maggie had to fight down an urge not to cover her nose with her hand. They were in a room with very little furniture, apart from a horse-hair sofa with the stuffing hanging out, a table made from two orange boxes pushed together, and a mattress in one corner with a couple of brown blankets thrown over it.

Maggie blinked, and when her eyes became used to the darkness, she saw that a small fair-haired girl was sitting on the sofa, a girl who hung her head in shyness, then turned away.

'Belle.' Joe spoke quietly and urgently to his sister. 'Where is she? Through there?'

The girl nodded.

'With him?'

Another nod. Joe glanced at the door leading into the back room and raised his eyes ceilingwards. Then as if remembering that Maggie was there he led her forward.

'Belle, love. This is Maggie. You remember I told you I was bringing her?'

Belle looked up and Maggie saw that the pale eyes were filling with tears which spilled over and ran slowly down her cheeks. She stared at Joe with a pleading expression as if begging to be forgiven.

'She was ready, Joe. Honest she was. All waiting like you said. Dressed, with a frock on and everything.' The fair head dropped again. 'Then *he* came.'

'The big one that says he's a sailor from Liverpool?'

'Aye, an' he had a bottle with him, Joe, and he started laughing and he tried to make me have some.' Belle turned her head from side to side in distaste. 'But I wouldn't open me mouth, then they went through there.'

Joe went to sit beside his sister and put his arms round her, pulling her to him. 'He didn't try to, you know . . . to touch you? Like last time?'

'No, he didn't. I think you frightened him with what you said you would do to him, Joe. I think he thought you meant it, Joe.'

Maggie stood a little to one side, watching, listening to Joe speak to Belle in a low resigned sort of voice.

But what Belle had just said made him shout in sudden anger. 'I should think I bloody did mean it. If he tries to touch you again I'll swing for him.'

Maggie glanced round her. Oh, dear God in heaven, she knew what it was to be poor. Sometimes of a Thursday there was nothing left in her purse but her key, and Clara was poor because Arnie's wages did not amount to much. And she could remember the poverty of the women in the farm labourers' cottages, women who when their boots were worn out had to stay indoors until the money could be found for another pair, and them usually handed down from somebody else. But this poverty was a different kind. This place was a slum, a *hovel*, and now she had placed that strange sweet sickening smell.

Once as a small child, her mother had taken her into a cottage where an old woman had recently died. Hannah had gone to rescue a terrified cat, and in reply to Maggie's outspoken query about the 'horrible' smell had explained:

'That smell is bugs, love. Once they've got in the walls you can't shift them without a stoving.'

And Joe lived here. He had laughed with her, and kissed

her, then come back to this place. Maggie was staring at him with pity when a burst of loud laughter came from behind the closed door.

'I'm sorry, Joe,' Belle said again.

When the door was banged back almost to the plaster, the man framed in the opening was the biggest man Maggie ever remembered seeing. Heavy-jowled and unshaven, he was buckling a wide leather belt round the top of his trousers and laughing with his head thrown back, showing brown uneven teeth. Behind him was a young-old woman, so like Joe in the set of her features and the way her dark hair sprang back from her forehead that Maggie blinked.

For a moment, as Joe stood up from the sofa and faced her, Annie Barton knew a moment of sheer panic. Her glance went to the girl standing there beside her son, a fresh-faced bonny girl with country pink cheeks, wearing a clean print dress.

That was the way she used to look. That was the way Belle should look now, not shriven up like an old woman before her fourteenth birthday. Anger suddenly took the place of fear.

'Wait for me outside, Ned,' she told the big man. 'I'll not be long.'

'You heard what she said.' Joe's voice was low but firm.

Maggie held her breath as the big man's darting glance went from Joe to his mother then back again. Then she let it out in a sigh of relief as with a shrug of massive shoulders the man went to the front door, opened it and stepped outside.

'Now!' Annie Barton said before Joe could speak. 'Let's get it over with, our Joe.' She jerked her head in Maggie's direction. 'All right, so I shouldn't have gone in there when I knew she was coming, should I? But Ned came unexpected like, and afore you jump on your soap box, just you go through there and see what he's brought this time. Enough food to last us a month.'

41

'I provide for that.' Joe's hand shot out as he gripped his mother's wrist. 'We could manage if you'd try.'

With a twist of her thin body she broke loose from his grasp, rushed over to the cluttered mantelpiece and snatched a piece of paper, thrusting it in front of Maggie's horrified face.

'See, lass! See here what he makes me do! Every mouldy penny he expects me to write down afore he'll hand over another. See! Have a sken at that. Rent half a crown. Gas fivepence. Two candles a halfpenny. Soap a penny and a tin of milk twopence. Go on, tek it, and see for thyself what a skinflint tha's courting!'

The sound that came from Belle frightened Maggie more than the loud shouting of the dishevelled woman. It was the cry of a small, wounded animal, ashamed to the point of collapse.

'Oh, Mam, stop it,' she moaned softly. 'You know if it wasn't for our Joe there'd be days when we didn't eat at all. Stop showing him up, our mam. Just go!'

Then as the front door slammed behind her mother, Belle lifted her head and smiled a tremulous smile at her brother.

'Soon I'll be living in at me new job, then you can stop fretting about me, our Joe.' She turned to Maggie. 'He has to try to make her write it down or else she spends every penny on drink.' The watery smile widened. 'And if you hadn't been here he'd have clouted her one. He's not always as quiet as this. If you hadn't been here I don't know what would have happened.'

'I do. I'd have thrown that big lout outside for a start off,' Joe muttered.

'You and who else?'

And incredibly they were laughing, the pair of them, pulling Maggie down to sit beside them on the moulting sofa, the three of them shaking with a laughter bordering on hysteria.

'And I'd got the best tea-set out,' Joe grinned, pointing to four saucerless cups set out on the rickety makeshift table.

'And Mam was going to crook her little finger when she drank, like this.'

Joe's eyes met Maggie's with an expression that cut straight through to her heart.

'It doesn't matter,' she whispered. 'It doesn't matter, truly.'

'Wait till you meet my father,' she kept saying in the weeks that followed when Joe refused to even consider a return visit. 'He won't shout at me, I admit, but he'll probably close his eyes and carry on rocking himself in his chair when I take you in.' She touched Joe's arm. 'Neither of us come from what anyone could call a *stable* background, Joe. My father won't make any friends, and your mother makes too many, that's all.'

She clamped a hand over her mouth. 'Oh, I'm sorry, I really am. I didn't mean it like that.'

'But it's true,' Joe told her, his young face dark and anguished. 'My mother's a whore, a drunken whore. If just one of Mam's men even tries to touch Belle, I'll kill him. Stone dead.'

Maggie nipped his wrist as they walked along, so that he had to turn and look at her.

'Stop talking like that, Joe Barton. You're not going to kill anybody, and one of these days you're going to come to tea, and Belle too. See?'

'You're the boss,' Joe said, but he was smiling again, and that was enough for Maggie.

'Jesus wants me for a sunbeam,' she sang at the top of her voice on the afternoon of the following Sunday. The sun was still shining, and she had managed to push Thomas out

43

through the front door, making him promise to walk to the top of Foundry Street and back.

She was happy, because unless things were terrible, she felt she owed it to herself to be happy.

She knew, of course, that Sunday was supposed to be a day of rest, and that if she disobeyed the rules of her Chapel she might end up in hell-fire, but surely, she argued, cleaning the little house and stopping in with her father, her *earthly* father, was doing more good than going with Clara to Chapel in the morning and the evening? Surely her heavenly Father would understand?

And Joe was coming to tea soon. He'd promised.

Sometimes, on the very rare occasions when Thomas was out of the house, she had this overwhelming urge to shout and sing, to climb on the table set squarely in the middle of the room and dance on it.

'Jesus wants me for a sunbeam, and a flippin' fine sunbeam I'd be,' she sang, standing on tiptoe and staring at herself in the large mahogany-framed mirror over the mantelpiece. She stuck out her tongue, and all at once she was little Maggie Craig, six years old, pulling faces in class and goading Miss Hepinstall to fury. Once, too impatient to reach for her cane, the teacher had grabbed Maggie's slate from her hands and clouted her over the head with it.

She wasn't fed up, not really. It was just that her father was always *there*, following her around the house, lurking behind her like a doleful shadow, a shadow with more substance than himself. He was so *negative*. Maggie was sure that the messages Doctor Bates had said could not reach his brain would be all the wrong ones even if they got there.

'Go and have your rest, Father,' she would say.

'The only rest I want is my eternal one,' he would answer back.

If it wasn't for all the larking about that went on at the mill, and Joe's return to good humour, she bet her face would have forgotten how to smile. She stretched her mouth into a wide grin, then still watching herself, she said:

'You are not a very nice person, Maggie Craig. Carrying on like a mad woman just because your father's gone out of the house for a bit. He's ill and he can't help being as miserable as sin, and one day you'll be old and I bet you'll be a miserable old faggot.'

She sucked in her lips as if over toothless gums, chewing wildly on nothing, then burst out laughing, feeling the laugh catch in her throat as the front door opened with such force that it banged right back to the plaster wall.

Clara's voice rang out like a clarion call.

'It's all right, love. Don't worry now. We're fetching your dad back. He fell off the kerb and couldn't get up, that's all.'

Carried into the house between two men – Arnie and Mr Isherwood, a blacksmith-striker from number fifteen, Thomas lolled like a filleted corpse, his eyes closed, and his face the colour of putty.

'Put him on the sofa,' Clara ordered, her eye swivelling into the corner. 'You'd best run for the doctor, Arnie.'

'Or the undertaker,' she amended, not quite underneath her breath.

Maggie stared at her father's closed face, too shocked to move or speak. She had pushed him out into the street, and if he was dead it was all her fault.

Arnie stood, poised for flight, small and insignificant, neat head on one side, whilst Mr Isherwood, his part in the drama played out, moved towards the door.

'If there's owt . . . ?' he said vaguely.

'Thank you,' Maggie said, going down on her knees by the sofa, and Mr Isherwood went back to his own house to tell his wife that in his opinion Mr Craig was already knocking on the pearly gates.

Clara thought so too, and decided that she would make the funeral spread for Maggie. Ham and tongue, with a batch of her scones to follow. She felt heart sorry for Mr

45

Craig, of course she did, but he was a miserable old fella, older at fifty than her grandpa had been at eighty-two. She jumped at the sound of Maggie's voice.

'I'm going to make a pot of tea. Would you like a cup?'

Her voice as she got to her feet was bright and cheerful. Clara stared at her as if she had not heard aright. Then she saw the way her eyes twinkled as she exchanged a glance with Arnie, and her bewilderment increased.

They were tickled about something, those two, laughing while Mr Craig was on his way out, lying there with his eyes closed, and his jaw hanging loose and slack.

'Father? Would you like a cup of tea?'

Maggie repeated the question, and this time there was no doubt about it. She *was* winking at Arnie, and he was winking back at her. Clara sniffed. Well, all she could say was she wished they would let her in on the joke, that was all.

'I think you will have to fetch the doctor, Arnie,' Maggie was saying now, her voice low and mournful. 'There'll be nothing for it but the Infirmary.'

'Or the Workhouse,' agreed Arnie.

'Ah, the Workhouse,' said Maggie with a deep sigh.

Clara stepped back a pace as the recumbent figure on the horse-hair sofa raised a languid hand up to his forehead, opened his eyes, and said in a weak but clear voice:

'Where am I?'

'In your own house,' Maggie told him briskly, swinging the kettle-stand over the flames with a deft flick of her wrist. 'And now I'll make that cup of tea. I could do with one meself.'

'You mean the old devil was shamming?' Clara's face was a study as she faced Arnie in the living-room of the house next door. 'Upsetting Maggie like that, and letting you and Mr Isherwood carry him in. I can't believe it. He looked as if he was at death's door, you can't deny that.'

46

Arnie nodded and stroked his sparse moustache.

'Oh, aye, he looked a right gonner, I'll grant you that, but he'd made up his mind he wasn't going to walk up the street no more, and now he's won. Well, hasn't he?'

'Well, I suppose he can't keep having to be fetched back.' Clara still sounded doubtful.

'He's a crafty old sod,' Arnie said, and Clara winced as a look of pain ran like a reproachful shadow over her flat features.

'I wish you wouldn't swear like that, Arnie. I know you get it from some of those Irishmen you work with, but it doesn't sound nice. Me mother was only saying yesterday that she's seen some of them rolling drunk down by the market. Rolling about and cursing and swearing. They should have stopped where they were, me dad said.'

She gave the oilcloth on the table an unnecessary wipe with the edge of her apron.

'I'll just go next door for a minute. There's plenty of time before we start getting ready for Chapel.'

'Don't know why you don't have a door cut through the wall,' Arnie muttered as the front door closed behind his wife. 'Save you going out in the wet, that would.'

Still muttering he went out into the backyard, and stood for a while, his thumbs tucked into his waistcoat pockets, staring with a blank expression at the soot-blackened walls flanking his tiny garden. Over the wall to his right he could hear his wife's voice as she talked to her mother. Their voices were loud, strident, as if they were rowing, shouting a normal conversation to each other. Arnie bowed his head. Mother and daughter, thicker than the thickest of thieves, thinking alike, two minds as one, with Clara's father chipping in just now and again like a forgotten echo. Agreeing with them because he daren't do nowt else.

'They only tolerate me because I married their Clara,' Arnie told himself out loud. 'They knew that mugs like me didn't grow on trees. . . .'

He jumped as if suddenly prodded in the back as the

knocker on the front door rapped three times, and immediately his expression changed.

'It's Maggie,' he told himself, and hurried back into the house to ask her in.

He knew it was Maggie because everyone else in the street just lifted the latch, called out 'yoo-hoo', and walked in. But not Maggie. Clara had been right when she had said that the Craigs were out of a different drawer, and it was funny but even when Mr Craig had been lying on the sofa with his mouth agape, he had still looked like a gentleman. Arnie stood back to allow Maggie to walk past him, through the parlour and into the living-room. He jerked his head.

'She's next door. Gone to tell her mother what she missed by not being out on the flags when your dad fell down.'

Maggie smiled and gave Arnie a look that said she was not going to take sides, then or ever. She looked so pale that Arnie pulled a chair forward and told her to sit down, then stood in front of her stroking his moustache and trying to think what to say.

If he told her she looked tired she'd deny it; if he told her what he really thought about that miserable old father of hers, she would be up in arms. If he offered to make her a cup of tea she'd say she'd just had one, and if he told her he was sorry, she would ask him what for.

But he was sorry for her, and it was a sorrow that went far deeper than pity. It was, all at once, a terrible anger, taking him unawares, and making him sweat. He ran his finger round his starched Sunday collar.

By the left but she was growing up into a bonny lass. Her brown hair was so tightly raked back that it might have been scragged into position by a garden fork, but there were little curly tendrils escaping round her forehead, and more wisping down behind her ears. From where he stood he could see the sweat standing out on her upper lip, in the tiny soft groove, the sweet hollow from her nose to her mouth. Funny him noticing that. . . . And she wasn't as innocent as

48

she looked. She had a boy, Clara said so, and a rough sort from Montague Court at that.

'I've persuaded me father to go upstairs and lie down on his bed,' Maggie was telling him now, then she leaned forward, and the bit of unbuttoned blouse at her throat fell away to reveal the suspicion of soft curves. Arnie swallowed hard.

'You knew it wasn't a proper faint out there in the street, didn't you, Arnie? He looked awful though.' She sighed, pressing her lips together in a childish gesture. 'I wish you could have known him before we came to live here, Arnie. He was such a *clever* man. He had over fifty children in his class and he could put his arms on his desk and recite poetry to them, and they would just sit listening, not a fidget between them.' She shook her head. 'It's such a *waste* him being like this. I sometimes wonder if I'm treating him right, you know? If I ought to be a bit firmer with him? Then when I have been, like this afternoon, he makes me feel guilty, and a bit ashamed.' Her head drooped. 'It was a bit cruel mentioning the Workhouse, because he's always going on about ending up there, as if I would let him.'

She got up from the chair, and smiled. 'I'd better go. You'll be wanting to get ready for Chapel, and I've got me ironing to do.' A rounded dimple deepened at the corner of her mouth. 'I'll never go to Heaven like you, Arnie. You'll be playing your harp up there, and I'll be fetching the coal in down there.'

'Nay, that you won't.'

Arnie's normally quiet voice was loud and assertive, and Maggie looked at him in surprise. He was staring at her with his eyes sort of glittering, and he hadn't said much come to think of it. She'd done all the talking. Maggie turned towards the door. Well, there was nothing unusual in that. He often sat there listening to Clara talking without saying a single word. Arnie was one on his own, as her father often said.

'Don't go yet!' he said abruptly.

She smiled at him. 'But I have to go, Arnie. I didn't tell me father I was going out, and if he wakes up and finds himself alone . . . besides you're going to Chapel.'

'I'm fond of you,' Arnie said, blurting the words out. 'Right fond.'

Maggie felt an embarrassment so acute it was a pricking sensation in her stomach. She had no idea what to say back. . . .

'Well, I'm fond of *you*,' she said at last, her face hot, 'and of Clara. You've been good friends to me since we came to live next door. It's been like having someone of me own.' She took a step backwards and found she was up against the hard edge of the table. She steadied herself with her hands.

'I'll have to go now, Arnie.'

Arnie was breathing heavily with his mouth slightly open. He looked so funny she wanted to laugh, even as she knew this was no laughing matter. Then he came right up to her, and putting both hands on her shoulders, brought his face close to hers. His breath had a musty smell about it, and she could see the way the hairs of his small moustache were stained yellow with the smoke from his pipe.

Maggie brought her hands up and tried to push him away, and as if he had been wanting her to do that, he slid his hands down to her waist and jerked her towards him so his body was pressed close to her own.

'Let me kiss you, Maggie! *Please*! You've got to let me!'

His mouth was over hers, open and wet, and with a strength she wouldn't have given him credit for, he held her clamped against him as his tongue probed determinedly against her clenched teeth.

'Let me, Maggie . . . oh let me, I bet you let that boy of yours do it,' he moaned, and to her horror, she felt one of his hands leave her waist and grip her breast hard. He began to rub himself up and down against her, forcing her legs apart with his knee, then the hand squeezing her left breast crept down and started to hitch up her skirt.

In a wild anger, torn between humiliation and fear, Maggie acted instinctively. Bringing her knee up to his groin as hard as she could, she raked her nails down the side of his face, causing him to stagger back.

Then to her horror, he slid down to his knees, sobbing incoherently into the folds of her long skirt.

'I'm sorry . . . oh I'm sorry, Maggie, love. I don't know what made me. . . . Oh, Maggie. She won't let me near her, and if I try anything on she tells her mother, I know she does, and they look at me as if I was dirt what the cat brought in. Oh, don't tell her, Maggie. Promise me you won't . . . promise. . . .'

Shaking with hurt pride, and almost retching with disgust, Maggie prized the clinging hands from her skirt.

'I won't tell anyone,' she promised, 'not anyone. Ever.'

Then she ran out, through the parlour, wrenching open the front door, clutching the edges of her blouse together, and praying that no one in the street was watching.

In her own house, she ran straight up the stairs to her bedroom, and sitting on the edge of her bed, rocked herself backwards and forwards, holding the tears inside her as she stared down at her bared breast and saw the imprint of Arnie's fingers on her flesh.

With a shudder she remembered the terrifying hardness pressing itself against her stomach, then she unbuttoned the torn blouse with fingers that shook, and rolled it up to hide it away at the back of a drawer.

She poured a little water out of the jug into the bowl on the marbled top of her wash-stand, and making a lather with the soft water and the cake of mottled soap, she washed the top part of her all over, pulled on a clean bust-bodice, and buttoned a fresh blouse over the top.

Then she lay back on her bed, and stared at the ceiling, trying to hold back the tears which spilled out at the corners and ran sideways down her cheeks. 'Oh, Joe,' she whispered. 'You'd kill him if you knew, wouldn't you? Oh, Joe. . . .'

Then Maggie's vivid imagination took flight as she pictured Arnie, divested of his trousers, clutching the stout reluctant Clara to him in bed, slavering over her, with the yellow-stained moustache pricking her face, one hand squeezing her enormous breasts, whilst the other . . . here Maggie gave up with a shudder. Swinging her legs from the bed she leaned close to the mirror and wiped away all trace of tears. Then with her back straight she opened the door, stepped across the tiny square landing and went into her father's room.

'Feeling better now?' she asked him.

Thomas turned a face violin-shaped with self-pity towards her, and failed to see the recent torment on his daughter's face.

With the selfishness of a man for whom the problems of others had ceased to exist, a man who would grumble that he hadn't finished his dinner if the world came to a sudden end, Thomas noticed nothing.

Indeed, if he had noticed any trace of tears on Maggie's face he would have assumed that they had been on his behalf.

She had made him go out when he did not want to go out, because what was there to go out for in these mean streets? There was no chance of a bird rising suddenly from a hedgerow, or seeing a clump of primroses, their petals wet from a shower of spring rain. Here there was nothing but grey streets, and people with faces as grey as the washing perpetually hung across the backs, flapping wetly against sooty walls.

'I've got you some tea in the oven. Would you like it, Father?'

Maggie's usually clear young voice was subdued as she stood at the foot of his bed. Just for second Thomas felt the tiniest twinge of conscience.

It must have upset her seeing him brought back like that. She was only a young lass after all. About the same age his Hannah had been that day long ago when he had seen her

52

coming towards him down a country lane, wearing a blue frock with the sleeves rolled up above rounded elbows.

'What was that you said, Hannah, love?' he said.

Maggie clenched both hands on the rail at the foot of the bed.

'Father, it's me, and you know it's me. You can't go on living in the past. Nobody can.' She shook her head in tired resignation as Thomas stared at her with the bewilderment of a little boy chastised for something he had not done.

'There's a dish of finnan-haddy in the oven, Father. I've done it in milk, just the way you like it.'

'With an egg cracked into it?' The dark eyes narrowed with greed.

'With an egg cracked into it.'

Thomas spoke with stumbling hesitation. 'Well, I suppose I'll have to eat it if you've gone to the trouble, though it will likely lie like a lump of dough on my stomach, the way I feel.'

'I'll bring it up.' Maggie turned towards the door, then as she groped for the rail bracketed to the wall at the top of the dark stairway, she heard Clara's voice calling out from downstairs.

'Yoo hoo! It's only me, love.'

Entirely without volition Maggie's hand crept to the breast that Arnie had kneaded with hard fingers not half an hour before, then running quickly down the stairs, she parted the curtain and faced Clara with her head held high.

Anger was taking the place of distress now, and if Arnie had given the game away, and if Clara had come to say anything, well she was ready for her.

But Clara's voice was as stridently normal as usual.

'You've changed your blouse, love. Does that mean you're going to Chapel tonight?'

Keeping her face averted, not quite ready to stare Clara

straight in the eye, Maggie skirted the table and taking the oven-cloth down from its hook, opened the door of the fire-oven.

'No. I just felt a bit hot in the other one. I always get hot when I'm ironing.' She took out the steaming dish of fish. If she was blushing now then it would not matter – not with the afternoon sun still streaming through the window, and the fire blazing away in the grate. The room was like a furnace anyway.

'What I've come for,' Clara said suddenly, her voice brisk and full of purpose. . . .

'Excuse me,' Maggie said, apprehension tightening itself into a knot in the pit of her stomach. 'I've got to take this upstairs to me father. He's much better, but he still looks awful. Could you pass me that plate warming in the hearth, Clara, please?'

Why should she feel guilty when she had no cause for feeling guilty? Maggie asked herself. But Clara was obviously leading up to something.

'That looks good.' Clara peered into the dish. 'You've been busy this afternoon, haven't you, love?'

Maggie held her breath, but continued with what she was doing.

'Whoops!' Clara said. 'The way you're slapping that there fish on the plate, there will be more on the floor than in the dish. Nay, what I came in for was to ask if you would like to come to Chapel tonight with me and me mother and dad? Arnie says he will listen next door, and your father only has to knock on the wall if he wants owt.' She sniffed and jerked her head towards the dividing wall. 'He's in one of his moods, Arnie is. Tripped over a loose edging stone round that flamin' garden of his and scratched his face on his flamin' rose bush. Serve him right if you ask me for messing about with them of a Sunday.'

Maggie pulled open the knife drawer set into the front of the table.

'Yes, serve him right,' she smiled, weak with relief. 'And

yes, I think I will come with you to Chapel. It'll get me out of the house for a bit.'

'Then you can come with us to the prayer meeting after,' Clara said over a plump disappearing shoulder. 'It's a Mrs Carmichael what lives with her son up Hodder Street. She's bad with her legs and her chest, and can't get to Chapel. They say she served her time to millinery in the Hat Market.'

'Then I'd best put me new hat on,' Maggie said, with a flash of her usual smile. 'We don't want her thinking we don't know what's what down Foundry Street, do we?'

Kit Carmichael reminded Maggie of an elephant. Big and soft and grey-suited, the skin of his neck hung in flabby folds over his high starched collar, and he shook hands with her in the flabby gesture of an extended waving trunk.

'It's good of you to come, Miss Craig,' he told her in a strangely high-pitched voice, a light voice at variance with his size. 'Mother will be right glad to see a fresh face.' He inclined his big head in a conspiratorial whisper. 'She's never had her foot over the doorstep for the past year. This half-hour is the highlight of her week.'

He led the way through the front parlour, its glory reflected in a large round wooden-framed mirror tilted slightly forward from the wall above the high mantelpiece. Like every front room in the street, it smelt of cold soot and years of being unused, and the delft rail was lined with blue china plates.

'This is Miss Craig, Mother,' he said, leading them into the back room. 'She lives next door to Mrs Preston. You know Mr and Mrs Hobkirk, Mrs Preston's mother and father, don't you?'

The woman sitting up in bed was as small and intense looking as her son was large and mild of manner. She threw

55

Maggie a darting glance from beneath well defined dark eyebrows.

'I thought Mr and Mrs Hobkirk lived next door to Mrs Preston. Nobody told me they'd flitted.'

Her voice was deep and throaty, and at least an octave lower than her son's. Maggie averted her eyes from the invalid's flourishing moustache.

'No, Mother. They haven't moved. Miss Craig lives the *other side* of Mrs Preston, dear.'

Mr Marsden, the minister, cleared his throat, and in a determined voice, because he had four other visits to make, said:

'Let us pray.'

The little group round the bed lowered their heads obediently, and folded their hands together.

From beneath downcast eyelashes Maggie studied them with interest.

The Reverend Marsden and his wife, small, grey-haired, almost a mirror image of each other, devout and pious as befitted their standing in the Chapel community. Clara's parents, Mr and Mrs Hobkirk, eyes squeezed so tightly together with heavenly fervour they appeared to be suffering the most exquisite torture. Mr Elphick, the tiny dwarf man who pumped air into the newly installed organ behind the choir stalls, and Miss Birtwistle, crossed in love, so it was rumoured. Clara, with her clasped hands almost hidden beneath the shelf of her matronly bosom.

And Mrs Carmichael's large son, Kit.

Studying him carefully, Maggie decided that he was 'nice'. In spite of the fact that only a little while before she had decided that all men apart from Joe were less than the beast of the field, she knew, without being told, that Kit Carmichael was different. A mother's boy, no doubt about that. Head on one side, and tongue protruding slightly, Maggie set about calculating his possible age – difficult because of his bulk – but around thirty-five she thought. Yes that would be about right.

Maggie blushed and lowered her head as he opened his eyes and stared straight at her, but not before she had seen the kindly gleam of amusement in his eyes.

Yes, she wasn't mistaken. He *was* nice. . . . Not as nice as Joe, but *nice*. . . .

The Reverend Marsden threw his head back so that his face was parallel to the ceiling.

'Save this our sister from the ravages of the flesh,' he intoned. 'Lift her up so that she shall see Thy face and know that Thou art beside her. Comfort her in the dark watches of the night, and sustain her in her cruel affliction, until the day she comes into her glory, when she shall know pain no more.'

'Amen.'

'Amen,' Maggie said, stealing a glance at the small woman with the dark gypsy colouring, her high-necked nightgown decently covered by a high-necked bedjacket, topped with a three-cornered shawl.

Then as if to justify the prayers on her behalf, Mrs Carmichael began to cough, a great bark of a cough, so shattering to her thin frame that her face turned purple, and the deep-set eyes bulged forth. Maggie started forward with outstretched hands as she flung herself backwards on her pillows, tiny hands clutching the air as if she clawed for breath.

But Kit was there before her, taking his mother's scrabbling hands into his own, talking softly to her, calming her, smoothing the black wiry hair back from her forehead.

'You're all right, Mother,' he told her firmly. 'I'm here, and there's nothing to be afraid of. These are your friends come to pray for you. . . .'

Mrs Carmichael stopped coughing with dramatic suddenness. Her contorted features relaxed, and the Reverend Marsden resumed his praying.

'Hear our prayer, oh Lord,' he commanded.

'And let our cry come unto thee,' answered the Hobkirks, whilst Kit Carmichael patted his mother's face with

57

one hand, and plumped up her high-piled pillows with the other.

'Amen,' said Miss Birtwistle with such deep feeling that Maggie had to swallow hard to rid herself of the giggle rising up in her throat.

'No, you're not a nice person, Maggie Craig,' she told herself for the second time that day, as in the wrong key, and with Mr Hobkirk raising his tenor voice in a shaky descant, the short service was ended by the singing of the twenty-third Psalm.

It was no good. More than one person singing without accompaniment always made her want to laugh. She stared fixedly at the wall, not risking a glance either to the right or the left as she joined in the singing.

What was she doing in that overheated room anyway? Standing there with her best Sunday hat on round a complete stranger's bed. A woman who in spite of her recent coughing fit was now singing in a husky baritone?

Mrs Carmichael and her father. Trying it on the both of them. Touting for sympathy, even though some, she supposed, would call it a cry for help. Maggie stood on one foot then eased herself on to the other. There was tomorrow's dinner to prepare, and her father to make comfortable, and Arnie to avoid . . . she stole a sideways glance at Clara singing away at the top of her voice.

Arnie had made her feel *diminished*, yes that was the word, he had spoilt an easy undemanding friendship, and if he ever tried anything like that again . . .

Maggie's expression grew so fierce that Kit Carmichael, watching her, decided that she was making up her mind never to come again. He sighed, head bowed as the Reverend Marsden pronounced the Blessing. . . .

'Seems funny,' Maggie told Clara, as they hurried back down the street, with Mr and Mrs Hobkirk following at a more leisurely pace. 'Him seeing to his mother, and me seeing to me father.' She laughed. 'She came round from her coughing fit almost as quick as me father came round

58

from his fainting do.' She steadied her hat with one hand as a sudden gust of wind threatened to blow it away. 'Did you notice how *gentle* he was, Clara? More like a woman than a man. You'd never expect such a big man to have such a high voice, would you?'

'They say he does *everything* for her,' Clara said darkly. 'It seems all wrong to me somehow to think of a man seeing to his mother. I mean she is a woman after all.' She sniffed. 'Arnie's never seen me properly undressed, but they say Kit Carmichael washes his mother down twice a week.'

'Can't she get out of bed at all?'

'On her good days she sits out in a chair. Her son does all the housework, and the cooking and what not, as well as working as a day servant to an old man in a house up North Park Road. I've heard the old man thinks the world of him, and won't let a woman come near him, not for love nor money.'

'He's a good man,' Maggie said, her interest in Kit Carmichael completely evaporated. They turned into the row of shops leading to Foundry Street. 'But not my cup of tea somehow.'

'They say he doesn't bother with girls, and never has,' Clara volunteered, wondering if Maggie would understand what she only vaguely understood herself, but Maggie was walking quickly now, twitching her long skirt up as they crossed an uneven place in the road.

Her conscience was troubling her as she told herself her father ought not to have been left alone for so long, even though she had left him comfortable in bed, with a warm fish tea settling in his stomach.

He hated her going out at the weekends, even though she had told him all about Joe, about how nice he was and how she was bringing him to tea one day.

'I'm on my own so much during the week,' he'd say.

'Steady on, love. Where's the fire?'

Clara was panting along at her side, but Maggie walked even more quickly. She ought not to have left him, but when she got in she would make him laugh, describing the prayer meeting to him. As deeply religious as he was – as he *used* to be – Maggie corrected herself, her father could always find the over-sanctimonious amusing.

'I'm sure God Himself has a good laugh sometimes,' he'd once said.

Clara said goodnight to her and pushed open the door of number four.

'That you?' Arnie called, as she stopped to unpin her wide hat and tidy it away neatly in the sideboard cupboard.

Then as Arnie turned a vacant face towards her, and as Clara opened her mouth to ask him what he thought he was doing sitting there and watching the fire go out, through the thin walls dividing the house from number two, they heard the scream.

'It's Maggie!' Arnie said, and moving more quickly than Clara had ever seen him move before, he started for the door.

Maggie kept her best coat and hat upstairs in the walnut cupboard in her room, so she went up just as she was, deciding against calling out in case her father was asleep. Sleep was all he seemed to want to do these days, she told herself as she ran lightly up the uncarpeted stairs. Sleep and eat, and grumble in a voice which had no light or shade. Almost like the voice of a deaf-mute, she told herself.

The door of his room was closed, properly closed, not just left ajar as it normally was. Maggie frowned, feeling a small trickle of fear in her stomach as she turned the knob, pushed at the door, and felt something holding it from the inside.

'Father? Let me in! It's me, Maggie,' she added absurdly, heaving and straining at the door, then with heart pounding, putting her shoulder against it, leaning on it till it gave so suddenly she almost fell inside.

For a moment she lost the power to move, to make a

sound, to even breathe as she looked on what was left of Thomas Craig. For a moment it seemed as if the man lying on the floor by the side of his bed had two mouths. Both of them spilling blood and grinning at her.

So great was her shock that at first it did not register what had happened. Blood was everywhere, staining the cotton bedspread and spreading in a sticky shiny pool by her father's head, down on the cold linoleum.

Then she saw the open razor by one outstretched hand, and knew that he had slit his throat, slashing it from ear to ear.

She knelt down beside him, and screamed. And screamed. . . .

For just that one night, and then only because the shock seemed to have driven her willpower away, Maggie slept next door in Clara's spare room. If it would not have shocked people and been an insult to her father's memory, Maggie would have gone straight back to the mill.

Back in the house she made herself walk upstairs. She was going to sleep alone that night, no matter what anyone said. So she forced herself to open the door of Thomas's room, to see for herself that there was nothing to be afraid of.

Immediately her glance went towards the empty bed, but she walked over to the bedside table, and there was her father's leather-bound copy of Wordsworth, a book he had once carried around with him on his country walks as if it were his second skin.

Maggie picked it up and held it against her cheek for a moment, feeling the rush of tears to her eyes. A slip of paper, concealed in the leaves, fell to the floor, and as she picked it up she saw he had written a sentence in his neat school-master's print:

'A power is gone, which *nothing* can restore.'

The word 'nothing' was underlined, then underlined again, as if he was trying to tell her something.

She backed towards the door, trying not to see the stain on the mattress, stripped by Clara and her mother the night before. Downstairs the fire was giving off little sluggish puffs of smoke, as if it needed and missed Thomas's constant attention with the brass-handled poker. As she knelt down to see to it, Maggie's foot caught in the rocker of his chair and set it into silent motion.

'Oh, Father,' she sobbed, catching the chair and holding it still. 'You would not even *try* to let me make you happy. And now you'll never see Joe, and I wanted you to like him. I thought he might have made you laugh. . . .'

'Our father started to die the very day our mother left us,' she wrote to her brothers, sitting at the table, with a new Waverley nib in her pen. Then she pushed the writing pad to one side and covered her face with her hands. . . .

And in the days that followed, she saw to the things that had to be seen to. She failed to convince herself that what her father had done was a sin in the eyes of the Lord, and she went to his funeral against all advice, holding on to her hat in a corner of the windswept cemetery, with Clara lending a solid arm of support.

When Doctor Bates came over to see her, a little older and a lot more stooped, but with the nose still in glorious bloom, she listened to him gravely.

'You have no cause to feel remorse,' he said, as everyone else had said. 'Your father had a mental condition that meant he could not even try to overcome his depression.'

Maggie nodded.

'But on the day he died he had collapsed in the street, Doctor, and I mentioned the Workhouse to make him come to.'

'And I bet as soon as you said that, he *did* come to?'

'But I ought not to have said it.'

Her head drooped, then she lifted her eyes and gave him her straight and candid gaze.

'I looked after me father, Doctor Bates, and I . . .' She hesitated, finding it impossible to talk openly about love to

62

the nose. 'I was right fond of him, but till I die I'll wish I'd made more fuss of him when he was brought in from the street. I knew he was trying it on to force me to stop talking about fresh air.' Just for a moment her voice wavered on the verge of lost control. 'He said he *hated* fresh air! Me father, who knew the call of every birdsong.' She blinked the unshed tears rapidly away.

'He wanted sympathy. . . .' She spread her hands wide. 'Oh, Doctor Bates, me father wanted sympathy every day; he wanted to talk every day about how unfair it was me mother dying. And there were some days when I just hadn't any more sympathy to give.'

The doctor moved his big head up and down in a motion that said he had heard it all before.

'Maggie, love. Listen to me. If you had talked to as many bereaved folks as I, then you would believe me when I tell you that we always, yes *always*, wish we had said this, or not done that.' He wound his heavy gold watch-chain round his fingers. 'What we have to think about is your future. . . .'

He looked genuinely worried, so worried that Maggie put out a hand and touched his arm.

'I can take care of myself, Doctor. As long as I keep in work, my wages cover the rent of this house and give me enough to eat. I've got three looms now.' She smiled to cheer the doctor up. 'And I could always take in a lodger or two. Arnie Preston next door works at the bottle factory, and he says there's always Irishmen looking for a good place to live.'

It was terrible, the doctor told his wife that evening, terrible seeing that young girl, pink-cheeked and dry-eyed, calmly telling him that she would manage.

'Talking about having Irish navvies living in, and her no more than seventeen and as bonny as a morning in spring. I remember her mother as a bonny woman, but young

Maggie Craig is a real beauty, and as innocent as a new-born babe. I'd stake my life on that.'

His wife shook her grey head. 'It's to be hoped she doesn't take up with the wrong one now that she is entirely alone. That girl has got to find love and affection from somewhere, it stands to reason.'

Doctor Bates fingered his watch-chain.

'There was a whisper about a boy at the mill, but I don't think there can be anything in it. Maggie's only a child.'

'That's something she has never had a chance to be,' Mrs Bates said sadly.

Joe Barton walked down Foundry Street and knocked at Maggie's door the day after the funeral.

When he saw her white face and the way her eyes filled with tears when she saw him standing there, he walked straight in, kicked the door closed behind him, and took her into his arms.

It was the first time they had been alone, in a house, by a leaping fire; the first time he had seen Maggie cry, and the sight of her tears moved him so deeply that he drew her down beside him on the sofa, tangling his fingers in the soft weight of her hair, loosening it from its little high-pinned bun so that it fell clean and sweet smelling round her face.

'I love you,' he whispered, almost in tears himself. 'I love you . . . love you . . . love you.' Then to try to still the trembling of his own body, he held her closer, listened as she told him in jerky halting sentences how it had been.

'There was blood everywhere,' she sobbed, and Joe covered her mouth with his own, kissing the words away.

When they slid down on to the rug together, Maggie's arms were round his neck, and as their bodies fitted closely together as they lay side by side, Joe told her he was going away.

'Tonight,' he whispered, then as her arms clutched him tighter he told her why.

'Belle had to have dresses and aprons and caps for her new job, and I'd earned a bit more by staying on late at the mill, you know that.' He lifted his head and looked down at Maggie's flushed and tear-stained face. 'I hid it away in a place where I thought me mam couldn't find it. But she'd had it, Maggie. She'd got her thieving hands on it, and spent the lot on drink. It was for Belle, and she still took it, knowing.'

'Oh, Joe. . . .'

Maggie raised a hand and stroked the thin and earnest face bending over her. 'Poor, poor Belle. What will she do? She was looking forward to that living-in job so much. What will she do now?'

Joe grinned. 'Oh, Belle got her things all right, love. Me mam's big man stopped the night and left his money in his back trouser pocket, so I took it and gave it to Belle, and now she's safe, and I'm off, because when that loud-mouthed sod finds out he'll have the police on me. As sure as my name's Joe Barton he'll have me put away.'

They kissed again, a slow lingering kiss, and when Maggie spoke her voice was slow and dreamy as though what she was saying bore no relation to the meaning of the words.

'Where will you go, Joe? I can't bear it if you go away. . . .'

Joe was going away and she didn't want to believe it. He was kissing her and swearing he would come back, that he would marry her when he had a decent job.

'And we'll live in a house like this,' he was saying.

He was whispering into her cheek and turning her mouth into his, and his teeth were hard against her lips so that she opened her mouth, and his hands were moving gently over her.

Not like Arnie's, nothing like Arnie's. Joe was moving with a fierce protective urgency, lifting her clothes, murmuring to her, broken words, moaning sighing whispers of love.

There was one sharp swift pain, when for a moment, she

65

saw her father's dead face and cried out, then it was all rushing comfort, soothing, straining movements of love.

'Maggie . . . Maggie. . . .'

Joe's voice lingered in her ears, even long after it was over and he had gone, leaving her alone in the empty house with what she was sure was her father's sad little ghost waiting for her at the top of the stairs.

3

Kit Carmichael read the short piece in the *Weekly Times*. It was flanked on one side by a full column advertisement of Carter's Little Liver Pills, and on the other side by a report of a meeting at the Teetotal Mission.

'You remember Miss Craig coming to our prayer meeting, don't you, Mother?'

Mrs Carmichael's small black eyes filled with dislike.

'Navy blue hat with dog daisies on it. Aye I remember her.'

Kit leaned over the bed rail and read the piece aloud in his high-pitched voice, then tapped the paper with a podgy forefinger.

'It must have happened the very night she came here. Perhaps at the very time she was joined with us in prayer.' He smoothed back his tightly curled hair. 'I think it would be the right thing for me to call and express our sympathy, Mother.'

'They wouldn't be able to take his coffin into the Chapel, not with him having done away with himself.' Mrs Carmichael spoke with some satisfaction.

'He was *insane*, Mother. He wouldn't be responsible for his actions.'

'They always say that.'

Kit saw the way her right hand crept to her throat, but before she could begin to cough, he was beside her, holding on to her hands and talking quickly.

'Mother. Miss Craig will be all alone now. I believe she has looked after her father ever since she was a tiny girl.

67

Now surely there's no harm in me going to see her and telling her how sorry I am? How sorry we both are?' He stroked her face. 'You won't be by yourself because it's the Sewing Ladies' Class.' He gave her chin a little tweak. 'See, there's one of them at the door now. I'll let her in on my way out.'

All the way down the street, he muttered to himself, as he had been muttering to himself for many years now. . . .

It was ridiculous that a grown man of thirty-five should have to be beholden to his mother for his every movement. He had started all wrong when his father went off to live in Liverpool with that soprano he'd met in the town's Operatic Society during the rehearsals of one of Messrs Gilbert and Sullivan's pieces. He hoped she had not seen that the same company were doing *Sorcerer* at the Theatre Royal that very week. It would bring it all back to her. And every time it was brought back to her, she had an attack.

Kit stepped off the kerb without seeing it, and twisted over on his ankle. He was too soft, that was his trouble; too inclined to let his sympathy run away with him.

Turning into Foundry Street, he walked with his short tripping steps down to the house at the bottom. A curtain twitched as he went past a house, and for a moment he wondered if he had perhaps been a bit hasty in coming to call on Miss Craig.

Not for a moment would he dream of besmirching her reputation. But it was too late to turn back now. . . .

When Maggie opened the door to him, dressed from chin to ankles in mourning black, her face a pale oval above the frilled neck-line of her blouse, Kit hardly recognized her as the girl with the twinkling eyes who had stood round his mother's bed so short a time ago.

Quite without volition, his innate kindness overcoming his shyness, he held out both his hands.

'You poor little thing,' he said. 'You poor poor little girl.'

68

'You'd better come in, Mr Carmichael,' Maggie said, and stood aside to let him pass.

Kit Carmichael was well aware that there were those who found him an object of amusement, considered him to be a mother's boy, but he did not care.

His not caring was in no way derived from apathy, but rather from the fact that his complete lack of conceit made the sly jibes at his lack of masculinity of no importance whatsoever.

'Our Kit hasn't got a mean bone in his body,' his mother was fond of boasting, and she spoke the truth. Kit poured affection and generosity on to everyone he met, so that even those who laughed behind their hands at his high squeak of a voice and his girlish complexion, laughed with tolerance rather than with spite.

'Has your Kit never walked out with a young lady?'

Mrs Earnshaw lived next door, and often came in to keep his mother company, and her voice carried through into the front parlour where Kit was taking the willow pattern plates down from the rack and giving them a bit of a dust.

He stiffened, the duster held still in his hands.

'As a matter of fact, Mrs Earnshaw, he's got a lady friend coming for her tea on Saturday. Miss Craig from the Chapel. Lives by herself since her father came to a sad end.'

'Not the Mr Craig what . . .?'

Kit saw in his imagination the first finger of Mrs Earnshaw's hand drawn across her turkey throat in a revealing gesture.

'Aye, that one.'

'Serious then, are they?'

Not wanting to hear any more, Kit walked over to the dividing door and closed it none too gently.

It wasn't that he was annoyed at his mother discussing him like that with the neighbours, he was used to that, but he had to smile the way she had made out it had been her idea about Maggie coming to tea. Kit put a plate back and took down the one next to it. It was surprising the dirt on these plates, especially as there had not been a fire in the parlour grate since last Christmas. . . .

It had taken him almost two months to get his mother to agree to meet Maggie again. Two whole months, two attacks, and countless arguments about the foolishness of giving a 'girl like that' ideas.

'I knew the minute I set eyes on her what she was after.'

'Now, Mother, don't talk daft. I bet you can't even remember what she looks like.'

'Cheeky face and a hat with too much trimming on it.'

It was no good. He would never get his mother to think any different. Kit breathed on a plate and rubbed it hard, smiling with tolerance. You could never blame his mother for being afraid he might leave her one day. Not after what his father had done to her.

Kit sat down for a minute, taking his weight off feet too small for his bulk. Then he leaned his curly head back against the antimacassar, and closed his eyes.

There had been a girl once. He shuddered with the remembering of it.

He would be perhaps eighteen, nineteen, something like that. He had gone with a lad called Harry Burton to the Theatre Royal to see Billy Thomson's Concert Party.

He would never have gone if Harry had not taunted him about being tied to his mother's apron strings, backed up by the other lads from down the street.

'Go on, Kit. Be a devil.'

'Tell her you're going to the Mission to sign the bloody pledge.'

They were jeering at him, caps pulled down over laughing faces, and so he had gone with Harry Burton, a grinning Harry with larded-down sideboards gleaming, and his Prince Albert moustache combed into neatness.

And the Concert Party had been enjoyable, and the

inside of the theatre not quite the den of vice his mother had made it out to be. The second half was in the form of a Nigger Minstrel Show, with the men's faces blacked, and Bones asking Sambo:

'Who was that lady ah seen you walkin' with las' night?'

And Harry had loudly joined in the reply, much to Kit's embarrassment:

'That was no lady. That's ma wife.'

Then at the end Harry had actually put three fingers in his mouth and whistled his satisfaction.

'I'd have a pennorth of hot potatoes if I wasn't dressed up like a bloody toff,' he said as they walked back along the Boulevard. 'Just look at that poor little donkey. It's fast asleep between the shafts, and don't look round,' he continued in exactly the same tone of voice, 'but there's two girls I know behind us. Want an introduction, Kit?'

His eyes were sly, and as they stopped beside the cart, he turned round, pretended to be overcome with surprise, beamed all over his whiskered face, and made the introductions with great aplomb.

'Agnes. Florrie. This is Kit, a mate of mine, and if you smile at him nicely he'll buy you a paper of spuds. Won't you, Kit?'

Kit winced as he remembered the way they had paired off. Harry with Agnes, and Florrie taking his arm and swaying along beside him, teetering on the tiny heels of her high-buttoned boots.

At first they kept more or less together, then as they turned off the main street down an alleyway leading to the canal, Harry, with his arm round Agnes's waist, dropped behind.

'We'd better wait for them, I think,' Kit said.

Florrie laughed, taking his arm. 'Don't be daft. They'll be glad to be shot of us.'

Kit persisted. 'What have they gone round that corner for? Does your friend live down there?'

Florrie pressed his arm into her side, leaning so close that he caught a whiff of strong scent mixed with sweat. She grinned up at him showing small uneven teeth.

'You are a caution, honest you are. I've never met a lad like you before. Why have I never seen you before? I know most of Harry's mates, but I don't know you.'

Kit tried to pull his arm away, but realized the only way he could do that would be to wrench it from her grasp, and he could not face the indignity of that. He was sweating slightly, and ran his free hand round his collar.

'I'll see you home, Florrie, then I must leave you.' He said her name with difficulty, stuttering a little. 'I told my mother I was going . . . well, I told her I was going somewhere else than where she thinks I've been. She gets herself worked up if I don't come home when she expects me to.'

At this Florrie did exactly what he had been praying she would do. She moved away from him, swinging round to face him.

'Your *mother*? Did you say your mother?'

Utterly without guile, more naive than a cosseted girl of seven, Kit explained with serious politeness that his mother was all alone; that she was not at all well. And that he normally stayed in with her of an evening because she had been on her own all day.

'She would be really upset if she found out that I had been to the theatre.' He wrinkled his forehead earnestly as he tried to explain. 'My father used to go to places like that, and it led him into bad ways, so she's a bit biased, you see.'

Florrie stared at him as if she could not believe he was quite real, her head on one side, and a tip of pink tongue protruding between her lips.

'How old are you, Kit?'

'Nearly nineteen.'

'Where do you work?'

'For a man up North Park Road. I keep house for him, but only on a daytime basis.'

'So you can be with your mam at nights?'

'Yes.'

'And you always tell her where you are going when you go out?'

'I've told you, she gets worked up when she doesn't know where I am. There's only me can quieten her down.'

'Well, stone the flamin' crows. . . .'

Florrie was walking towards him now, and the only way he could try to avoid her bumping into him was to step backwards. And behind him was a wall, a dirty wall that would make marks on his jacket if he leant against it.

She came forward relentlessly, and Kit forgot about getting marks on his checked jacket, his neatly patterned, nipped in at the waist jacket, as her arms slid round his neck.

'How many girls have you been out with, Kit?'

He clamped his mouth tight shut, waves of horror washing over him and making him feel sick.

'How many girls have you kissed, Kit?'

The smell of her was in his nostrils, turning his stomach right over as Florrie peered up into his face, laughing at him with her mouth wide open, showing her tongue.

'I don't think you know nowt about owt, do you, Kit what's your name? I think you're still a great big baby.'

Then, before he could stop her, she had clamped her mouth over his own, and he could taste her spit, and feel the whole length of her body pressed up against his own. She was wriggling like a little eel, and suddenly Kit forgot to be polite. Forgot that he was 'Sonny' Carmichael, the apple of his mother's eye, a boy who never forgot his manners, especially when there were ladies present.

'You dirty little . . . you dirty little *bitch*,' he shouted, using a word he had never used before. Then gripping her by the arms he thrust her from him so violently that she almost fell.

Her hat, a silly flat purple straw, one his mother would not have given house-room to, came off in the struggle, and in the frenzy of his humiliation Kit kicked it away from him, then as she bent to pick it up he pushed her so hard that she fell sprawling on the greasy cobbles with her hair coming down.

Kit moved his head from side to side on the antimacassar as he remembered the way he had waited for her to get up without stretching out a hand to help.

'You great soft 'aporth!' she had shouted, actually dancing up and down with rage. 'Go on. Run home and tell your mam. Most likely she'll kiss you better, and you'll like that, won't you, you great sissy!'

Mrs Earnshaw opened the door and stood there, pulling her shawl into position round her shoulders, and watching him with her foxy pointed face.

'Your mother's waiting for you, Kit,' she said, and it seemed to him that her eyes were sly.

Sly in exactly the same way Florrie's eyes had been.

4

When Maggie missed the first month she was not unduly worried. There could be many reasons why nothing had come on the day it should. She told herself the shock of finding her father lying there, his white hair all matted with blood, could be the cause, or it could even be she was inwardly horrified at what had happened between her and Joe lying by the fire.

The more she went over that in her mind the more impossible it seemed to be. She wasn't like that. She wasn't like some of the girls at the mill who talked about what they did with boys. She had more sense.

And more than once she had suspected that the girl weavers were just showing off, because look what happened when Elsie Arkwright suddenly went to live with her auntie down in Sussex. Everybody had been shocked out of their minds. They had talked about it for days in whispering and horrified disbelief.

'I have this friend,' Maggie told Essie Platt, a big girl with her hair fluffed up into a frizz at the front. 'She's a bit scared she might be going to have a baby.' Then she hung her head and felt the blush creep up from her throat, making her eyes water. 'But she . . . it was only the once.'

Essie nodded firmly. 'Then it's all right. Nothing can happen the first time, especially if she's never been with anyone before.'

'Oh, she hasn't!' Maggie was shocked at the idea. 'She's not like that. It was . . . this friend says it was the first time in her whole life.'

'Then tell her to stop worrying.' Essie smiled a sly smile. 'Worry's the worst thing out for upsetting the system.'

Maggie saw the way that from that day onwards Essie's circle of friends eyed her up and down then looked quickly away. For another few weeks she deliberately lulled herself into a sense of false security, repeating to herself what Essie had said during the times when the worry almost paralysed her with its implications.

Every day she looked for a letter from Joe, telling herself that maybe he could not write well enough to compose a letter.

'I was off school more than what I was there,' he'd said.

She remembered Thomas saying that the proportion of children leaving school unable to read or write was a disgrace.

'Half-timers in the main. Children who somehow, through no fault of their own, get left behind in a big class of brighter pupils. Children who move from one place to another and slip through the educational net somehow.'

'We're always doing moonlight flits,' Joe had grinned. 'Once we escaped through a top window and over the roofs.'

Maggie, oblivious to the deafening clatter of the weaving shed machinery, bit her lip and nodded. Yes, that would be it. Joe was proud, above all else he was proud. He would never have admitted that he could not write. Somehow he would have covered up. Her father had explained that too:

'They master the ability to print their own name and that's all.'

Then with a sinking of her heart Maggie remembered Alice Barton taking the slip of paper down from the mantelpiece and thrusting it in front of her face. All written in Joe's neat handwriting . . . Rent, tea, candles, tins of milk.

That night she took down one of her father's books from the shelf in his room, running her fingers over the leather binding. Always, even towards the end, Thomas had tried to find solace in poetry, but when she tried to read the print blurred before her eyes.

'Oh, God,' she prayed, down on her knees, holding the book close to her chest. 'Don't let it be true. Please don't let it be true. If it is I don't know what I'll do. I keep thinking about what I *could* do, and there's nothing to show, nothing wrong with me really but the worry going round and round in me head till it feels it might burst open. And Kit Carmichael's asked me to tea, and oh God I have no interest in going anywhere or doing anything. I can't seem to talk to anyone with this great black cloud on me. An' I know that worrying like this is the very worst thing, so just for a week I'll stop fretting to give it a chance. I'll put my trust in Thee,' she ended. 'For Jesus Christ's sake, amen.'

'If Kit Carmichael has asked you there for your tea, then he's serious. He hasn't bothered with girls before, you know, love.'

Clara's eyes were sly. 'You keep quiet, I notice. Not been upsetting you has he, love, this Kit Carmichael?'

'He's kind,' Maggie said, moving the lamp so that it shone directly on to the sewing in her lap. 'I can't ever remember meeting anyone so kind. I think if I asked him for the moon he'd climb up and get it down '

'His mother looks like something what's dropped off a flitting.'

Maggie lowered her head over the blouse she was feather-stitching without smiling, and Clara sat forward.

'You feel all right, don't you, love? You've been acting different lately. Are you sweet on him?'

Maggie wished Clara would just get up and go. She could not talk naturally, it was no good. Oh, dear God. . . . Apart from the one thing there were no signs. No being sick in the mornings, nothing. Oh if only Clara would go back next door. . . . She was better left alone, like they were

77

leaving her alone at the mill now. She merely stood at her looms, willed herself into a state of numbness, even as her fingers busied themselves with the cotton threads and the intricate machinery. She ran home when the hooter went and half the time did not even bother to make herself any tea. She made herself go to Chapel because there in God's house she could pray to Him with all her heart and mind not to let it be true. She was anaemic, she was imagining the worst, and one day, perhaps tomorrow, it would come right and this terrible anguish would all be over.

'*Are* you sweet on Kit Carmichael, love? He walked you home from Chapel again, didn't he?'

Maggie pricked her finger and sucked at it furiously.

'If you don't mind, Clara, I think I'll go upstairs and have a bit of a lie down. I keep having these headaches coming on.'

'Doctor Williams's pink pills,' Clara said at once, but getting up and going just the same.

The room where the sick woman lay was smaller than Maggie remembered; smaller and more oppressive, with the inevitable coal fire burning high in the grate.

'Do I look all right?' she had asked Kit nervously when he called for her, and he had nodded without really looking at her, muttering that they must hurry.

'Mother is having one of her off days,' he explained. 'I ought not to have left her alone, but I knew you would be waiting for me.'

Maggie sighed. She had willed herself to make the effort, even told herself that getting out a bit might take the worry off for a while, but it was still there, tightening her chest, smudging dark shadows underneath her eyes, and pinching her face into lines.

'It might be better if we waited for another time then?'

Kit licked his lips. 'No. She says she wants you to come. She's like that, is Mother. One minute you would think she was dying, but she never gives in. I could hear her panting for breath when I was upstairs getting ready.'

And hating me with every panting breath, Maggie thought, as after a silent walk through the streets, silent because she was feeling the worry starting up again, and because Kit was urging her on so quickly there would not have been breath to talk anyway.

'We're here, Mother!' he called out the minute the door was open, and for the second time Maggie stood to attention at the foot of Mrs Carmichael's bed.

The old woman lay, propped high with pillows, dark eyes sending out shafts of stabbing dislike, busy fingers smoothing and pleating the turned-down sheet.

'I'll take your hat and coat,' Kit told her, and as Maggie obediently unpinned her hat, divested now of its daisies, and unbuttoned the long coat, she was conscious of the unwinking stare from the bed.

'Take them upstairs, Kit. I don't like the front room being untidy. Then stop up in your room for a bit. I want to have a few words with Miss Craig on my own.'

He hesitated, but only for a moment, then with an apologetic glance at Maggie, he did exactly as he was told.

Mrs Carmichael pointed to a chair. 'Sit down, Miss Craig.'

Her beady eyes were on Maggie's blouse, and perching on the very edge of the chair Maggie wondered for a wild moment if she had guessed something was wrong and was looking to see if her shape was any different.

She told herself not to be so silly and glanced surreptitiously round the room when Mrs Carmichael closed her eyes.

Hardly a touch of colour brightened the drabness of the heavy, suffocating furnishings. Brown fringed mantel-border, maroon bobbled tablecloth, oilcloth the colour of beef tea, covered with two rag rugs pegged from pieces of black cloth. Sepia pictures framed in black, two ebonized vases each corner of the mantelpiece, and a marbled clock dead centre. Flat iron resting on the range and a dark mahogany chest of drawers covered with a brown runner, and overall the powerful smell of camphor.

Maggie noticed a tray set on top of the chest, with three flowered cups and saucers, a milk jug covered with a net weighted down with beads, and a plate covered with a tea cloth.

Everywhere signs of a woman's touch, and yet she realized that the thin spare little woman in the bed had had no part in it. Her heart warmed to the gentle man waiting upstairs.

The minutes grew and lengthened.

Mrs Carmichael took note of the way this girl sat with her back ramrod straight and her head held high. The black eyes narrowed into calculating slits. No milk-pobs mill girl this. Not one she could send packing with a flea in her ear.

A beauty too, with a complexion that looked as if her cheeks had been newly scrubbed, and heavily fringed eyes that met hers with unwavering frankness. Just for a fleeting moment the old woman was back in time, seeing herself as she had once been. A young woman, with cloudy dark hair, breasts high and proud. Entirely without volition she put a claw-like hand over her own wasted, stringy breasts, and felt a stab of jealousy so acute it felt as if a dagger had been thrust into her chest.

'Kit tells me you live on your own,' she said suddenly in a hoarse growl of a voice, startling Maggie into a nervous betrayal of her feelings by the quivering of her long eyelashes.

'Yes, that's right, Mrs Carmichael.'

The dagger in her chest gave an extra twist as the old woman pushed herself higher on her pillows. This girl had a refinement in her speech that had never been learnt down Foundry Street. The flat vowels were there all right, but there was breeding there somewhere, she would swear to it.

'How old did you say you were?'

'Just seventeen, Mrs Carmichael.'

So this young madam thought she was going to give as good as she got, did she? Well, she would see about that.

'Have you nobody of your own? No family?'

'Two brothers. Twins. They joined the army years ago. I don't hear from them often.'

Mrs Carmichael digested this for a moment, then she pulled at the high neck-frill of her calico nightdress before saying:

'And your father cut his own throat?'

Maggie's head drooped. 'Yes, that's right.'

'What drove him to that, do you suppose?'

'Nothing *drove* him to it, Mrs Carmichael. He was ill. He had been ill ever since my mother died of the diphtheria years ago. He wasn't himself when he did it.'

'Not himself? Do you mean he was mental?'

Maggie's eyes met her own with a directness that would have made a lesser woman flinch, but the old woman was fighting for what she considered to be her very existence, and only the constant pleating and re-pleating of the turned-down sheet betrayed her agitation.

'My father had a stroke, then he developed an illness of the nerves that affected his brain. The doctor explained it to me. It was a kind of depression he had no control over.'

'Doctors know nothing.'

'No, Mrs Carmichael.'

This was getting them nowhere fast, and any minute Kit would be coming back down the stairs, and brewing the tea, and passing round the potted-meat sandwiches he'd taken such a time over, slicing off the crusts and cutting them into triangles, just as if the Queen herself was coming for her tea.

'And you think you're going to get my son, do you, Miss Craig?'

Maggie drew in a sharp breath.

'I don't think nothing of the sort, Mrs Carmichael. But

81

Kit is a good and kind man. I've never met a kinder man in the whole of my life. You must feel very lucky to have a son like that.'

With an abruptness that brought Maggie swiftly to her feet, the old woman slumped back on to her pillows, her eyes wide open, her fingers clutching the air as she gasped for breath. It was like the time of the prayer meeting, but worse. There was a loud rasping sound as Mrs Carmichael fought for breath. Her face turned blue, and the deep-set eyes seemed to fall back in their sockets, rolling right back with the whites gleaming like milk-jelly.

'Kit. . . .'

The cry was a strangled groan, and even as Maggie moved, she heard his running footsteps down the stairs.

Pushing her to one side, he lifted his mother, held her hands, reached for a piece of cloth and sprinkled something on it.

Even in the middle of her distress Maggie found she was reading the lable on the bottle with complete detachment.

'Mr Himrod's cure for even the most distressing cases of asthma.'

Kit held the cloth to her nose. 'It's all right, Mother. I'm here.'

She pushed the cloth away, and pointed an accusing finger at Maggie.

'She . . . she. . . .'

Horrified, Maggie stepped back a pace, then another, her eyes wide and startled. 'I didn't say anything,' she gasped. 'I said nothing to upset her, Kit. Nothing.' She felt the blood drain from her face, as for the first time in weeks she forgot her own frantic worrying.

Mrs Carmichael was dying; she was going to peg out right there before her eyes, and it would be all her fault.

She ought not to have stood up to her and said that about her being lucky to have Kit. She was too outspoken and always had been. Anxious to make amends she forced herself to approach the bed again, but even as she stretched out a hand Mrs Carmichael knocked it away with a slicing motion of her own.

'Go through there, Maggie,' Kit whispered, jerking his head towards the dividing door, and willing to do *anything* that might help, Maggie walked through into the parlour, and stood trembling by the net-shrouded window, looking on to the quiet afternoon street, placing her hand over the pin-tucks to still the fluttering of her heart.

There was an aspidistra plant in a pot standing on a bamboo table in the window, and without knowing what she was doing, Maggie stroked a shiny dark green leaf, then drew her hand back as its coldness gave her no comfort.

The room was very damp and smelt of chilled soot and beeswax polish, and as the laboured breathing coming from the living-room showed no signs of easing, she faced the truth.

Kit would never marry her nor anyone whilst his mother was alive. He was more than a son to his mother; he was the husband who had deserted her, the daughter she had never had, the lover she needed to ease her sense of rejection. It was dreadful and it was also terrible, but it was true. . . .

Maggie rubbed her arms and shivered as the minutes ticked by. She wondered if she dare creep upstairs and retrieve her hat and coat, and quietly let herself out of the front door? It would be the best thing all round, she thought, with resignation.

When at last, Kit came to her, closing the door behind him, she looked at his face and saw that there was a man who could take no more.

Not a weak man, nor even a dominated man, but a man bowed down with responsibility, with a kindness and a compassion he could not and never would deny.

He came straight to her, and put his arms round her, holding her up against him, so that she felt the warmth and the gentleness of him, the *softness* of his undeclared love for her.

'I've got her off to sleep,' he said. 'Oh, Maggie. I'm that sorry. I can't begin to tell you how sorry I am.'

His hand was on her neck, beneath the heavy weight of her hair, stroking gently, caressing. . . .

'Oh, Maggie, what am I going to do? Tell me what I ought to do?'

Because she pulled away from him at that moment and saw the suffering in his eyes, the words she had meant to say were stilled.

What she had wanted to say was:

'Stand up to her, Kit. Make her see that she can't have an attack just when it suits her. Harden yourself! Tell her if you want to go out with me then you will go out with me. . . .'

But it was no good, and she knew it. The ailing woman in the next room had bound the big kindly son to her as surely as if she had tied him to her with steel ropes. And he was too kind to do anything about it. . . .

Wearily Maggie put up her hand and tucked in a stray wisp of hair.

'Fetch my things from upstairs, love. I'm going home, and I'm going on my own, because I know now that your mother needs you far more than I could ever do.' She half smiled. 'And it might be better if you stopped coming down to see me, Kit. After all, it's not as if we were courting seriously or anything, is it? Anyway, you don't know me, not really.' Her voice rose as she fought for self-control. 'One of these days you might be ashamed of me. You might wish you'd never walked me home from Chapel, or brought me to see your mother.'

'Oh, Maggie,' he whispered, not understanding. 'Oh, Maggie. . . .'

And the cry that came from him was more like a groan, and it was a sound that filled Maggie with anguish and exasperation. In her own agony she was not sure which. . . .

At the end of three months Maggie gave up hope and gave up looking every day for a letter from Joe. Although she wasn't sick in the mornings, there were signs now that she was definitely pregnant. Her breasts were rounder and fuller, and she had to lace her stays tighter to hide her slowly thickening waistline. Her cheeks were so pale that she had to pinch and pinch at them to make them glow rosy again, but the warm colour faded in a matter of minutes.

Even as she stared at herself in the mirror it went, leaving her as pale as a little frightened ghost.

Clara came in one day, without knocking as usual, and after watching Maggie drag herself listlessly from her chair to swing the heavy kettle on its stand over the coals, she said straight out:

'There *is* summat up, isn't there, Maggie?'

The tone of her voice was kind and caring, but there was something in the way Clara's left eye glided into its socket that told Maggie she knew.

'There's nothing wrong! Nothing!'

She was shouting without meaning to, and it felt as if her heart had moved up from her chest and was beating wildly in her throat.

'I'm tired, that's all, Clara,' she said more softly. 'It's been that warm lately I've been off me food, and since Father went I haven't felt like cooking much, not for one, it doesn't seem worth it.'

Clara wasn't listening. What she said next proved that.

'What about that black-haired boy who was always hanging about at the top of the street? Standing there whistling with his hands in his pockets? I was always seeing you running up to meet him at one time.'

Maggie was sure now that Clara would be able to *hear* her heart beating, or even *see* it pounding away, boom, boom in her ears, rushing and thumping as if it would burst her head wide open.

'He's gone away. He went away a while ago. To get a job, a better job. I thought I had told you.'

Clara leaned forward, podgy hands on podgy knees.

'You told me nowt. But you're going to tell me now, aren't you, lass? That Joe's gone away because he did something dirty to you, and he's not going to stand by you. I'm right, aren't I?'

Maggie jumped up so quickly that her chair fell over with a clatter. Standing sideways on to Clara, twisting her hands she presented a perfect view of her gently swelling stomach, no bigger than the soft curve of a throat but enough to convince her of the truth.

'You're going to have a baby, Maggie Craig.'

'No, it's not true!' Maggie's cry of anguish was torn from her trembling lips. 'Yes it is true, but Joe went away because if he'd stopped the police would have been on to him. He doesn't know . . . oh, Clara, he doesn't even know.'

And just for a moment, a wild impossible moment, it seemed to Maggie that it was her mother sitting there in the rocking chair. Hannah was holding out her arms, and enfolding Maggie in them, telling her to have a good cry and get it over with.

'There, there, l'al lass,' she was saying in her Cumberland accent, as soft as the water trickling down from the hills. 'It will be right, you'll see.'

Maggie bowed her head and let the tears roll down her cheeks, feeling the salt taste of them as they trickled into the corners of her open mouth.

'Don't tell anyone, Clara,' she sobbed. 'Promise me you won't tell anyone. Joe will come back any day now. He said he was coming back when he got a good job, and we'll get married and then it won't matter. *Promise* me, Clara.'

'As if I would tell,' Clara said, 'I can't think of what to say. I'm flabbergasted, that's what I am.' She got up heavily from the chair and nodded towards the kettle. 'I won't stop for a cup of tea, now, love, but I'll tell you something for nothing. If I got my hands on that Joe I'd throttle him till his tonsils burst out of his collar stud. Nay, I can't credit it, no way I can't. As if you didn't have enough trouble, but

86

then they say trouble always comes in a three, so you've one more to go yet.'

Her flat plain face working with an emotion and a sympathy quite genuine, Clara walked splay-footed to the front door, closing it quietly, almost reverently, behind her.

Passing her own door without a glance, she went into her mother's house, walked through the front parlour and into the living-room.

Ignoring her father she spoke directly to Mrs Hobkirk.

'Aye, it's true, Mam, but I've promised not to tell, so think on you keep your mouth shut at the Sewing Class tonight.'

'As if I would tell. That poor little lass. That's what comes of having no mother to guide her.'

Mrs Hobkirk was already pinning her hat on to her wiry hair, her mouth a grim line of satisfaction at having her suspicions verified.

'But that's one secret no woman can keep for long, and to think Maggie Craig looks like butter wouldn't melt in her mouth. Thank God her father is no longer alive to see his daughter's shame.'

'Think on what I said,' Clara reminded her.

Mrs Hobkirk sniffed, then meeting one of the sewing ladies on her way to the meeting she had the pleasure of passing on the news without even having had to wait till she got there.

They were all at Chapel that Sunday evening. All the sewing ladies grouped together, with Clara and Arnie in their usual place at the back. Mrs Hobkirk darted a sidelong glance at Maggie, turned round and whispered something to the pew behind, and Maggie lowered her head over her folded hands.

'Oh, God, dear loving Father of Jesus, Clara's mother knows, and if she knows then everyone else will know. And I'm asking you what to do, oh my loving Father, because I don't know where to turn. Help me, please, and show me what to do. Help me to go on working at the mill for a long time yet, and help me to try somehow to put a bit by, because when there's no money coming in, what will I do? Will I have to go to the workhouse or to one of those places for fallen women?'

The tears gathered in her eyes and splashed down on her cotton gloves.

'Am I a fallen woman, God? I don't feel like one . . . oh, Joe. . . .'

Maggie lifted her head then quickly lowered it again. It felt as if every eye in the Chapel was upon her, and when a woman carrying a bible started to edge her way along the pew and saw it was Maggie, she turned swiftly away, going to sit three rows in front.

But not before she had hissed a single word.

'Jezebel!'

Maggie felt a cold shiver trickle down her back. Her hands trembled so much she could not find the place in her hymn book, and though she held her head high and tried to sing, no sound came from her lips. Though the Chapel was full she was alone in the long pew, and when the hymn was over and they sat for prayers, bending heads over folded hands, a woman's voice behind her said distinctly:

'Praying won't get thee nowhere, Maggie Craig. You being here is an insult to God. Make no mistake about that!'

Maggie wanted to put her hands over her ears. She wanted to rock herself in her misery, but most of all she wanted to get up and walk out. Back down the aisle with the steel tips on her boots ringing on the metal grids, back to the house in Foundry Street where she could pull down the blinds and shut herself away.

When Mr Marsden went to stand behind the pulpit to give his sermon he banged with his fist and called on God to punish the wicked, and Maggie was sure he was speaking directly to her.

Frozen, with tears like slivers of ice inside her, she told herself that Mr Marsden knew too. He had been so kind to her when her father died, and now he would think she had been wicked even as Thomas lay scarcely cold in his grave.

The sermon was over, and Mr Marsden bowed his head.

'Let us pray for those who fall from grace,' he intoned, casting his closed gaze to the high ceiling, speaking slowly because he was, as usual, making up the words as he went along. 'Let them repent of their evil ways. Let them hide their shame from the godly, and walk from henceforward in the paths of righteousness.'

Completely carried away by the flow of the high-sounding phrases, Mr Marsden's beautiful voice droned on. Maggie bowed her head even lower, the tears inside hardening into a tight knot in her throat. The minister's prayer was bouncing back at her from the walls; she knew that if she lifted her head and looked around, every eye in the Chapel would be upon her. Now all desire to get up and walk out had gone. She merely wanted to slide down from the hard seat and lie on the wooden floorboards, hidden from sight.

When it was over Mr Marsden announced the last hymn, and there was a rustling of pages as the congregation found their places. It was one of Maggie's favourite hymns, but as the voices swelled to the rafters, she heard nothing. Mr Elphick might be pumping the organ till the sweat ran down his little wrinkled face, and the tenors in the back row of the choir stalls were giving of their best in the soaring descant, but still Maggie sat there.

All through the first verse she sat huddled in her seat, conspicuous now as she had never meant to be, tittered at from the row behind, and stared at from either side.

'We thank Thee that Thy Church unsleeping, while earth tolls onward into light. . . .'

The congregation, led by the choir, started on the second verse, and suddenly Maggie felt a light, a feather-light, touch on her arm.

'Stand up, Maggie,' a familiar voice whispered, and looking up she stared straight into the kind brown eyes of Mrs Carmichael's big son Kit.

Some courage he had not known he possessed had moved him to do this thing. Some well of pity deep inside him had made him leave his own pew, and go to stand by her side.

'Is it yours?' his mother had demanded when Mrs Earnshaw had departed in triumph after imparting the shocking news.

Then she had nodded with satisfaction, the blank amazement on her son's face telling her what she knew already.

'I could have told you what she was,' she went on. 'I tried to tell you, but you wouldn't listen. I knew from that first time Maggie Craig stood round my bed what sort of a girl she was. *Now* will you listen to me? I bet she doesn't rightly know which lad it is herself.'

She had raised herself up on her pillows and pointed a finger at him. 'Keep right away from her, sonny. She'll be looking for some mug to pin the blame on, you mark my words.'

'Poor little Maggie.' Kit had left her sitting up in bed, the three-cornered shawl round her shoulders. He had climbed the stairs and sat on his own bed, staring at the wall.

'Why?' he asked himself. Not who, but why? Because he knew who it was. He had seen them together once in the park, and their joined hands and their mingled laughter had filled him with inexplicable anger.

When Kit walked by Maggie's side out of the Chapel there was a little knot of people already gathered on the pavement outside. Clara Preston, red-faced and looking as if she was giving her mother a piece of her mind, and Arnie, turning his cloth cap round and round in his hands. Then four or five of the sewing ladies, staring at Maggie with a terrifying stillness that made Kit's blood run cold in his veins.

He held tightly to Maggie's elbow, feeling sure she would

fall down if he let go. His heart was thudding madly, and he knew that when his mother heard about this, as hear she surely would, there would be the very devil to pay.

One of the women drew her long skirt aside as they passed, and another – no, he must have imagined it – turned her head and spat on the cobbles.

'You ought to be ashamed of yourself, Kit Carmichael!' a woman shouted.

'Have you no shame?' another called out, and suddenly Kit could bear no more.

'Let them cast the first stone!' he cried in his shrill voice, knowing he was identifying himself with their vulgarity, but unable to stop himself.

'You shouldn't have done this, Kit.'

Maggie's voice was low as he led her away, and she was so small, so desolate that her concern for him made him feel at least ten feet tall.

'You mustn't come in,' she said when they stood at the door of the bottom house in Foundry Street. 'You've stuck your neck out for me enough tonight, and I won't have you talked about, not when you've done nothing to deserve it.'

Kit coughed, shuffled his feet, ran a finger round his stiff white collar and blushed like a young girl.

'Will he see you right, Maggie? I know it's none of my business, but will he do right by you?'

She was fitting the key into the door so that he did not see her face as she answered.

'He's gone away, but I'm expecting him back. And thank you, Kit Carmichael. I'll never forget what you did for me, not till the day I die.'

Then, with a swift glance up and down the deserted Sunday evening street, she stood on tiptoe and kissed him gently on his smooth cheek. 'God bless you, Kit. Always.'

She opened the door, turned briefly, smiled at him with her mouth, but with despair clouding her eyes, and stepped inside.

Kit walked slowly back up the street, his heart already

in his boots at the thought of the scene with his mother. He saw her, in his mind's eye, ranting and raving, and he told himself that as this seemed to be his night for sticking up for people then he would have a go at sticking up for himself.

But his resolution wavered even as he reached the top of the street, and turning right instead of left, he decided to take the long way home.

5

'Is what I did the worst sin of all?' Maggie asked Clara in the weeks that followed. 'Is nagging and meanness and vindictiveness not just as bad? What do you think, Clara?'

But Clara, who had never been taught to think, just shook her head.

'I don't rightly know, love,' she said.

Now the pattern of Maggie's days was set. It was getting up when the knocker-up rattled his wire-tipped pole against the window. It was raking last night's ashes from the fire, laying it ready for the evening, then running to the mill with her tea and sugar screwed up in a piece of paper for the brew-up at eight o'clock.

Lacing her stays as tightly as she could and letting out the fasteners on her skirt, the signs of the baby were only there if they were looked for. True her breasts were fuller, but then she had never been lacking up there, she told herself, and by moving the buttons on her blouses she managed.

At dinner time she ran home, always alone, forced herself to eat a slice of bread and jam, then it was back to the mill and standing in the damp atmosphere by her looms all through the long noisy afternoon until the hooter went and she was free.

Free to go back to the house, light the fire and force herself again to eat something a bit more substantial, an egg or a slice of ham. Freedom to Maggie meant isolation, a shutting herself away from other people, the way Thomas had done. But she refused to think about that.

One evening when she was just over four months pregnant she waited until it was dark, then she took her coat down from its peg behind the back door, pushed her hair up into a tammy, and walked out of the house, round the corner on to the canal bank.

She had promised Joe she would never go down that part of the town alone, but he had gone away and she had to see for herself.

It was a night of shifting clouds and pale glancing moonlight, turning the canal into a glistening ribbon of silver.

'One in the family's enough,' Maggie muttered, looking away from it. 'That's the easy way out, and besides, I'm not done yet, not by a long chalk. Joe will write when he's found a good job. He will . . . he will. If he knew he would be back for me like a flash, police or no police. An' if we had no money then I'd take in sewing. I could if I set me mind to it. . . .'

She walked even more quickly as she entered the maze of streets leading to Montague Court. In the middle of one narrow street a small crowd had gathered round two drunken men who were fist fighting with the ferocity of a pair of hungry tigers. One man had blood streaming down his face, and his opponent, a man twice his size, was ramming his fist repeatedly into the battered face.

One of the watching men shouted at the top of his voice:

'Police! The bloody rozzers are coming!'

Maggie watched, holding a horrified hand to her mouth as the small crowd disappeared, dragging the victor with them and leaving the bleeding man lying in the middle of the street being loudly sick. The awful retching sound made her clutch her own throat, and when the policeman puffed and lumbered round the corner, she walked away.

When she reached Montague Court she was panting for breath and there was a stitch in her side like the thrust of a sword. To catch her breath for a moment she clutched at a lamp-post, and as the wavering light shone down on her upturned face, two women crossed the street and stood in front of her with arms folded.

One of them put out a finger and poked Maggie in the chest.

'We've been watching you, we have. We saw you trying to speak to them men at the fight. This is our beat so bugger off!'

Maggie straightened up, holding her hand to her side, as the second woman, well into middle-age, gave her a push that almost sent her sprawling.

'Bugger off then, or we'll have your guts for garters. See?'

Trembling in every limb Maggie walked on and knocked at the door of number four, seeing, out of the corner of her eye, the two night women watching her. She knocked again.

From the dim yellow light coming from behind the blind she knew there was someone in, and just for a moment she imagined the big unshaven man opening the door, reaching out a hand and pulling her in. She glanced down the street to where the women still stood, and as the sweat broke out on her skin she raised her hand and knocked for a third time.

'Who is it?'

The voice was a woman's voice, thin and wavery, threaded with fear, and as the two night women began to walk towards her, nudging each other and laughing loudly, Maggie called out:

'I've come to see Mrs Barton. It's Maggie Craig.'

There was the sound of a bolt being drawn back before the door opened for about six inches. Maggie smiled, then the smile faded as she saw that the woman standing there bore no resemblance to Joe's mother. This was a woman who looked as if she was dying where she stood, with sparse grey hair pulled back from a face as yellow as the buttercups Maggie remembered from her childhood.

'I thowt it were the rent man,' she said. 'Come on in, lass, and tek your coat off. Did you say as 'ow you wanted Mrs Barton?'

The sweet smell in the tiny room was even worse than Maggie remembered, but the bits and pieces of makeshift furniture were the same. The wooden boxes still stood in the middle of the floor, and from the way a brown blanket was pushed back on a single bed Maggie realized that the woman had been lying down.

Her face seemed no bigger than the perimeter of a teacup, and the flesh had dropped away from her face so that it resembled a skull, with forehead, nose and chin jutting out. The effort of getting up to open the door had proved too much for her, and now she sank back on to the bed, staring at Maggie from sunken eyes.

'Mrs Barton's dead, love,' she said. 'They came and took her off to the Infirmary, but it were too late. She had choked on her vomit, they said, drunk as a lord.'

'And Belle? Can you give me the address where she works now?'

Maggie wondered why the stitch in her side wouldn't go. She'd stopped running, and what the woman was telling her wasn't exactly a surprise. She would have been more surprised to see Joe's mother sitting there, staring at her with Joe's eyes.

It all fitted in somehow. Joe had never existed, Belle and the big rough man had never existed, and what she was left with now was a dream-like memory of coming here. And what she was left with now was Joe's baby inside her.

'She was a bad lot that Mrs Barton,' the sick woman was saying. 'I hope I'm not treading on any toes, but she was a real wrong 'un.' She shook her head wearily from side to side. 'I'm not much help, love. I'm sorry. I'm not much help to nobody because I'm on me way out.' She smiled, and it was as though the skull parted its lips in a hideous grimace. 'We was lucky to get this place to rent.'

'We?' Maggie wished she could say something to comfort the bird-like woman lying back against her pillows, but she was struggling against a desire to give way and slide down on to the floor in a faint. She forced herself to stand upright, though the pain in her back drained the blood from her face.

'Me husband. He'll be back soon, and then we'll have a nice drop of stout. He's a good man. One of the best, and good men don't grow on trees, not round these parts.'

Maggie backed towards the door, trying to smile. She heard her own voice as if it came from a far-off place.

'I hope you soon feel better, then,' she whispered.

She saw a man turning into the Court as she closed the door gently behind her. He was walking quite steadily, carrying a jug held in front of him. She hoped the stout would help, because the part of her that was all her mother made her want to go back, to see to things, to fill a bucket from the tap out at the yard, and scrub the filth from the floor.

'Maybe I'll go back tomorrow with some gruel,' she told herself aloud, but even as she said it she knew she wouldn't.

'When we're in trouble we behave like animals,' Thomas had often said, and he was right. 'We just curl up in a corner and let the rest of the world get on with it.'

Maggie walked as quickly as she could without actually running. Out of the Court, out into the dark labyrinth of streets, past a corner pub with the clinking sound of glasses and the smell of beer and sawdust coming from an open window. The stitch had come back, but not as bad; the night women were nowhere to be seen, and down on the canal bank the silver water still shimmered and rippled as though beckoning her in.

She stood for a moment, swaying, her eyes fixed on the gleaming width of water. Oh, it was true . . . Joe had behaved like an animal. He had been threatened so he had run away. He had made love to her because she was warm and soft, and just for a while he needed softness and warmth badly.

Now she would just have to settle her mind to what had

to be and get on with it. And getting on with it did not include jumping into that deceptively attractive stretch of water. Once she was in she would feel the dirt and smell the stench, and down at the bottom there would be dead dogs and cats, and she was young. She was Maggie Craig who had defied Miss Hepinstall, and given her brothers back as good as she had got.

For the first time since the terrible thing had happened, Maggie knew real blazing anger. Not the wild tempers of her childhood when she had snatched her tammy from her head and stamped up and down it, but a deep revulsion at the way she had allowed this thing to happen.

She remembered a book she had once read, where the heroine, faced with the same situation, had actually banged her head against a stone wall.

'You fool! You fool! You fool!' she had cried.

'An' if I thought it would do any good I'd do the same,' Maggie muttered, turning away from the water and climbing the bank up to the bridge.

When she woke in the night and discovered the first signs that she might be going to miscarry, Maggie got up, the white-hot anger somehow sustaining her. Some instinct, maybe some far-off memory of the village women, worn out with constant child-bearing, made her get down on her knees and start scrubbing the living-room floor. By the time she had finished, the pain in her back had moved round to the front and was a dragging agony, but she emptied the bucket, re-filled it at the slopstone, and without bothering to heat the water from the kettle, she pulled down the blind in the parlour, carried a single candle through and began to scrub again.

She knew exactly what she was doing. She knew that if the baby was meant to be then no harm would come to it, but she knew equally that the sign she had been given was going to be interpreted by her as a definite nudge.

Every pore in her body was pouring sweat when she had finished the front room floor. Her hair was sticking to her head, ends wisping down her neck, and when she held the candle up to the mirror, it was the face of a woman well into middle-age staring back at her.

When she crawled into bed again she knew she was not going to keep the baby, so she faced the truth fair and square.

One part of her had wanted Joe's baby, oh yes, no doubt about that. There were moments when she had put her hand over her stomach and imagined how it would be when the baby started to kick. She had wondered whether it would be a boy or a girl, and she had imagined Joe coming back and marrying her, and the three of them living together in the house. She would keep on with her sewing and Joe would learn to weave, and she would set a good dinner before him every single day.

But life wasn't like that. Life did not tie up knots neatly and manufacture happy endings. Joe had gone, and she would have had the baby all alone, with the Chapel folk looking down their noses at her, and the neighbours eyeing her up when she went out with her stomach all sticking out.

Where would the money have come from when she had to stop work at the mill? She would have had to put the baby out to mind, and its milk would come out of a two-penny tin, and she wouldn't have liked to see her baby bowed with rickets or catching the cough because it wasn't nourished enough.

No, her baby wasn't going to be bearing the stigma of illegitimacy for the whole of its life . . . not now. Thank God, not now.

'Oh, Joe. . . .' Maggie felt the anger drain from her, and at last knew the relief of tears. When the knocker-up came down the street she was moaning to herself, turned on her side with her legs drawn up.

But when he came the morning after, she got up, washed herself all over, dressed herself, and went to the mill.

6

When the telegram came from the War Office Maggie folded it neatly back into its envelope, placed it behind the clock on the mantelpiece and told no one.

The official wording informed her with deep regret that the troopship *Himalaya* had left Cape Town for Natal with drafts of the York and Lancaster Regiment, and had run into heavy weather. The captain had hove to with the intention of dropping anchor in Durban, when Private Jonathan Craig had been swept overboard. Private Benjamin Craig, his brother, had immediately gone to his rescue and had perished when a life-line thrown to them had snapped in two.

A week now since it came and Maggie had come home from the mill, gone upstairs without bothering about the fire, and was sitting on the edge of her bed studying her face intently in the swing mirror atop her chest of drawers.

It was strange, but her face looked just the same as ever. A bit peaky since she lost the baby, and still pale, but that was all. Now that the nights were drawing in she went to work in the dark then came home in the dark, so pale cheeks were only to be expected. No, the trouble was in trying not to think, trying not to *realize*.

So if she went on mapping out each day, planning every hour in detail, it was possible that the time would go on till the pain in her chest would dissolve away. At least she slept . . . oh God, how she slept!

'Sleep has always been Maggie's salvation when she's ill,'

Hannah used to say, but oh no, she must not think about her mother, or her father, or Joe, or the night she lost the baby, or the message from the War Office. She must not think of *anything*. She had to go to the mill and she had to buy enough food to keep her from starving, and she had to remember to order enough coal to keep the lean-to shed in the yard filled. Apart from this there was nothing else she needed to do.

And today in particular she must ignore the stabbing pain in her chest and the way her head throbbed, because it was all in her imagination.

But what were the boys doing sailing out to Natal? She had thought they were safe from the war over in Canada. How could they go to fight in a war and never even let her know?

'Now they are dead,' Maggie told her reflection, 'and you must go up to the shops before they close. You know that, don't you?' So, quietly and thoughtfully she went downstairs and put on her coat and hat.

Clara always wore a shawl when she bobbed out to the shops, but she wasn't Clara Preston. She was Maggie Craig, and her father was the schoolmaster at the village school. Her mother wore a blue dress with the sleeves rolled up, and she baked apple-pies with shiny brown crusts, and fatty-cakes, stiff with currants, and oatcakes she laid over the rack to dry.

Miss Hepinstall was cross, but she wasn't afraid of her. Little Maggie Craig was not afraid of anything. Of owt, as Clara would say. Her hat was slipping, so lifting her arms up with difficulty – what was wrong with them? – she pinned it on more firmly, then whimpered as a strand of hair refused to be tucked back out of sight.

Then with back erect, and head held high, she set off up the street, and as she walked the cobbles seemed to blur together and become one.

She was not ill. She could not afford the *time* to be ill. There was no buzzing in her ears, and the little hammer tapping away in her skull was all in her imagination. No, she was just a bit dizzy, that was all.

What she had to concentrate on was how lucky she was to have the house with the rent book all paid up to date. No hiding in the stairs when the rent man came on Friday nights like some of the women in the street.

'Never spend a penny unless you can cover it with another,' her father had always said.

No, she would never get into debt. Never.

See, she was doing all right telling herself about the good things and not dwelling on the bad. It was just a matter of concentrating.

Conditions at the mill were good compared to what they were at some of the others. Yes, that was something to be glad about. Why, only a while ago she had read one of Thomas's books telling what it was like in some of the Manchester mills. She had never been there, but the book told of workers living in narrow alleys, in one up and one down houses, with next to no sanitation. Irish workers in the main, and it was no good Clara telling her that they had been brought up like pigs, and lived like pigs, blaspheming with every other sentence. Owing allegiance to the Pope, and using Jesus and his mother Mary as swear words.

Clara's horizons were indeed set no further than her own front doorstep. Dear Clara. Kind Clara. Salt of the earth Clara.

I love her, Maggie thought. In spite of the fact she couldn't keep a secret longer than two minutes. She is my one true friend.

It was funny how heavy her basket was, especially as there was nothing in it yet.

No, that book had been written by a writer who had never experienced the aching grind of poverty, never slept ten to a room, never sent his children out to play bare-bottomed, to paddle in their own dirt. He was reporting, not identifying.

Maggie opened the door of the shop, and the pinging of the bell set the hammering up behind her eyes again.

She could not think what it was she had come for, so she asked for some sugar, and watched through a swirling mist as it was weighed into a three-cornered poke. Then she asked for some Monkey Brand for the simple reason that she could see it there on the shelf. She pointed to the tall butter-pat with a design of a girl in a summer dress stroking a cow on it, and finished off by asking for a slice of cheese. She swayed as the shopkeeper pulled a piece of wire through it and thought how clever he was.

When she came out of the shop, it had started to rain, heavy drenching rain. Nothing like the rain she remembered from her childhood. Surely the rain then had been sweet and gentle, falling like a soft mist, not bouncing up like this from the cobbles and blinding her when she turned her face up to the sky?

Here was where she turned to go back down Foundry Street. There was where she lived, right at the bottom, in the house exactly like all the others, and inside it was cold because she had forgotten to bring the coal in from the yard.

She stopped, puzzled, and put a hand up to her forehead, and was even more puzzled to feel that her skin was dry and burning as if on fire.

No, she had been quite wrong. She could not possibly live down that mean little street, with the tall mill chimneys standing sentinel over it. She was little Maggie Craig, and she lived in the School House, and there were fields, and hedgerows thick with hawthorn, and her father was the schoolmaster. She had three brothers, and they teased her and pulled off her beret, and threw it over the low stone wall, and she climbed over to get it back, showing her bloomers.

It had landed in a cow-clap, and she had taken it into the house, holding it at arm's length, holding her nose. Her mother had rinsed it out, then washed it, but it had never again been quite the right shape. Maggie put up a hand to her head and was surprised to find a hat pinned to the slippery bulk of her hair.

What was she doing wearing a hat? Oh, yes, now she remembered. She had been dressing up in her mother's clothes, and she had walked to the gate to meet her father with her mother's weekday coat trailing behind her, and her mother's shopping hat balanced on top of her cloud of unruly hair.

Her father had carried her inside perched on his shoulders, and her mother had only pretended to be cross when she saw the mud-trimmed hem of her coat.

'Maggie Craig, you'll be the death of me!' she'd said, and when her father had kissed her, Maggie had put her arms round them both and squeezed and squeezed, and they had all finished up laughing . . . and laughing.

Oh, no, she did not live down there, not down there. Maggie put the basket down, and lifting her aching arms, unpinned the hat, then dropped it into the streaming gutter.

'I'm coming!' she cried, then picking up the basket again, she turned her back on Foundry Street, and walked away with little stumbling steps, in the opposite direction.

When Arnie knocked at the door of Kit Carmichael's house and saw the big man standing there on the step, waiting patiently to hear what he had to say, the breath caught in his throat, and he had to swallow twice before he could get the words out.

The fact that the bloke was wearing an apron over his trousers did nothing to help either.

'Oh, my God, what are we coming to?' Arnie thought.

It was all very well Clara and her mother making him come out in the pouring rain on what he was sure was a fool's errand. He knew this was the last place Maggie would be. Full of pride Maggie was, and anyroad Clara would have been the first to know if she had taken it into her head to call on Kit Carmichael. Wasn't Clara capable of wheedling the truth out of anybody? Aye, she were that. There were no secrets kept from Clara.

'Why, Mr Preston!' Kit's voice was higher than usual with surprise. He smiled and whipped off the apron. 'I was just setting things to rights before I locked up for the night. There's a lot to do with having to leave my mother alone during the day.' He looked up at the dark sky. 'And what a night it is! Come in . . . come in.'

'I'd rather not.'

Arnie's diffidence was like torture to him at times, and now the enormity of what he was doing overwhelmed him. He stepped back a pace.

'It's Clara. Mrs Preston. You know? Me wife. She and her mother went next door to Miss Craig's house – she's been locking herself in lately, and sitting in the dark they think, and well, she hasn't been looking well you see, so they went to try to persuade her to go to the doctor's. The last few nights we've heard her coughing through the wall.' Arnie coughed himself, and stuck his hands deeper into his pockets.

'Maggie's ill?'

Kit asked the question quietly, but his words rang out like a pistol shot. He opened the door wide. 'Come in, Mr Preston. I'll get my coat, right this minute. Come on in.'

'No, it's more than that. At least she is ill we think, but . . .'

Arnie gave up, and remembering to pull his dripping flat cap from his head, stepped inside, and guided by the light from the back room, followed Kit with reluctance, telling himself that once again Clara and her mother had stuck their noses in where they'd no business to.

To further his acute embarrassment, there was a bed in the small and cluttered room, and in it an old woman with the face of a tired monkey. Arnie held his cap in front of him, twisting it round and round in his hands.

Eyes as black as two lumps of shiny coal looked from him to Kit, then back again.

'Mother.' Kit's voice held the kindly tolerance Arnie felt would have been more in keeping when speaking to a backward child.

'Mother, this is Mr Preston from down Foundry Street, and I am going out with him for a little while.' He raised his voice. 'Miss Craig has been taken ill and I am going to see if there is anything I can do. I will leave the lamp turned up like this, so you will be all right, and I'll get back as soon as I can.'

The old woman plucked at the bedclothes, eyeing Arnie with narrowed eyes.

'I know who he is. You don't need to tell me who he is. He's married to that stout woman what skens, the one who sometimes comes to the Meetings. Wears a brown coat and a hat like a chamber-pot, and sings out of tune.'

'Mother!' Kit looked across at Arnie apologetically, then as he took his coat down from a peg behind the door, Mrs Carmichael put a hand to her throat and began to cough.

Kit hesitated, but only for a moment. Giving Arnie a little push he followed him out of the room, calling out as he went.

'You'll be all right, Mother, as long as you stop in bed.'

Then before Arnie knew what was happening they were out in the street with the front door pulled to behind them.

'It may have seemed cruel,' Kit explained, starting off down the street with such long strides that Arnie had to take little running skips to keep up with him. 'But my mother just did not want me to come out. You could see that. She *plays* on me, Mr Preston. Oh, she is very sick, I grant you that, and of late her mind wanders, and her memory is shocking, but if I had not got you out quick she would have seen to it that I never got away.'

He slackened his pace a little. 'I am so grateful that you thought to come to me, Mr Preston. But I must ask you this. Is it Maggie herself who has asked to see me, or is it your wife's idea? You see the last time I saw Maggie she gave me the impression that she did not want to see me again. Not that I blame her, mind. Not with things as they were then.'

Then, without waiting for an answer, he set off again.

Arnie tried to talk and to run at the same time, without much success.

'Mr Carmichael! I never said she was ill in bed or anything. It was you what jumped to that conclusion. Nay, the missus sent me to see if Maggie was at your house, because they went in and she wasn't there. In her own house, I mean. There's no fire or nothing, and not much food . . . Mr Carmichael! You'll get yourself locked up for running like that at this time of night.'

Arnie gave up trying to keep up with Kit's flying, lumbering figure. It was no good anyroad. He dug his fingers further down into his coat pockets, and bent his head against the sweeping driving rain.

He still felt guilty whenever he remembered that summer afternoon when he had tried it on with Maggie. He had scared the living daylights out of her, and to the day he died he would never know what had come over him. He trudged on. But he wasn't responsible for this carry-on. Not by a long chalk he wasn't. And it were more than likely that Maggie would be there when he got back, and they would feel right fools then. . . .

He turned into Foundry Street and saw something lying in the gutter, and bending over it, recognized Maggie's hat because of the way she had tied the black ribbon in a whacking great bow at the back.

'Cheers it up a bit,' she'd said.

'Oh, my sainted aunt!'

Arnie picked it up, his slow mind working out the possibilities, each one more terrifying than the last.

She had been set upon and carried off. She had gone to drown herself in the canal. She had taken after her father. Clara always said that sort of thing ran in families. . . .

Bearing the ruined hat aloft like a morbid trophy, Arnie lifted the latch of his own house and walked through into the living-room. To see his father-in-law sitting by the fire, in *his* chair, drinking tea out of *his* favourite pot.

'They've gone in next door, lad,' Mr Hobkirk said, jerking his head towards the dividing wall. 'By the gum, but tha's wet. It's a nasty neet all right.'

'How long has she been missing?' Kit stood on the rag rug in front of the grate with its heap of dead ashes, and asked the question calmly, only the urgency in his high voice betraying his distress.

'We don't know but what she *is* missing, Mr Carmichael,' Clara said, exchanging a significant glance with her mother. 'It's just that I didn't hear her moving about since she came home from the mill tonight. You know, raking the fire out or anything. So I came in to see if she was all right.

'She doesn't *look* herself,' Clara added. 'And she doesn't do enough cooking for herself. When her father was alive she was always taking something tasty out of the oven to tempt his appetite, finicky fella that he was.'

'Never a smile for nobody *he* hadn't,' Mrs Hobkirk said.

Feeling nervously impatient, but too polite to show it, Kit said:

'Have you been upstairs, Mrs Preston?' He coughed discreetly. 'And out to the back? She might have gone out there then been taken ill.'

'We've checked,' then after exchanging another glance with her mother, held out the telegram.

'I know it might seem like noseying, but we found this.'

'And after . . .' Clara's eye flickered. 'After what her father did, and with her well, having that other trouble in the summer, and now looking so poorly we thought we ought to read it.'

With obvious reluctance, Kit took the telegram from the

envelope and read it. Then, with hands that had been stiff with cold, and were now suddenly clammy, he muttered. 'And you thought she might have come to tell me?'

'With you having been friendly like,' Clara said, and was nudged into silence by her mother.

'So we sent Arnie.'

When the front door opened and closed, the three faces turned eagerly towards it.

Arnie held the hat in front of him.

'I found this,' he announced.

'Oh, that poor child.' Mrs Hobkirk took it from him and handed it to Clara. 'See, the pin's still in it.'

'As though it had been snatched from her hand.' Clara stared at it, her mouth working with emotion.

'Where did you find it? Where, Mr Preston?' Kit picked it up and turning it round and round in his hands, walked over to the window.

Out there, in the dark and rain, over there was the canal. He turned swiftly and threw the hat down on the table so that it covered the telegram completely. His teeth dug into his bottom lip.

'*Where* did you find it?' he asked again. Curse the man. Did he have to think before he could answer even a straight question like that?

'Lying in the gutter. At the top of the street,' Arnie told him, moving his head in that direction.

Kit nodded to them.

'Try to get the fire going. And put the kettle on,' he ordered, then leaving them standing there, an open-mouthed trio, gazing helplessly at the bedraggled hat, he ran from the house. Banging the front door behind him so that the little house shook to its very foundations.

Maggie had no thought in her feverish mind of walking to her death when she left Foundry Street behind her. No melodramatic desire to end it all. Just a feeling of need. A terrible hurting need to be back in the country once again, to get away from the dirt and the meanness of the streets, from the terraced houses that grew in rows like a regiment lined up on parade. To forget that she ever knew Joe Barton – just to be back in the lanes where the hedges grew, where cottages were fronted by gardens overgrown with moon-daisies, marigolds, and night-scented stock. Where fields were thickly carpeted with yellow buttercups, and her brothers ran in from the pump, their brown hair flattened and wet against their heads.

If only her chest did not hurt so much, she could walk more quickly. And she needed to hurry because Hannah, her mother, was waiting for the jug of blue milk from the farm to make into a pudding stiff with rice.

And oh she loved going to the farm, in spite of the wild cats that sometimes streaked across her path from the barn. There were great hams curing in the rafters, and inside the dairy it was cool with its scrubbed stone table with the groove in the middle filled with water. There were milk dishes and wooden pails neatly arranged in rows, and everything smelt clean and sweet.

She had to go slowly now in case the milk spilt, but one day she had put it down carefully on the grass to lie on her stomach as she watched an army of ants going methodically about their daily task. And Benjamin had come up quietly on tiptoe behind her, and tickled her neck with a piece of grass so that she had jumped up and knocked the jug over.

No, this was not the right place. Even the sky was wrong. This sky was dark and heavy, and there were puddles in the road with the gas lamps reflected in them. She must hurry, and yet she could not hurry, and in spite of her slowness there was a trickle of sweat running down her face, and down her back. She was panting as though she had been running for a long long time.

Her hair had come loose when she wrenched her hat off. It hung in heavy wet strands down over her shoulders into her eyes, and it was a basket she was carrying, not a jug of milk.

She put it down because it was heavy and the heaviness was making the pain burn harder in her chest, so she left the basket there and tried to cough the pain away.

She stopped trying to run after that. She just put one foot in front of the other and stumbled and fell, then picked herself up and stumbled on again. She turned into yet another street filled with the darkened windows of unused front parlours, and for a moment she knew who she was and why she was out there in the dark, wandering aimlessly in the rain.

A door opened and a woman stood on the step, straining her eyes into the blackness, her body etched against the dim light coming from the back room. A child clung to her skirts, and two more children clustered behind her.

'Is me dad coming yet, then?'

'Nay I can't see no sign of him yet.'

'Can I have a sugar butty, Mam?'

'You can have nowt if you don't stop that moithering.'

Maggie stood quite still in the shadow of the wall, her coat and the darkness of the night rendering her invisible. Then the woman went inside the house, pulling the children after her and closing the door with a slam. For a moment they were silhouetted there in the dividing doorway, then that too was closed, and the house fell into darkness again.

Maggie remembered how her mother had always kept the lamp burning in the front window of the School House, sending out rays of welcome to whoever walked up the path. A sob caught up in her throat, then more sobs crept up, till her whole body was shaking, then she was crying with her mouth wide open, the tears pouring down and mingling with the rain on her face.

She was crying, not because she was lost and could not find the School House. She knew now that it was miles away with someone else living in it.

What she was crying for was the fact that it had come to her that she was alone, entirely alone in the world, the only one left, without even the right to think of the boys marching down a foreign road, climbing a foreign hill, or sailing on a foreign sea.

For the space of a terrible second, she saw with vivid clarity a towering wave carrying Jonathan away; she saw his face as he cried for help, and she saw Benjamin trying to reach him, stretching out a hand before they disappeared for ever.

'Oh, God!' she moaned, feeling her way along the wall because her legs no longer seemed able to support her. She turned into a back alleyway, and sliding slowly to the ground, closed her eyes.

'I'll manage,' she muttered. 'I've managed before on me own, and even if I'd had the baby I would have found a way. It's just that I feel so ill, and I daren't be ill. I can't *afford* to be ill.'

She craved a drink. More than anything else in the world she wanted a drink. Her throat was parched and burning, and if she lay there with the rain-wet cobblestones underneath her, she knew she would die.

And she did not want to die. In spite of everything she did not want to lie here and die. . . .

Painfully, slowly, working herself up the wall with hands gripping the sooty uneven stones, she managed to stand upright, and now her mind was clear. She had to get into the warm. She had to get where it was dry.

With the unerring instinct of a sick animal she stumbled forward in search of warmth and shelter, and help.

The street lamps were out now, but all at once she knew where she was. She recognized the tall houses on her left, each with its own little paved front garden. Here the better-off lived, the men with a trade in their fingers, and two streets further along was the street where Kit Carmichael lived with his mother.

Maggie made herself go on, fighting for every breath

now, her hair hanging loose and her coat stained with mud.

Every single house was in darkness, and she felt a recurring wave of panic. Oh, dear God, what was she doing out in the streets, in the dark, in the rain at this time of night?

Was she going to be like her father with his black depressions, his slipping mind? She put out a hand to steady herself against a window bottom before moving painfully on.

No, it was not that. There was blackness in her mind, it was true, but now she could see the substance in the darkness. She was ill. Ill in her body, not her mind. And yet if that were so, how did she come to be out here, walking when she had no strength to walk, burning hot and shivering with cold at one and the same time?

She would never get to the bottom of Kit's street. Never cross over the wider one, never make her way along the flat to Foundry Street. She lifted her head and saw, through the mist before her eyes, that she was directly opposite to Kit's house, and through the black square of window she saw the soft glow of lamp-light shining through from the back room.

Kit . . . kind, considerate Kit Carmichael.

He was there, only a few steps across the street, and behind that closed front door would be warmth, and a drink, a hot soothing drink to hush the pain burning her breathing away.

The door was not locked.

Feverishly Maggie's mind registered surprise at this. The town people always locked their doors at night. But it was too late to wonder. Too late even to bang the heavy knocker against the door in case she woke the street up.

All she wanted was help and warmth, and a drink. . . .

She was inside, groping with outstretched hands to the light, going towards it, stumbling, falling through the dividing door, and seeing the old woman with black picking eyes and the skin of a wrinkled crab apple, staring at her from the high-piled nest of white pillows. . . .

The rain had stopped, and the sky was slowly changing from black to a sombre grey when Kit decided there was no point in searching the surrounding streets any further. No point in standing on the canal bank and once rather foolishly calling Maggie's name, his eyes narrowed as he tried to identify the floating debris in the murky water moving sluggishly against the canal banks.

Clara had kept a solitary vigil back at the bottom house, dozing in the rocking-chair, and going through into the parlour every now and again to stare through the window at the glistening cobblestones and the sleeping houses across the street.

'There's nowt else you can do, Mr Carmichael,' she told Kit when he came in defeated and wet to the bone. 'You've let the constables know, and they'll send word if owt turns up.' Her left nostril twitched upwards in a resigned sniff. 'They always let the families know first.'

He glanced towards the table where Maggie's sodden hat still covered the telegram, and a great knot of sadness tightened itself round his heart.

'But Maggie has no family, Mrs Preston. She hasn't got anybody, and it's killing me to think she had nobody to turn to.' He shook his head from side to side. 'Oh, I know there was you, and there was me, but she didn't come to us, either of us, did she? Not even when she was – you know.' He gave her a piteous glance which pleaded for understanding. 'I stopped seeing her, Mrs Preston, because I thought she never wanted to see me again. I'm not much of a catch, Mrs Preston. I've always been *torn*, you see. I've not wanted to upset my mother, and then I've ended up upsetting everybody. For as long as I can remember there have been terrible rows and scenes if I tried to get friendly with anybody. She's always been delicate, you see. . . .'

He had been up all night without sleep; he was wet through, muddy and anguished, and his exhaustion led him to admit something he had never admitted before.

'I've always been a bit afraid of her, my mother, you see. Not physically afraid, not when I could pick her up with one hand, but afraid of the "bother" she makes.' He rubbed a hand over his curly hair in an apologetic gesture. 'My mother can make bother quicker than anyone else I know, but it's only natural when she had my father to put up with. I used to hear her shouting at him when he came in the worse for drink, and I got frightened. He hit her once.'

Clara nodded. Maggie had been right about this man. He had a heart as big as a football – a great soft football at that. He'd be like a piece of putty in the hands of a woman like old Mrs Carmichael, old witch that she was.

Leaning forward, she raked the slack over the flames, and pulled the guard round the fire. When she looked at him the dough-like features of her flat face were softened into compassion.

'You're tired out, lad. Go back home and get some rest, and see to your mother. She'll be wondering what's been going on. I'm going in to see to me husband's breakfast, but me mother will take over here. There's got to be somebody here when Maggie comes back.'

'You're very kind, Mrs Preston.'

Kit put out a hand and laid it gently on her shoulder, almost as if he would draw her to him, and Clara was only mildly surprised to find that she had no instinctive urge to flinch away from his touch. This was no man with wandering hands. Kit Carmichael's touch was the touch of a woman comforting another woman in their mutual distress. She would tell her mother that Mr Carmichael was a gentleman. A proper gentleman.

'Get off with you, then,' she said, and her voice held a gentleness Arnie had never heard.

When old Mrs Carmichael opened her eyes and saw Maggie come through the door, the jealous hatred smouldering in her mind enveloped her in a flame of white-hot rage. She would never have believed that Kit could leave her all alone and neglected to go off with that peculiar little man from down Foundry Street.

It was as though Maggie Craig had appeared like a vision in direct answer to the evil dwelling of her thoughts. It was as though she had managed to conjure her up herself out of a filthy cloud of ectoplasm.

So overwhelming was her uncontrolled rage that it failed to register on her mind for the first minute that the girl swaying on her feet, clutching now at the bedpost to keep herself upright, was ill.

And when the anger blotting Maggie's features out from her sight cleared a little, she saw the straggling wet hair, the fever-flushed cheeks, the chest that heaved and rasped with the effort of breathing.

'You're drunk, you little dirty whore,' she said, and even as she said it she convinced herself that she could smell the drink on Maggie.

Raising herself in bed with an ease that would have astonished her son, had he been there to witness it, she pointed a finger, jabbing it into the air.

'How *dare* you come into my house at this time of night? How dare you, without even **as** much as knocking at the door? This is a decent house. Get out! Get out back on the streets where you belong. Get out!'

There was a chair over by the window, and Maggie saw it through a mist of pain. If she could just manage to get there, she could sit down, and she would be warm, and Kit would come. He would come downstairs from his room the way he'd done before, that other time. She could almost hear his footsteps on the stairs. Light, tripping footsteps for so big a man.

116

Yes, it had all happened before, just like this.

The old woman had been shouting at her, just as she was shouting now, and Kit had come . . . as he would come now.

Holding a hand straight out in front of her, like a sleep-walker, Maggie took one step, then another towards the chair. She felt for the arms with her hands, and lowered herself into it.

It was a hard chair, and the arms were wooden, but she laid her head back and closed her eyes with thankful relief.

Now there was no more rain on her face, no tearing wind chilling her very bones. She was warm and safe in Kit's house, and she could sleep, and when she slept she would be better. 'Sleep is her salvation,' someone had said once, a long long time ago.

'Kit?' she whispered before she drifted into unconsciousness. 'Kit?'

The old woman pushed at the bedclothes, pushed at them with scrabbling hands so that she could swing her feet slowly round and place them on the floor. She stared at her feet for a moment, at the bent toes, the ridged yellow toe-nails, then raised her eyes to stare at the girl lying back in the chair.

Even with her hair hanging in wet rat-tails round her face, Maggie Craig was beautiful. She was beautiful, and Mrs Carmichael was ugly and old. Sonny had left her all alone, with the heavy rain beating down and bouncing off the corrugated roof of the shed outside. He had left her to go after that girl, but she would show him. She would show him . . . and her. . . .

She advanced towards the chair, and stretched out her hands.

'I'll do for you,' she muttered. 'You'll not get him. I know your sort. I'll kill you with me own bare hands before I'll let you get him!'

But even as she reached out for Maggie's throat, her

117

hands were stayed as her wandering mind registered the fact that this girl was ill, not drunk. She was running a fever so high that the heat from her face could be felt even before she had touched her.

Maggie Craig's lips were dry, and she was mumbling something, turning her head from side to side, her breath coming up from her chest as if it was being forced through a bag of rusty nails.

'Kit . . .' she was saying. 'Kit. . . .'

Mrs Carmichael stepped back a pace, her own breathing, in spite of her agitation, as free and easy as that of a healthy child.

She knew what she had to do now, and it was going to be so simple she had to chuckle at her own cleverness.

It was a struggle unfastening the catch on the sash window, then sliding the window up from the bottom, but she managed it.

The rain and the wind rushed in, and a pile of papers on the dresser fluttered to the floor. The old woman grunted her satisfaction, but Maggie did not move.

She never thought she would have had the strength, but it seemed as if something outside of her was pouring strength into her, giving her the feeling that she could have put the flat of her hand on the wall, and given no more than a little push for it to have crumbled away.

Even the pan of water poured on the fire, sending a cloud of smoke out into the room, failed to make her cough. True she was shivering when she climbed into her bed, and pulled the blankets up over her head, but the shivering was with excitement and not with cold.

It was like a cocoon of comforting warmth inside the bed, and the feather mattress seemed to come up and wrap her round. She reached to the bottom for the copper hot water bottle, and it was still hot. With a sigh of contentment, Mrs Carmichael placed her feet on it.

She could be warmer though, much warmer. The old woman chuckled as she stuck a skinny arm out from underneath the bedclothes, and groping around on the bedside table, felt her fingers close over a small bottle of brandy.

'If you hadn't been in such a hurry to go out and leave me, you would have put it away in the cupboard like you always do after I've had me hot milk with two teaspoonsful in it, wouldn't you, Sonny?' she whispered.

Then back inside the warm tent of heavy blankets, she tipped the bottle, and felt the fiery liquid stream in glowing comfort down her throat.

'When you were born,' she muttered, 'I used to cuddle you up, young Kit, nice and warm, just like this. I suckled you for two years, and even when you were a big boy, we would sit on the couch, just you and me, and you would put your arm round my shoulders. We would sit there of an evening when your father was out doing God knows what. Spending good money on beer; money what should have been for providing us with a good meal.'

A tear ran down her cheek, and she tried to lift a hand to wipe it away, but the hand had grown suddenly too heavy. She was crying in earnest now, just letting the tears fall.

'What about that time the man came down from the Guardians and said I would have to go up to the Committee after your dad had gone and left us and we had no money? Do you know what he said, that man from Guardians when he saw we had proper chairs and a table instead of orange boxes with covers on them? "You're not quite destitute, Mrs Carmichael" he said. He had a walking stick, and he pointed it at you. "He looks well nourished, doesn't he?" he said. So I didn't waste me time going up to the Committee after that, did I, Sonny? No, I took work in and trimmed hats till me eyes were coming out at the back of me head. I remember one hat took me five hours, and she give me twopence for it. . . . And her in the chair thinks she has more right to you, Sonny, than what *I* have?'

The brandy bottle was empty, and with her case made out and now rested, Kit's mother slid comfortably into sleep. . . .

She was abruptly jerked awake to see Kit's face staring

down at her. Whimpering, she reached out for the bed-clothes he had wrenched away.

'Don't do that, love. You're making me cold.'

But the beloved face, the face she only knew as a smiling face, was contorted with an anger so terrible, she could only shrink back and close her eyes again.

'Get me stuff,' she gasped, clutching her throat, and disciplined by years of ministering to her, Kit thrust what she wanted into her hands.

'Now get out of bed!' he said, 'and put this round you.'

The shawl he gave her was torn from its nail behind the door. She heard it tear, and when the inhalant dropped from her fingers, he made no attempt to pick it up.

'Kit . . .?' she whispered, and it was flung on to her lap.

'See to yourself,' he said. 'It would serve you right, Mother, if I let you choke yourself to death.'

And the way he said the word 'Mother' was an insult in itself. . . .

Faces came and went each time Maggie opened her eyes. Hands held her, stripped off her wet clothing, wrapped her in blankets, and piled yet more blankets on top of her. A hand smoothed the hair back from her aching head, a voice bullied her; more hands held her head over a steam-ing bowl with a pungent aroma that made her turn her face weakly aside in useless protest. Held her there and made her breathe. Forced her to take one rasping breath after another.

Once she thought she saw Clara, then Clara's mother, sitting by the bed, and once an unknown face above a bib of a white starched apron lifted the hair from the back of her head. She heard and felt the snip of scissors.

'It was taking your strength, love,' an unfamiliar voice told her, and she submitted because she was in too much pain to do anything else.

'Kit?' she whispered, and he was there, always there, holding on to her, tucking the blankets round her chin when all she wanted was to push them away. He stripped them off when the crisis came, and she sweated so much it ran down her sides, into her eyes, stinging with the saltiness of it, running down her legs and soaking the sheet.

'The fever's broken,' she heard Kit say, but he was saying it from a long way away. The room was filled with steam from the steam kettle set permanently on the kettle-stand at the front of the fire, and Kit was sponging her naked body, patting her dry, sliding a clean sheet beneath her, murmuring all the time.

'It's all right, Maggie, love. You are getting better. Do you hear me? You are going to be well and strong again. Soon. Do you hear me?'

Into sleep and vaguely out of sleep again. Too weak to smile or speak, or even think. Opening her mouth obediently so that the carefully held spoon could trickle broth into it. Beef-tea. She recognized that, and it tasted good.

'Good,' she managed to say, as a child would say it, then she drifted into her first real sleep for days, a healing natural sleep with her breath coming even and unforced.

'Hello,' she said, and Kit's face was there, close to her own, and there were tears streaming down his cheeks.

'Don't cry,' she thought she said, before she fell asleep again.

'She's been sleeping all day,' Kit said when Clara came in, appearing through the door with a covered basin in a basket. 'No, I won't go up and get some rest, Mrs Preston. She is going to need me here when she wakes up and finds out she is in my mother's house, in my mother's bed. I've got to be here to tell her that they took my mother away.'

'To the loony-bin,' Clara said with relish, speaking in what she considered to be a whisper. 'And what else could they do with her carrying on like a mad woman? What else was there for it when you'd found that poor lass half dead with the double pneumonia sitting half dead in a chair by an open window? A window your mother had opened with her own two hands? And the fire out,' she added, moving over to the hearth and setting the covered basin down. 'A nice drop of pigeon broth here, Mr Carmichael. That man that's a blacksmith striker across the street wrung the neck of one his own birds specially. All the street keeps asking about Maggie. Knocking on the door all the time for news. Seems some folk have short memories seeing what they was like with her in the summer.'

'I could not have done anything else but let them take my mother away,' Kit said, putting a square slab of coal on the fire, then tipping what was left of the coal bucket round it. 'I wasn't thinking straight. Maggie would never have lasted as far as the Infirmary. It was warmth she had to have, and her wet things off. There wasn't time to waste.'

Clara's good eye held a sly expression; the other one seemed to be non-committal.

'People will talk all the same. You know what they was like when she . . . when she had that other trouble. The poor lass is after getting herself a bad name without deserving one. An' what about your job, Mr Carmichael. How's the old gentleman you do for managing?'

Kit smiled as if it was of no consequence whatever. 'Oh, he's told me not to go any more. Said he had got someone more reliable. A younger man, a boy straight from school, but I'm not bothered. Shop work's what I've always wanted, and there might be, there might just be an opening . . . but I'm biding my time.'

'She's still a terrible colour,' Clara said, shaking her head at Maggie lying quiet on her pillows.

Maggie was awake and yet not awake. She could open her eyes if she wanted to, but the effort was too much. The lids felt as if they were weighted down with pieces of lead.

'Kit?'

But before he had time to move over to the bed and take her hands in his own, she was properly awake. Terror made her cry out as she saw she was in the downstairs room of

Kit's house, the dark brown room, and oh God, help her, she was in his mother's bed!

Suddenly the sweat was breaking out on her forehead, pricking in her armpits as she tried to raise herself up. When she lifted her head from the pillow the ceiling dipped towards her, and Kit's face blurred out of focus. Her heart began to beat wildly as memory flooded back. The telegram, the pain in her chest, the rain and her hair straggling dripping over her face, the feel of the slimy wet cobblestones against her face. A woman at a door with children clutching at her skirts. The telegram, and old Mrs Carmichael pointing at her with a bony accusing finger. Shouting at her to go away when all she had wanted was to sit down and close her eyes.

'Last night,' she gasped. 'I came looking for you . . . oh, Kit.'

She was held safely in his arms, held up against his shoulder, and he was all warmth and softness, and somehow it was as if she was back in the kitchen at the Schoolhouse, held in the cushiony comfort of her mother's arms. Having her hair stroked back from her face, and being promised that there was nothing to be afraid of.

'There's nothing to be frightened of, Maggie, love,' Kit said. 'My mother isn't here. She has gone away. To a special kind of hospital.'

'She's fallen asleep again,' he said, and laid her gently back on the pillows. 'She'll sleep herself right,' he added, then as Clara nodded, putting a finger to her lips, and picking up the empty basket, he followed her through into the parlour, and ever polite, stepped in front of her, and opened the door on to the street.

'Thank you for the broth, Mrs Preston. I know I don't need to ask you again not to repeat what you know about what my mother did.' He pulled the lapels of his jacket together, and it was a gesture that said plainly, 'I *forbid* you to gossip about what happened. You did enough damage with your clacking tongue before.'

123

'As if I would talk,' Clara said insincerely. 'Things is bad enough as it is.'

She walked flat-footed down the street, going over in her mind the things she had to tell her mother. It was a right to do an' all. The Chapel lot would have something to say when they found out that Maggie Craig was stopping at Kit's house, just the two of them. And with his mother screaming and tearing her hair out in a padded cell. It was a real caper, it was 'n all. . . .

Two days later Kit pulled up a chair to Maggie's bed and sat down. She looked, he told himself, about twelve years old. Her eyes were enormous in the small oval of her face, and her cropped hair curled round her ears and fell over her forehead in a fringe.

'Well, love?' he smiled, and suddenly shy, Maggie smiled back.

She knew he was going to ask her to marry him, and there was a little niggle in her mind that kept her wondering if he would have asked her if his mother had not gone away. Or if she had gone on and had the baby?

And yet it had seemed to her, lying on her side these past days, too weak even to lift a hand to brush her short hair, too weak to hold a spoon at first without Kit guiding it to her mouth, that here in Kit Carmichael was all the kindness she could ever ask from life.

Someone she could rely on, not someone she was responsible for.

He spoke into her thoughts, 'Maggie, I am old enough to be your father, I suppose.'

'You'd have to have started a bit young, Kit.'

He rubbed a hand over his clean-shaven chin. 'Aye but I didn't, did I, lass? I wish I could make you see what my mother was like in those days. She could have been a very different woman if she had not married the wrong man. She told me once he made so many promises to her about the way it would be if only she married him. Went down on his knees, she said, with tears rolling down his cheeks, swearing he would give up the drink and go to Chapel Meetings, and sign the pledge.'

'What a prospect,' Maggie said, and when he saw the twinkle in her eyes, Kit shook his head and smiled.

'Aye, put like that, it does sound a bit sanctimonious, but it wasn't long before he lost his job at the factory.'

'What for?'

'He turned up for work dead drunk and pushed his foreman's face into a vat of water kept for tempering hot steel.'

'Why?'

'Because he said he hated the man's guts. Then he got taken on at the Brewery, and they had to wheel him home one day on a handcart, so drunk he could not stand. That was when my mother started taking work in from the big Manchester shops. She lost three babies before I was born, you know.'

Maggie put out a hand, and Kit covered it gently with his own, rubbing his thumb up and down the thin blue vein at the front of her wrist in an absent-minded way.

'Aye, she had a rough time, my mother did. Then she took to having her bed downstairs because of her chest, and he took to going with other women. He was too uncouth to realize that after three dead babies, and a delicate son like me, any man with a decent bone in his body would know that his wife had had enough.'

Maggie blushed and hoped Kit would not notice. She wished he would stop telling her about his mother's life, and making excuses for her. She wished he would talk about *them* for a change.

She hoped he wasn't going to try to get her to say she was sorry for his mother, and that they could have been friends if things had been different. Nobody but a saint straight down from heaven could have made a friend out of Kit's mother, and she doubted if even an angel could have managed it.

'Nobody would believe what it was like during those years, Maggie. Once, when the hat trade fell off a bit she opened a shop through in the front room. She sold candles and odd bits of grocery – things I could fetch from the warehouse on a handcart. She used to have customers from down Montague Court way.' Maggie caught her breath, but Kit wasn't looking at her. 'Real rough they were, and some of them so poor they had to take the stuff home held in their pinnies because they couldn't afford the price of a basket. At one time the shop was open sixteen hours a day, closing Christmas Day, and that was all. And do you know what my father did? He took the tin where she kept the takings, and ran off and drank it away. He'd found that tin where she had hidden it away, and through it all she insisted I went to school, refusing to send me into the mill when I was nine, then even when the little shop had to close she went on with the hats and went out and scrubbed other people's floors.'

He gave her a pleading glance. 'So what I mean is, I don't want you to think she was all bad, even though what she tried to do to you was so terrible, it doesn't bear thinking about.'

'What *did* she do, Kit?'

He winced away from the softly spoken question, but it had to be told. Told now and never referred to again. He squeezed Maggie's hand hard.

'She opened the window, love, and she unbuttoned your coat, and then she put the fire out, and got back into her own warm bed, and if I had not come in when I did, back from looking for you, you would have died.'

His voice was very low as he told her, and his head was sunk deep on his chest. 'So if you can't forgive her, love,' he said as if reading Maggie's horrified reaction into her silence, 'at least I hope that some day you will learn to forget.'

He touched her cheek lightly with his forefinger. 'What I have been leading up to, really, is trying to make you see that I'm hoping that in spite of what my mother did, you can still find it in your heart to be fond of me.' He nodded as if to give added importance to his next words. 'Aye, I am asking you to marry me, even though I have lost my job, and am not qualified for anything but a glorified nursemaid.' He turned his head and stared steadily through the window.

'And there's something else that must be said. I am not like my father. There is nothing in me that comes from him, thank God. What I am trying to tell you, Maggie, is that I won't *bother* you if you don't want me to.' His back was now almost turned on her. 'There is more to a marriage than what I just said. There is friendship, and tolerance, and pulling together, and even though you could have anybody with looks like yours, there is nobody in the whole world who could think as much of you as I do. Nobody, not even that other one . . . that Joe,' he added softly.

'And your mother, Kit?'

It had to be said. There would never, she felt, be another time, and so she had to say it now.

'Suppose she gets better and comes out of that place? There's not the room for both of us under one roof, you must know that.'

A shadow crossed his face. 'She won't come out, Maggie. I am afraid that my mother is less than an animal now, crawling about in her own dirt on a stone floor, with her food pushed at her in a wooden bowl. She eats it as if she was a pig at a trough.'

'Oh, my love. . . .'

With an effort, Maggie held out her arms, but ever considerate, he shook his head gently at her.

'You look tired out, love. I've talked too much. Just slide down again, and when you wake up I'm going to try you with a bit of steamed fish.'

He stood up, tucked her hands in beneath the blankets, and bending down, kissed her forehead.

'And you will marry me, Maggie? Sweet Maggie?'

She nodded. 'I will marry you, Kit . . . yes I will. . . .'

Even as she spoke the desire to sleep was overwhelming, and it was surely the distorted meandering thinking of a dream that made her start awake, and ask herself the question again:

Would Kit have asked her to marry him if his mother had not gone out of her mind and been put away? Would he even have come to *see* her again if she had not run out into the wind and the rain?

And perhaps the most important question. Would she have agreed to marry Kit if she had had the slightest hope that Joe Barton might come back some day?

7

'I wish we could do something to make the wedding a bit more of a *cheery* occasion,' Maggie told Kit. 'Mr Marsden says that music at a Chapel wedding is a manifestation of idolatry, but you know, for two pins I'd take the black ribbon off my hat and put the daisies back on.' She sighed deeply. 'Nothing can bring Father back, or the boys, or undo what has been done, so why can't we be happy about the one nice thing that's happening?'

Kit looked away from her and coughed gently.

'Maggie, listen to me. I'm going to say this once, then never again, because it pains me. When we're wed I never want to hear the name of a certain person mentioned again. What was done can't be undone as you rightly say, but I want you to know that I have forgiven you from the bottom of my heart for . . . for what you did.'

'With Joe?' Maggie said quickly, her eyes widening with an expression that would have halted Kit's fumbling flow of words had he seen it.

He stared through the window. 'You were . . . you are . . . not much more than a child. He knew he had to get away from the town or be sent to prison, and yet he had his way with you, even knowing he would never see you again. You were more sinned against than sinning; you must always try to remember that.'

Maggie felt her face flame with anger. 'Kit. Kit Carmichael. It takes two to do what we did, and I can't, I won't marry you with you thinking I was set on by a lust-crazed boy fleeing from justice.' She went to Kit and put her hand on his sleeve. 'We were *unhappy*, love. So very very unhappy. Me because of what Father had done to himself, and Joe . . . oh, Kit, I know you and your mother had to struggle, but have you any idea how some of the people in this town have to live?'

She twisted him round, forcing him to look at her.

'Like pigs, Kit Carmichael. His mother was a drunken *whore*, and don't flinch away because you're surprised I know what the word means. There was no money coming into that hovel but what Joe earned, and his mother spent that on drink most of the time. He tried to set her weekly payments out and she took against him for that, and his sister looked as if a puff of wind would blow her over. That house smelled, Kit! It smelled of other folk's bugs in the walls, and I'll tell you something else. There was a man there, a big man on leave from his ship, and he'd tried to touch Belle. Oh, Kit, there were rough men working the harvest where I came from, swearing sweating men, but they wouldn't have laid a finger on a child. Because that's all Joe's sister is, even though she's gone living-in now and left school.'

Maggie felt the tears swim in her eyes. 'Joe took that money because his mother had pinched what he'd saved for his sister's caps and frocks and aprons. That was why he had to run.' Her voice dropped to a whisper. 'And he'd nowhere to run to, Kit. So when he came here it wasn't me and him being wicked. It was him and me putting our arms round each other and trying to make things right just for a bit. We were heartbroken, Kit, each in our own way, so we forgot ourselves and just comforted each other, that's all.'

She lifted her head high. 'Is *that* what you're so set on forgiving me for, Kit? Because if you can't accept the truth, then there's no chance for us, is there?'

Every feature on Kit's face seemed to be working with emotion. His Maggie was too honest. Couldn't she see that he *wanted* to believe his own version of how she had been ravaged against her will by a brutal boy running from the police? Why did she have to make him face a truth he did not want to face? She was brave as well as honest, this bonny Maggie. Even though the long speech had drained her face of colour she was still strong. Like his mother had been strong.

Kit lowered his head and kissed her tenderly on the forehead, leaning without knowing it, on the strength that came from this young brown-haired slip of a girl.

'I'm sorry, lass,' he said. 'And we'll not talk about it any more, I promise. It's me what should be forgiven for upsetting you.'

Maggie's smile was tinged with irritation.

'Now, there's no need to go *that* far, Kit Carmichael.'

He only saw the smile, so he smiled too. If Maggie was happy, then so was he. For Kit Carmichael it was as simple as that.

They were married quietly one blustery Saturday morning, wearing black arm-bands round their coat sleeves. The Chapel was so cold that Maggie could actually feel her nose turning red, and behind her, Clara's mother sobbed noisily into her handkerchief all through the simple ceremony.

Clara and Arnie stood in for them, and after Mr Marsden had pronounced Maggie and Kit man and wife, he gave a quite uncalled-for little homily on the evils of drink, trusting they would enter their new life together in a state of sobriety and with due regard to the solemnity of their union.

Kit had found a job as a grocer's assistant in a flourishing little corner shop in an area crowded with back to back houses and pawn shops. It was no more than twenty minutes' walk away from Foundry Street, and he was to be left in sole charge for most of the day.

They had decided to live in Maggie's house, not only because the rent was a shilling less a week than for the one he had shared with his mother, but because it had a bigger backyard, and fitted cupboards flanking the fireplace in the living-room.

'Small details, but worthy of consideration,' he had said, believing it was his idea and not Maggie's.

'I'm sure I'd have seen his mother bobbing out at me from every cupboard,' Maggie had told Clara, 'especially when I was on my own at nights.'

'I wish we were going away to the seaside for a bit of a honeymoon,' Kit said as they walked back to Foundry Street arm in arm after it was all over.

Maggie gave his arm a little squeeze against her side, and told him it didn't matter.

'It was very good of Mr Yates at the shop to let you have the morning off, especially as you've only just started there.'

'Yes, and Saturday is a busy day,' Kit told her, 'we get a lot of women coming in and stocking up a bit with food before their husbands can get their hands on what's left of the money.'

'Terrible,' Maggie said, so automatically that Kit looked at her with concern. She was still so very pale, and her face, beneath the wide-brimmed hat, was all eyes and dark shadows, with little hollows where no hollows had been before.

Without telling anyone, the week before starting his new job, Kit had paid a visit to the doctor's surgery, to reassure himself that Maggie's recovery was complete.

'She still coughs a lot. Especially in the mornings, Doctor,' he said, standing in front of the wide-topped desk, twisting his cap round and round in his hands.

'Bringing up phelgm?'

'Aye.'

'Streaked with blood at any time?'

Kit flinched away from the inference, hating the doctor for putting it into words. Consumption was more a way of life than a disease in the network of streets with their sunless houses, but the doctor shocked him by voicing his own terrified suspicions and anguished fears.

'No blood, but she is not getting any fatter, Doctor, and she always seems to be cold, even when I build the fire half-way up the chimney. She doesn't eat enough to keep a bird alive, no matter what I tempt her appetite with.'

The doctor stared hard at Kit. Then he got up from behind his desk and took up his stance by the window, hooking his thumbs into the lapels of his waistcoat, and watching Kit through narrowed eyes.

Dammit, he might just as well have been listening to a worried mother talking about a sick daughter. He turned his back and stared out at the view of a brick wall pitted with holes. Dammit, the man was an old woman, if not an out and out homosexual, and no more cut out to be the new husband of a young and spirited girl like Maggie Craig than a boy child recently breached.

The whole thing was obscene somehow. He tapped on the window with a short clean fingernail. At the moment the girl was weak, run right into the ground with the shock of all that had happened to her. How she had pulled through he would never know.

But what would happen when she fully recovered and looked around her and saw the world was full of men who were real men, not soft flabby mother's boys, like the man standing quietly and patiently behind him.

Sighing he turned round and caught the look of anguished anxiety on Kit's big face as he waited to hear what he had convinced himself must surely be bad news. News the doctor was steeling himself to give.

'The poor bloke is looking for another mother,' the doctor told himself silently, and shook his head sadly from side to side.

'Miss Craig has been very ill,' he reminded Kit. 'But I am sure there is nothing that good food and rest won't put right. She comes of fine country stock remember, and that will put her in good stead, but I would recommend that she stays away from the mill for a while.'

He sighed and asked himself what was the use? They

killed themselves, these working-class wives, running back to work before they were fit, having babies one after another, wearing themselves out before they were thirty years old. Oh, he knew poverty was to blame, and dirt, and apathy, and ignorance, and stupidity, but it was something else, something his training had not prepared him for.

It was a grit these Lancashire women possessed, a determination that kept them going on and on, as if they never knew when to call it a day.

'Miss Craig will not be going back into the mill, Doctor,' Kit was saying, in that tiny voice so much at variance with his size. 'I've got a job with long hours, but I'll still have time to help round the house if I can see she's not resting enough.'

Then he asked a question quite simply, taking the doctor by surprise.

'Shall I keep on with rubbing her chest with goose-grease every night? She says the smell makes her feel sick.'

'Then stop doing it.'

The doctor watched Kit leave his surgery, stepping as neatly as if he were avoiding the cracks in the oilcloth, then before he slammed the bell with the flat of his hand to summon the next patient, he leaned back in his chair, crossed his hands behind his neck, and addressed the ceiling:

'Oh, my sainted aunt! Rubbing that little lass's chest with goose-grease every night, and never, I'd stake my life on it, letting his hands stray as much as an inch. I thought I'd heard it all, but I was wrong. God help that bonny, funny, normal little lass. That bloke's still married to his mother, and always will be.'

And even though it was his wedding day Kit was there behind the counter of the corner shop until an hour before midnight. In the last two hours he had sold a dozen candles singly to the same number of customers, a paper of pins, and a jar of milk, remembering from his boyhood to tip the jar first so that the coin fell out.

'Once I had to scrape a jarful of jam off a penny,' his mother had said, and her warning came back to him so vividly that he could almost sense her presence. He could feel her standing there in the darkened shop, watching him, instructing him, praising him, devouring him with her smothering attention, so that in the end, all initiative wiped out, he would turn to her to ask how to do the simplest things.

But now his mother had gone, and soon if she kept on refusing to eat, and throwing her food at the walls, she would die, and he would have to will himself to remember her as she used to be, not as she was now.

Kit glanced at the round clock on the wall, longing for the time when he could put the shutters up outside, lock the door, and go home.

There was no way he could have closed early, even if his conscience would have allowed him to, not with his boss, Mr Yates, living in the two upstairs rooms.

Though you'd have thought he would have come down and stood in for me, just for tonight, Kit told himself, then immediately reminded himself how lucky he was to have a job at all.

'What can I get you, love?' he asked a spare little woman approaching the counter with her purse clutched tightly in her hand. 'We've some nice bacon pieces going cheap. Make a tasty Sunday dinner if you boil them up with a handful of peas. . . .'

It was a dark night, a night entirely without stars, when at last he stepped out into the street. It was the hour when the only people he would be likely to meet would be the tramps, the homeless, those without the twopence it would cost for a bed and a pot of tea in the dosshouse.

Turning up the collar of his jacket, Kit increased his pace, and when he saw the candlelight flickering in the upstairs room at the front of the bottom house in Foundry

Street, he knew that his bride was lying in bed waiting for him.

Maggie had ironed her long calico nightdress frilled at the neck and round the cuffs, as carefully as if she was going to wear it for a walk in the park, and had brushed her hair till it stood out round her white face like a halo.

'Hello, love.' Kit put his curly head round the door. 'Have you had your cocoa, or shall I bring some up? I know what you're like for neglecting yourself when I'm not there to see to things.'

Maggie smiled at him. He really was the kindest man she had ever known. Not a grumble about having to stand on his feet serving groceries on his wedding day, just a touching concern for her and her nightly mug of cocoa.

He took off his jacket and hung it carefully over the chair-back, pulling the sleeves down and smoothing the lapels with his fingers. Then turning his back on her, he slipped first one brace, then the other off his shoulders, unbuttoned the front of his trousers, and dropped them round his ankles.

Politely Maggie stared at the window, concentrating on the yellow blind, but when she felt the mattress move she shot a startled glance in his direction and saw that Kit was laying his trousers neatly underneath the mattress.

'A habit of mine. Saves a lot of pressing,' he explained, then, holding a fold of his shirt decently between his legs, he came round the bed, blew out the candle, and got in, causing the mattress to sag down heavily, and sliding Maggie straight into his arms.

For a moment she panicked, holding herself stiffly against him, and moving her feet away from the hard hairiness of his legs. Then as she felt the familiar touch of his hand on her hair, and heard his whispering voice telling of his love, she relaxed against him, and buried her head in the warm smell of him, a smell tinged now with cheese and salt and scrubbing soap.

'He's a funny man that Mr Yates,' Kit said. 'Hardly human if you know what I mean, but he told me today he has three shops altogether. Three shops and he dresses like a tramp, and when I took the money upstairs he was sitting in a room with just the one candle and sacking tacked over the window.'

'Do you see much of him?' Maggie asked, wondering when what was going to happen would begin.

Kit stroked the hair away from her face with an absent-minded gesture, then casually rubbed one foot up and down her leg.

'No, I don't see all that much of him, considering it is his shop, but if it was mine there are a lot of things I would change.'

'Mmm?' Maggie felt her eyelids droop, and quickly opened her eyes and stretched them wide.

'Mmm?' she said again as Kit moved her head a fraction to one side to ease his arm into a more comfortable position.

'Well, for a start off I would be more lenient with tick. Mr Yates says I must not hand over even a penny paper of pins without catching hold of the money first. He says the previous owner of the shop went bankrupt through handing over food in exchange for clothes which customers promised to redeem the next week. But of course more often than not, they never did. It's a poor district, Maggie, but the biggest part of them are God-fearing folks. So if a customer's money runs out before Friday, and if she has been a good payer and keeps her word about paying back, well, I feel we would attract more customers by showing we have a bit of heart.'

It was no good. Maggie was so warm, so relaxed, so comfortable, that Kit's words were blurring into a maze of sounds, like a soft and lazy lullaby. Her eyelids drooped, her breath came softly and evenly, and Kit, realizing that she was dropping off to sleep, turned her over gently and fitted her on to his ample lap.

'Spoons in a box, love,' he whispered. 'Sleep tight, and if I snore, just give me a nudge.'

He tucked the bedclothes in carefully round her neck.

'Good night, Mrs Carmichael,' he said.

Within seconds his leg jerked against her own, and perversely, the minute Kit fell asleep, Maggie was suddenly wide awake.

This was her wedding day. The only wedding day she would have, come to think of it. There had been no flowers, no music, no dressing-up even. She stared wide-eyed into the darkness.

But that was how they had decided they wanted it, under the circumstances. She sighed, and instantly Kit's hand clasped her own. There had been two rows of women at the back of the Chapel, two full rows, and every single woman come to gape, to gossip in the street after it was over. To pity Kit's poor mother shut away in an asylum, and to pity her big son for being such a fool as to marry Maggie Craig, a girl who had gone tarnished to her own wedding.

But Kit had forgiven her. He had said so, and she had shouted at him and defended herself, Maggie remembered with a touch of shame. She had told him how it had been with her and Joe, and she had seen the way his eyes had clouded over with pain. She squeezed Kit's hand.

This was the second time she had lain with her body stretched close to a man's. She closed her eyes and remembered how Joe's hands had caressed her, starting with her face, then tracing the outline of her mouth. How slow his movements had been, stirring her into an aching response. Then he had pushed her blouse from her shoulders, tearing at the buttons, and fastening his lips hungrily over her breast. . . .

Maggie sat up suddenly, staring down at the humped shape that was Kit.

In another minute she would have turned and covered his face with kisses, but it wouldn't have been her husband she was thinking about, it would have been Joe Barton.

Kit was sleeping so soundly, so exhausted, so kind, so *good*. Maggie bet he had never had a wicked thought in his

mind, whilst she. . . . Carefully she lay down again, fitted
herself back on to his lap, closed her eyes and willed a sleep
that would not come. An hour later, with Kit snoring
gently into the back of her neck she faced a bewildered
truth.

It was her wedding night and her husband was not going
to make love to her.

He did not want to, and nor was he going to. He had
acted as if they had been married for years and years and
were past it.

'I'd think it was funny if I didn't know it wasn't,' Maggie
told herself, then she slid quietly out of bed.

Padding bare-footed over to the window, she pushed a
corner of the blind aside and looked down into the dark
street. Making love wasn't the only thing that mattered,
she was ready to admit that.

With Joe it had been wonderful, and joyous, and filled
with the ecstasy of giving. Tonight she had not expected or
even wished for that. No, it was just that the whole day
had been grey, and drab, with no excitement in any part
of it.

She rubbed a place clear on the window and narrowed
her eyes. For a moment she had thought that someone, a
man, had turned the corner from the canal bank . . . but it
was a shadow, a trick of the shifting clouds wisping across
the dark sky. Maggie let the blind drop back with a click,
and immediately Kit was calling out to her.

'Come to bed, lass. What are you doing standing there?
You'll catch your death.'

Maggie, shivering now, crept back into the warm
hollow she had recently left, facing the window, feeling Kit
tuck her in for the second time.

She was the luckiest girl in the world to be married to a
man as unselfish and kind as Kit Carmichael. She was . . .
oh she was. After what had happened about the baby that
nearly was, it would have served her right if no man had
ever looked her way again.

And yet, even as she counted her wedding day blessings, she knew that if the shadow down in the street had been a man, and that man had been Joe, then she would have run out of the house in her nightdress to meet him.

There were no two ways about that. . . .

8

'I'm only human,' Kit told himself aloud when the letter with the London postmark came for Maggie the next week.

Insisting on her lying in bed in the mornings – just till she got her strength up – he caught the postman actually in the act of raising his hand to the door knocker.

'I'll take that,' he said, his pulse beating quicker as he pushed the envelope in his pocket. Then he walked with his light springy step up the street, muttering to himself as he went.

Kit knew who had sent the letter. Maggie had told him that Joe Barton had said he was going to London to seek his fortune. Besides, it was addressed to Maggie *Craig*. He patted the pocket as he crossed the main shopping street, then turned into the hilly web of streets he used as a short cut to the shop, passing late stragglers as they clattered their way down to the mill.

Once in the shop, he went straight through into the back, a small room kept for stores, and bending down set a match to the pile of shavings and wrappings in the grate.

He slid a finger under the flap of the envelope, took out a closely written sheet of paper, saw Joe's name scrawled at the bottom, and tore and tore until the letter was shredded into pieces not much bigger than confetti.

'And that's where they'll go till he stops sending them,' he said aloud, his anger as white-hot as the ashes which crumbled before his gaze. 'Every man Jack of 'em. Every single one!'

Although Wednesday was supposed to be Kit's day off, Mr Yates sometimes sent him down to the wholesale warehouse at the back of the station, preventing him from catching the train to the gaunt asylum built like a medieval prison.

When Mr Yates relented enough to allow his assistant to take what was, after all, no more than his due, three weeks had gone by since Kit's last visit.

'Let me come with you,' Maggie pleaded. 'I would wait outside, but at least I would be with you. I feel strong enough now. An' just look at my hair! It's growing fast!' She pulled hard at a strand. 'I'm getting fat on all that cocoa and the bits you bring home from the shop.' She patted her flat stomach. 'Fat and a lazy so-and-so, that's me.'

She stood in front of him, laughing. 'Do you know, Kit, I've never been as idle in the whole of my life. If the weather turns warm I'll be taking a chair outside and sitting on the flags with Clara and her mother.'

Kit smiled, adoring her, knowing that his Maggie would never do that. She was too ladylike to sit out at the front, and his mother had been just the same. In some ways Maggie reminded him of the way his mother had been a long time ago.

His mother had devoured the newspapers, every single word, and her movements had been quick and certain like Maggie's.

He watched her as she bustled about the room, laying a white cloth over the red chenille on the table, setting out knives and forks, her cheeks pink from the oven.

Aye, she was a grand little wife, and he wasn't going to have her upset by going with him this afternoon. He wasn't going to have her upset by anything, not if he, Kit Carmichael, could help it. . . .

Three hours later, Kit walked back down Foundry Street, a scarf held over his face, praying he could get into the house without being seen. Hoping he could clean himself up a bit before Maggie saw him.

They had tried to make him say he would stop the visits, but he could never say that. How could he when the emaciated, desperate, vicious little creature who had rushed at him, raking her nails down his cheeks, biting, mouthing obscenities, had once been his mother. So caring that she would take him into her own bed, soothing him with whispered words of love when he had the toothache bad?

But it was no use. Maggie was there even as he put his hand on the latch, drawing him inside with a smothered exclamation of horror.

'She did not know what she was doing,' he kept saying, as she bathed the long weals with water, dabbing at them gently. 'They told me she had been quieter for a while, that she had been eating better, and so they stopped giving her the dope for a while.'

Maggie winced as she bathed a nostril that looked as if it had been half torn away.

'You look as if you've been attacked by a wild animal,' she whispered, horrified, shuddering at the clear marking of teeth bites at the side of his neck. 'Maybe she is not as insane as they think? Maybe she has found out somehow that you have married me?'

'How could she do that, love?'

Maggie laid the damp cloth tenderly over a deep scratch. 'I don't know, but they say there's none as astute as the daft.'

Kit bit his lip. 'Sometimes I blame myself for her being in there. Perhaps I should have . . .'

Maggie suddenly exploded. Throwing the cloth down into the bowl of warm water, so that it splashed over the side, she said in her clear voice:

'That is rubbish, Kit! As far as your mother is concerned you have done nothing to reproach yourself for. Nothing!'

Making a mistake, turning his swollen face towards her, Kit tried to explain.

'But I have, love, don't you see? Many a night, without you knowing it, I've laid awake going over what happened that night.' He tried to find the right words. . . . 'To begin with, I was so upset when Arnie came round, I left her all alone in the house, with hardly a proper explanation as to how long I would be.' He put up a hand to his cheek and, wincing, took it quickly away. 'I was that upset, you see.'

'Go on.' Maggie's voice was ominously quiet.

'Then you walked in, hours later. Soaked to the skin and ill. But it must have frightened the life out of her, seeing you. As far as she knew, you had come to torment her.'

Now Maggie's hands were on her hips. '*Torment* her?'

'Aye, it wouldn't have been the first time. There was a girl once, a long time ago, a rather forward sort of girl, and she stopped my mother on her way to the butcher's, and said some awful things. Dreadful, hurting things. My mother had a terrible attack that night.'

Maggie walked over to the fire, bent down and picked up the poker, and found to her surprise that her hand was actually trembling. She dropped it into the hearth with a clatter.

'True things, I suspect, Kit. True, just the same.'

His swollen mouth dropped open into a wide O of amazement.

'What did you say?'

Maggie lifted her head. 'I suspect that girl said a few of the things I should have had the courage to say to you long ago, Kit. Listen to me. . . . Your mother tried to kill me that night. She was out of her mind with fear and jealousy because she thought I was going to take her precious son away from her. She wasn't daft enough or ill enough not to know what to do, was she? If you had not come in when you did I would have died, you've told me that yourself. And she would have won.'

Maggie started to pace up and down, almost beside herself with anger and frustration.

'And I'll tell you something else, Kit Carmichael. I am sick and tired of listening to stories about how wonderful your mother was, how self-sacrificing, how good. How she struggled to make ends meet. Wouldn't any mother do that for her child? Yes, she would, but she would never leave that child her slave for the rest of his life. She would do all that for nothing. *Nothing.* Expecting nothing in return, not even love if it wasn't freely given!'

Kit shifted uncomfortably in his chair, the blood oozing from his nostril again. So overcome with shock to hear her talk like that he let the blood trickle over his chin without raising a hand to mop it away.

Illogically the sight infuriated Maggie even more.

'You know something? You've told me how inconsiderate your father was. How he drank and went with other women; how he used to recite in pubs, and how he went off with a loose woman in the end?'

She gave a fierce little nod of the head. 'Has it ever once occurred to you, that between you, you and your mother emasculated him so much that he had to get away or be diminished?'

'He was a bad sort, Maggie. A real bad penny.'

So worked up that tears of frustration filled her eyes, Maggie stamped her foot.

'Well, it may surprise you to know that from the things I've heard about your father, I've decided I would have liked him. Yes, *liked* him, Kit. An' admired him an' all. An' I hope he spent years and years making passionate love to his lady friend. I hope she had bright red hair, and wore green corsets just to cheer him up, an' I hope they laughed and kissed so that he soon forgot the domineering old cow he'd had for a wife! That's what I hope, Kit Carmichael!'

There was silence for a long moment, then Kit shook his head at her in genuine and honest bewilderment.

'You don't mean any of that now, Maggie. It's upset you seeing me like this. It shows you're nearly better. . . . My mother always used to say that when . . .'

The bowl of water was on the table one minute and in Maggie's hand the next. Then the water was sloshing over Kit's head, running down his scratched face, dripping in rivulets down the towel she had placed with such concern round his neck not ten minutes before.

She stared at his astonished face, at his mouth, wide open like a fish gasping for air. But her anger was not ready to evaporate, not quite yet.

'If I hear once more what your flamin' mother used to say . . . if just once more you try to praise her to me after what she tried to do . . . the next time you'll get the bowl as well!'

Leaving Kit dripping, but with her own dignity intact, Maggie ran upstairs to sit on the edge of the bed, clenching and unclenching her hands, far too upset to cry. When Kit followed her upstairs, leaving the upturned bowl and the pool of water untouched on the floor, there was a new and unexpected urgency in the way he took her in his arms.

'Don't ever shout at me like that again,' he said, laying his swollen cheek against her own. 'I won't go and see my mother again if that is what you want.'

'It isn't what I want,' Maggie said wearily, but now, replacing her spent anger, was a languid tenderness, a floating weariness so filling her with pleasure she lay back and closed her eyes.

'Take my dress off for me, Kit,' she whispered, and his hands undid the buttons neatly, slid the dress from her shoulders, held it as she kicked her legs free of it.

'Now my bodice,' she said, and he started on the smaller buttons, feeling the silkiness of her warm flesh against his fingers.

'I love only you, little sweetheart, you know that. You must know that,' he told her.

'Kiss me here!' Maggie whispered, throwing her head back and pressing his curly head down on to her breasts. 'Kiss me here, *please*.'

And now as his lips caressed her nipples with an exploratory circling movement, the aching weariness spread to her stomach, to her thighs, so that with a fiercely desperate longing she pulled him over so that he lay on top of her. Then she tangled her fingers in his hair and murmured brokenly that she was sorry, that she was truly sorry. . . .

Almost, but not quite, he stopped what he was doing by repeatedly asking her if he was hurting her. Whispering he would stop if he was.

And hearing the apology in his voice, sensing the reluctance in his fumbling movements, Maggie held him tightly, willing him to forget himself and take her properly. Telling him to hurt her, pleading with him silently to assert his manhood, to stop, even in the act of making love, being so . . . maddeningly considerate.

When it was over, and he rolled away from her, still whispering shamed apologies, Maggie closed her ears to him and curled herself up into a ball. His hot face pressed into her neck as he slept, and she tried to remember, to recapture the floating quiet, the gentle feeling of tenderness she had felt for Joe when their love-making had ended. He too had slept, but that was the time she had held his dark head close to her breasts as a languid sweetness flowed through her.

This time she felt unclean, God forgive her. This time she wanted to slide away from him and wash herself all over at the wash-stand in the corner of the room

9

When Maggie told Kit she was sure, quite sure that she was going to have a baby, it put, as he said straight away, a stop to a lot of things.

It put a stop to her going back to the mill as she had been determined to do, and it put a stop to lifting anything heavier than a saucepan – at least when he was around to see.

And it stopped his sporadic attempts to make love to her.

Three or four times, since the row they had had about his mother, since her frustrated rage had forced him to lose control, he had made a valiant attempt, but his heart was not in it.

There was too much of the role of aggressor in the act for him to enjoy it, and the fumbling flabbiness of the part of him that should have been hard and erect, made Maggie imagine that the first time had been a figment of her imagination.

Yet somehow she had conceived, and Kit was showing almost childlike joy in the prospect of being a father. He worked even longer hours, for sometimes as little as an extra shilling in his wages, and his Wednesday afternoon visits to his mother were few and far between now that she no longer recognized him.

When she died, half-way through Maggie's pregnancy, his sadness was tinged with relief, and he told himself that she was better off, that it was a merciful release, repeating to himself the trite phrases trotted out by the Chapel members who remembered her as she used to be.

Considerate and kind as ever, he was careful not to grieve openly in front of his wife, even though she held him in her arms and comforted him. Not because the old woman had died – she was not such a hypocrite as that – but because if Kit was sad then she was sad also.

Yet it seemed to her that old Mrs Carmichael was still there, influencing her son from beyond the grave, Maggie thought one night as Kit held her close to him in bed. He had formed the habit of burrowing his head between the soft curves of her breasts, kissing each one in turn, gently caressing with his hands, groaning with pleasure, but making no attempt to carry his love-making any further.

So Maggie held him, telling herself that as usual, Kit was being his over-considerate self. She held him close, stroking his hair, totally unaware that he was reliving the times his mother had taken him into her bed as a small boy to relieve the stabbing pain of toothache.

'Mother . . .' he whispered to himself.

'Maggie . . .' he sighed aloud.

Three more letters came with the London postmark before Maggie's baby was born, and Kit destroyed each one of them. He burnt them without guilt in the fire at the back of the shop, and when they stopped coming he rejoiced.

'I've done the right thing, the only thing. No good upsetting her while she's like she is,' he muttered.

So fascinated was he by all the medical details of her pregnancy that he would kneel down on the rag rug, and lay his head against her stomach as she sat by the fire.

'I can feel it kicking!' he would say.

'The very minute you start in labour you must send to the shop for me,' he told her over and over again. 'I want to be there to look after you before the midwife comes. Think on and don't forget then.'

Maggie promised, but when, on a cold morning, with the wind rattling the frames of the sash windows till she thought they would drop out, her first pains began, the first thing she wanted was for Kit to be gone from the house. She managed somehow to keep her expression calm when the dragging sensation in her back made her want to moan. She prayed for it to be time for him to go downstairs and light the fire, and when he brought the usual cup of tea upstairs she took it from him and smiled.

'You had a bad night, didn't you, love?' he said, his face anxious and worried.

'The wind kept me awake,' she told him.

When he had gone she got out of bed, pulled a shawl round her shoulders and going downstairs knocked on the wall for Clara.

'It'll be a long time yet,' Clara said with the wisdom of a woman, with the know-all of a woman who had never given birth to a child.

'It won't.' Maggie shook her head, holding on to a corner of the table, her face draining of colour. 'I've been at it a long time.'

'And Kit's gone and left you to go to the shop?' Clara's eye shot straight down into its socket. 'That doesn't sound like him. You'd have thought it was him having the baby the way he's been carrying on.'

'I didn't tell him. I don't want fussing.' Maggie opened the bottom drawer of the chest and took out a pile of baby clothes, setting them out on the fireguard to air. 'And I don't want the midwife yet either. All I want at the moment is a nice cup of tea, Clara.'

'He would only have been in the way,' she told Clara's mother three hours later in the little front bedroom, clenching her teeth as she pulled hard on a roller towel fastened to the bottom of the bed.

'No, he's done his bit, and anyway it's no place for a man,' Mrs Hobkirk agreed, wiping the sweat from Maggie's forehead then going to sit by the fire.

The fire had been lit in the tiny grate in honour of the occasion, a smouldering fire that did little else but belch clouds of smoke into the room.

'You're going on nicely, love,' Mrs Hobkirk told Maggie from time to time. 'It's with being country bred like as not.'

Maggie caught her breath as pain gripped, and clamped her teeth down on her bottom lip to stop herself from crying out.

What she could not accept, what she must *not* accept, was that the other baby, Joe's baby, that half-formed embryo, had meant more to her than this full-term one did. Then, that awful time, she had been alone, all alone, not surrounded by attention and care, with the baby's things airing downstairs and a binder all ready to be wrapped round her stomach once the baby was born.

This baby had everything, and Joe's baby, the little one that had never had a chance, had had nothing. She drew up her legs and whimpered as another pain caught her unawares.

'I think it's time to send for the nurse,' she said quietly, 'and then perhaps Arnie could go and tell Kit. He'll never forgive me if it's all over when he comes home.'

'I was a full two days with our Clara, then it had to be the forceps,' Mrs Hobkirk said, but when Nurse O'Mara came into the house, taking charge even before she had climbed the stairs, she was able to tell Maggie that her baby had black hair.

'You left it long enough,' she scolded Mrs Hobkirk, then she turned her attention to Maggie.

'Right, love. Hang on to my pinny if you want to. Come on now! Right! That's a good girl!'

And as Kit opened the front door, the first real sound that Maggie had uttered, froze him to the spot with terror.

'How long has she been like that?' he demanded, glaring at Clara who was taking the kettle from the trivet, and starting with it for the stairs.

'Give that to me,' he ordered, his manners forgotten completely.

He had just reached the tiny landing when he heard the baby cry, a full-blown howl of outraged fury. Stopping transfixed in the doorway, the kettle still miraculously in his hand, he saw the nurse holding his daughter by the ankles and giving her a resounding slap between her shoulder blades.

'Get that man out of here!'

Nurse O'Mara's voice had the authority of a woman doing a woman's job, and Clara's mother, enjoying every minute, walked over to Kit, took the kettle from him with one hand, and with the other firmly closed the door in his face.

'How *dare* he!' Nurse O'Mara said, handing over the baby, and bending over the bed again. 'In all me born days that's the first man, not counting the doctor, who has ever set a foot in his wife's room before I've got her all tidied up like. Whatever is the world coming to?'

'Is the baby perfect?' Maggie's voice whispered from the rumpled bed.

'A fine girl, love,' the nurse said. 'Now just do as I tell you, and then you can see for yourself.'

'It wasn't all that bad,' Maggie said, lifting both arms above her head only to have them smartly pulled down by the nurse.

'No raising your arms my goodness me,' she said, reaching for the pile of newspapers at the foot of the bed. 'If all my mothers had an easy time as you've had, love, there'd be nothing for me to do. May you go on and have a dozen if they all come as easy as this one.'

'Catholic,' Mrs Hobkirk said with a sniff when the nurse had gone downstairs with the baby in her arms, bound and swaddled so tightly her tiny face had turned purple. 'A dozen indeed! They'd like that just so they can take us over. I've never had a good word for the Pope ever since that Bernadette Cleary from the top house used to cross herself every time she saw our Clara.'

Maggie raised heavy eyelids in silent enquiry.

'Because of her eye,' Mrs Hobkirk explained, tucking the bedclothes in so firmly that Maggie feared her ankles would never revert to their normal position again. 'Superstitious rubbish, that's all their religion is.'

'It's a girl, Mr Carmichael,' Nurse O'Mara said, standing before Kit and showing him the baby. 'A bonny little girl. Small to be sure, but with a pair of lungs on her like the six o'clock hooter.'

Kit looked at the tiny squashed face, at the blood-red pressure marks on the snub nose, at the forehead creased into lines of anxiety. Tears gathered in his eyes and rolled down his cheeks. All along he had been convinced that his Maggie would have a girl. He had seen himself walking up the street with a bouncy little girl holding on to his hand, staring up at him in adoration.

Kit didn't like little boys. The boys who played out in the street round the lamp standards were dirty and noisy, and often shouted rude things after him. They had black fingernails and permanent bruises on their knees and they played all the rough and tumble games he had never wanted to play.

'When can I see my wife?'

His tone was suitably humble and Nurse O'Mara, knowing she had asserted her authority and won, said he could go up straight away.

'We will call her Rose, because that is what she is, a perfect pink beautiful rose.' He looked at his wife and his daughter with the expression of a man who has just seen a miracle, and Maggie looked down at the tiny face, at the twitching eyelids and the furiously sucking lower lip.

There was nothing rose-like about this baby who stared cross-eyed up at her with the picking glance of the dead and buried Mrs Carmichael.

'She's like your mother,' she said, then closed her eyes before she could see the pleasure on Kit's happy face.

10

When the baby was almost four months old, the annual fair came to the town, and Maggie, on the evening of Kit's Wednesday off, suggested that they took the sleeping baby next door and then walked down to the market-place.

'Fairs are filthy places, full of gyppos,' Kit said, busy with the pipe he had taken to smoking, striking one match after another instead of using the tapers Maggie had placed in a jar in the hearth.

'Kit Carmichael,' she said, standing before him with her head on one side, and her eyes bird-bright. 'If I do not get out of this house I will die of boredom. No, I won't. I will run round this room pulling the pictures down from the walls. I will take the pots from the dresser and smash them one by one on the floor, and I will jump on the table and do a clog-dance in my bare feet. I will!'

She plumped herself down on his knees, setting the rocking chair into motion, leaning back, the narrow band round the neck of her dress unbuttoned to reveal the line of her throat, and the soft swell of her breasts.

'Kit, oh, Kit, do you never want to burst out of yourself and *do* something mad? Anything? Just to relieve your feelings?'

'Not really,' Kit said honestly.

He glanced down at her with affection, and thought what a child she was. In spite of her baby daughter asleep in her cradle upstairs, in spite of her growing hair pinned up into the semblance of a tiny bun with little tendrils escaping from it. As unlike most of the women who came into the shop as chalk from cheese.

Drabs most of them, with shawls round their heads and clogs on their feet, their babies fed on condensed milk at two tins for threepence-halfpenny. Terrible managers of money, unlike his Maggie who could make fourpence do the work of a shilling, and then have something left over.

He bent his head, and holding his pipe well away, kissed her gently at the side of her mouth.

'Kiss me *properly*!' Maggie gripped him fiercely to her. 'Pretend I am a beautiful woman with long red hair.' She pulled at a strand of her shortened hair and found that it just reached her mouth. 'This is the way I measure it every day. Look, Kit, soon it will reach my right ear and then soon I will be able to put it up into a proper bun, not a little scraggy thing like a hen's backside.'

He pretended to be shocked and failed.

'What if Clara comes in?' He shifted uncomfortably. 'She's in before you can blink.'

'She always calls out first,' Maggie reminded him. 'Yoo-hoo!' she called, in such an exact imitation of Clara's loud and ringing voice that Kit laughed in spite of himself.

Maggie got up from his knee, unkissed and restless.

'I don't like the way Clara comes in like that,' she confessed. 'I never have, but she has been so kind to me I would not dream of saying anything. Once I even tried putting the bolt on the front door, but she just came round the back.

' "What have you locked the door for? You been up to summat I don't know about?" she asked me, straight out. Kit. Let's go to the fair. Just to look, then?'

Knowing when he was beaten, Kit knocked out his pipe and went to fetch his jacket.

'All right then, Maggie, but not for long now. Bring the baby down and we'll go to the fair.'

Then, as he was enveloped in a bear-hug that almost knocked him off his feet, he smiled.

'I don't know about you wanting to put your hair up. It strikes me the way you behave it would suit you better floating down your back. Strikes me you're not old enough to behave like a married lady. . . .'

There was no need to risk waking the baby to take her in next door, because Clara offered at once to come in and sit.

'Arnie's gone out again,' she grumbled. 'So I might as well sit in your house as in me own. He's gone up to the Mother Redcap, to play dominoes he says, but he'll come back smelling like a brewery and swear he's had nowt but a pint of ale. I'd think he'd got himself another woman if I thought he had it in him.'

'Poor Clara,' Maggie said, as with her arm linked into Kit's, they set off for the market-place.

It was a warm evening, an evening anticipatory with the soft warmth of the summer yet to come. Maggie wore the hat with the daisies sewn back on to the wide brim, her navy-blue coat, and her much darned gloves buttoned neatly into place. Her eyes sparkled with excitement, and when they saw the fair, lit to splendour by naptha-lights, and when they passed the caravans and the weather-stained tents, she gripped Kit's arm even more tightly.

'Once, when I was a little girl, my father took me to a fair, and one of the fair-ground men took us inside his caravan, and I have never forgotten it. There were white muslin curtains with pink bows, and the beds were like berths on a ship.'

Then as the thought of ships came into her mind, her face was still, all the vivacity gone from it. 'Do you know, Kit, there are whole days now when I never even think about my brothers. I don't want to forget them, but I will, I know.' She looked up at him earnestly. 'Oh, Kit, doesn't it make you think that we owe it to ourselves to make the most of every day, of every minute, because we never know what is going to happen, do we?'

Used to her rapid change of mood and unable to follow

her swift and emotional reasoning most of the time, Kit patted the hand that lay on his arm.

'What a life for the fair people,' he said, wishing he was back home already. 'Packing all night, then moving on to another town. Collecting the horses from the inns they've been stabled at, and moving on. Not putting down roots, like us.' He smiled at his wife's glowing face. 'Not lucky like us.'

He held even more tightly to Maggie's arm, afraid to let her move away from his side by as much as an inch. Convinced that all the riff-raff of the town and the surrounding countryside were there that evening at the fair. Men with weasel faces, caps pulled down over shifty eyes, factory girls with their high shrill laughter as they moved from one side-show to another, linking arms. Fathers, who should have known better, in his opinion, with small boys riding piggy-back, the night women with raddled faces, and over there by the Bioscope, a woman known as the town's oldest whore, with only half a nose.

Maggie was pulling him towards a pea-boiling cart, the steam rising from its cauldron, then on to a hot-potato cart, the coals glowing red and the box of salt suspended from the side.

'Please, Kit,' she pleaded, and much against his better judgement, Kit handed over a penny and received in a double fold of newspaper, six small potatoes, roasted in their skins.

Then, as a father would indulge a beloved child, he watched as his wife unbuttoned her gloves, handed them over to him for safe keeping, and smiling broadly at the man in charge of the cart, put her hand into the salt-box and sprinkled the potatoes carefully, one by one.

'Oh!' she fanned her mouth with a hand. 'They're red-hot, but you don't know what you are missing, Kit.'

Just to please her, he took one, averting his eyes from the potato man's dirty hands, their nails broken and black-rimmed. His fastidious nature winced at the indignity, and what his mother would have called the 'commonness' of it all.

Never taking his eyes from Maggie's straight little back, he followed her reluctantly to a side-show where the dancing ladies shook their tambourines and wiggled their hips in time to tinny music from the hurdy-gurdy.

There was a man, a young, bold-looking man with a shock of jet-black hair, and a face as brown as a hazel-nut, standing on the makeshift platform, calling out to the crowd.

'Feast your eyes, ladies and gentlemen!' he shouted. 'What you are seeing now is nothing to what you will see if you come inside the tent. Straight from a London music-hall every man Jack of 'em. Chorus girls, ladies and gentlemen, in between their London engagements, and here to delight you with their abandoned dancing!' He winked at Maggie. 'Talk about the Can-Can. This little lot make the Can-Can seem like a ruddy minuet done in their sleep.' Unable to take her eyes off him, and seeing Joe Barton in the tilt of the black head, the boldness of the laughing eyes, Maggie pulled at Kit's sleeve.

'Let's go in,' she said, a hot potato half-way to her mouth.

Kit took her arm and tried to pull her away, but she stood firm.

'There aren't any ladies going in,' he pointed out, trying not to look at a blown-up picture of a girl lifting her skirts to show a wide expanse of bare leg encircled by a frilly garter.

'I've heard they don't wear no bloomers,' a man's voice said into a sudden silence, and the dark young man threw back his head, showing a strong line of throat as he burst into uninhibited laughter.

'Come in and see for yourself, mister,' he called out.

Although Maggie had given no sign of having heard, Kit saw that she had turned scarlet, and made no protest when he led her away.

'They're not like the Romanies who used to come round

to the house selling pegs,' she conceded, and Kit, taking advantage of her hesitation, handed her his clean handkerchief to wipe her hands, then the gloves, pulling her into the shadow of a tent as he helped her to button them on again.

'I *told* you you wouldn't like it, love,' he said.

She lifted her head and stared straight into his eyes.

'I *could* like it,' she flared, then biting her lips, was silent again.

What she had almost said was: 'I could have liked it if you had not been here spoiling it all for me.'

For a long moment they stood together, Kit miserably uncomfortable in surroundings he hated and mistrusted, and Maggie restlessly defiant, craving something she could not put a name to. Something far more than the loud blaring music, the happy, pushing crowd, the vulgarity of it all.

'Go home!' she wanted to shout at Kit. 'Leave me to be myself again! To be young again. To be winked at by the man with black hair who reminded me of Joe, to eat hot peas doused in vinegar, and brandysnaps straight from the bag.' She clasped her gloved hands together, the music filling her senses, almost as if it were a part of her.

'Let's go on the horses, Kit . . . oh, please. I haven't been on a roundabout since I can't remember.'

'It's coming on to rain,' Kit said, presenting his face with relief to the sky. 'I said it would.'

Even the fair people raced for shelter as the cloudburst caught them unawares, and within minutes the whole glittering display of stalls looked like some dingy squalid ruin, with tent flaps whipping back against the canvas in the strong wind. Girls squealed as their boots slithered and slipped over the greasy cobblestones.

Quickly Kit, with his arm protectively round Maggie, guided her across the road flanking the ground, and pulled her into the shelter of a wooden booth, specially set up for the three days of the fair.

'Let's go inside,' Maggie said, clinging on to his arm with one hand and hanging on to her hat with the other.

'Oh, Kit, it's not a public house. It's only a place set up just for the fair, and anyway, I haven't signed the Pledge, remember?'

'It's not right,' Kit kept saying, as sitting opposite to his wife round an upturned barrel, he watched her sipping a glass of ale, her eyes blazing with excitement, missing nothing as she watched the people crowding in out of the rain, the men shaking the raindrops from their caps, and calling out to each other.

'To think all this is going on while I sit at home with my sewing round the fire!' she marvelled.

'This place only has a three-day licence,' Kit reminded her, his face registering a mixture of pride in the attention she was attracting, and apprehension at what she might do next.

'I know. I know, Kit. But look over there. That little man hardly able to stand up is one of the door-keepers at the Teetotal Mission! It is him, it is, and oh, Kit, he's as drunk as a lord. Don't you think that's funny?'

'No,' Kit said, jumping up with dismay as the man, an old soldier, and a supposedly reformed character, started to weave his unsteady way towards them. 'Come on, we're going home,' he said.

The rain had stopped as quickly as it had started, and the stall-holders were taking the covers off the trays of ginger-bread, the Eccles cakes, the nuts and the brandy-snaps.

'Let's buy some and take them home for Clara,' Maggie said.

But Kit had had enough.

'We're going home,' he repeated stubbornly. 'How you could think that old man in there was funny, I don't know. He was maudlin and slavvery, and he reminded me of the way my father used to look when he had been drinking. Leering and then being sick over everything, and my mother having to mop up after him. You don't know what it was like, or what we had to suffer because he went in places like that!'

Maggie stared at him in astonishment.

'But we weren't going to get drunk, Kit. Just because you don't approve of something doesn't mean you have to run away from it.' She tripped and would have fallen but for his steadying hand.

'Not so quickly, Kit. I can't keep up.'

'That man made me feel sick,' Kit said.

Maggie stared at him. 'Kit, what's wrong? How do we know what that poor old man went through when he was serving his time in the army? He's old enough to have fought in the Crimean War. How do we know that just for once he wanted to sing and shout and pretend he wasn't cold and alone, with nobody left to care for him?'

'You just don't know what you are talking about,' Kit said.

He was walking along with his head bent as if the rain was still beating down. 'And look at you, Maggie Car- michael. Sitting there amongst them. *Enjoying* yourself!'

Maggie stopped dead so that he had to turn and face her. In her anger she slipped into dialect.

'Aye. Enjoying meself, Kit. Just for once enjoying meself.' She stamped her foot. 'I know what you would like to do.'

'And what is that?'

'Wrap me up in cotton-wool, and shut me up in the house like a prisoner. You don't even like me going to the market. You'd like me to be like me father, sitting by the fire, and only smelling the fresh air when I put me nose outside the back door. Wouldn't you?'

'Don't talk daft.'

'You're the one what's daft, not me,' Maggie answered childishly, hearing herself being childish, and not being able to stop herself.

Now the sounds of the fairground were receding, and

Maggie turned her head once or twice, but in silence, with his hand firmly on her arm, Kit urged her along.

His sense of what was right and proper kept him talking to Clara after Maggie had rushed upstairs to the bedroom.

'Had a few words, have you?'

Kit nodded miserably, knowing there was no point in taking offence at Clara when none was meant.

She came over to where he sat slumped in his chair and patted his shoulder.

'Aye, well, she's young, Mr Carmichael, and she's had a rough time taken all in all. She's different, tha knows.' Clara touched the side of her head with a stubby finger. 'Plenty up there, tha knows.'

Kit raised his head and stared at Clara's bland uninteresting face set above her thick neck, and saw the compassion in her sliding eye.

'I can't seem to follow what she's getting at sometimes, Mrs Preston,' he confided.

Clara sniffed. 'If she wants to go back in the mill I'd allus have the baby to mind. We'd manage her between us, me mother and me.'

Kit shook his head. 'There's no need for that, Mrs Preston. I'm not having my wife going out to work, not as long as I can provide.'

'Suit yourself,' Clara said, huffed, but determined not to show it.

When Kit went into the bedroom Maggie was undressed and sitting up in bed with a grey-fringed shawl round her shoulders, feeding the baby.

He hovered in the doorway, uncertain what to say or do next, getting no lead from his wife, her face hidden by the fall of brown hair, long enough now to cover her eyes.

'I'll take the nappy downstairs and put it on soak, and fetch your cocoa,' he said in a humble tone.

'Thank you,' Maggie said. 'You are very kind.'

The completely detached tone of her voice hurt him so much that he went to sit by her on the bed, his weight causing the mattress to sag down as usual. He stared at her in misery, biting his lip.

It was no good, he could not bear it when she was funny with him, like this. He had not been able to bear it when his mother had been cross with him either. It left him stranded and unsure of himself, unsure of anything.

'Are you not speaking to me?' he asked, putting out a hand towards her. 'Are we not friends, then?'

Maggie sighed and took her time about prizing the fiercely sucking mouth from her breast. The blue veins contrasted with the whiteness of her skin, and in spite of his misery Kit felt the stirrings of a kind of desire. He knew a sudden sharp jealousy, a hatred almost for the baby, its head lolling back on a neck that appeared to be broken, milk dribbling down its rounded chin.

'All right then, I'll tell you,' he said, his voice sounding alien even to his own ears.

'Tell me what?' Maggie said with studied indifference, moving the baby over to the other side.

'I'll tell you why I wanted you home, and quick. Because I saw that gyppo looking at you and winking at you. Him shouting the odds about those girls being chorus girls and coming from London.' He snorted with disgust. 'London! That lot have never been no further than Todmorden. Dirty fast little pieces, and as for him, I saw him staring at you with his eyes standing out like chapel hat-pegs, an' I saw you smile at him, and wink back. So don't deny it. An' another thing. He reminded you of someone, another one with a cheeky grin. You think I've forgotten, but I haven't. You think I'm daft, but I'm not. I have feelings like anybody else.'

'Oh, Kit. . . .' Maggie smoothed her daughter's round head, her hand moving in a gentle circular movement that quickened Kit's heart-beats. 'That boy reminded me of when I was a little girl and the Romanies used to camp on the edge of the wood.' She refused to meet his eyes lest he saw that she was lying. 'I remembered a young man just like him who rode with his family on a cart pulled by a painfully thin donkey. I was fetching the milk and he winked at me, and when I tried to wink back he burst out laughing.' She lifted the baby and held her over a shoulder. 'There now, she's drunk herself to sleep.

'Never be jealous, Kit,' she whispered later, 'but I like it when you are. I do.' She wound her arms round his neck, and bewildered by the frenzy of her passion, half aware that even as he struggled to comply, she was thinking of the man at the fair, Kit moved away from her as soon as it was over.

He didn't want to look at his wife, because he did not like what he saw. This was not the young girl with daisies on her hat, and the demure expression that could change in a flash to twinkling mischief. This was a flushed and beautiful woman, eyelids heavy over dream-filled slumbering eyes.

'You won't have another baby on account of you're feeding,' he muttered, backing away from the bed, and tripping over the worn oilcloth by the door. 'But we'd best be careful . . . I'm not having you knocked up again, not just when you're picking up.' He rubbed his finger across his chin, wondering how he could put it best.

'So I'll go through into the back. The bed's made up. It's only fair . . . only fair.'

And as he slid between cold sheets in the single bed in the room where Thomas Craig had killed himself, he failed to hear his wife's muffled sobs as she wept for a man she never thought to see again.

Only one letter came from Joe Barton during the next year, and Kit marked the envelope NOT KNOWN AT THIS ADDRESS, and posted it back into the letter-box.

Rose walked before she was one, but made no attempt at

talking, and Maggie, exhausted by the tantrums of the little doll-like child who would throw herself on the floor, kicking and screaming if her will was denied, took her to the doctor to ask him if her daughter was tongue-tied.

'She'll be talking your heads off. You won't be able to get a word in edgeways,' the doctor reassured Maggie, smiling at her anxious concern.

'Her father seems to be able to understand the sounds she makes,' Maggie told him, prizing a pencil from off the doctor's desk out of Rose's twitching fingers.

Darting a look of uncontrolled fury at her mother from beneath black eyebrows, Rose immediately flung herself backwards on to the doctor's carpet, kicking her heels in noisy fury.

'Sometimes I think the devil himself gets into her,' Maggie apologized, scooping up her daughter and carrying her, still kicking, out of the surgery.

11

The death of Queen Victoria in 1901 – t'owd Queen, as Kit's customers called her, was commemorated by every column in the local paper being outlined with a thick black line.

'Today,' the paper's readers were told, 'the nation is mourning the loss of the best Sovereign in British History.' They were also told that when the Queen came to the throne sixty-four years ago, her people were neither educated or free.

'Aye,' Kit said when Maggie pointed that bit out to him. 'That's true enough.'

Her answer was to raise her eyebrows in eloquent exasperation.

'Kit Carmichael! When will you learn not to swallow every word you see in print? Do you really believe that the majority of the people in this town are both educated and free? What chance have most of your customers had to take advantage of what little knowledge they got from school when they go straight into the factory to work as unskilled labourers?'

She faced him squarely. Up on her soap-box, he thought with amusement, eyes flashing and determined chin jutting forward.

'How much do you get for the hours you work in Mr Yates's shop? A pound for six days a week from seven till sometimes eleven o'clock at night!' Her fierce expression softened as she looked at him.

It wasn't fair to shout at this mild and gentle man, whose

voice was so rarely raised in anger that she had to laugh out loud when it was.

She sighed. It was just that it got her down sometimes thinking of that Mr Yates with his long face and a beard on him like a billy-goat, counting his takings in the upstairs room.

'Most weeks, like last, we only took eight pounds,' Kit reminded her, 'and most of that in halfpennies and farthings. It's a right run-down area, Maggie. Most of the men, even when they are in full-time work, don't bring home more than fifteen shillings.'

'And some of that gone in the pub on their way home of a Saturday dinner-time,' she said, quick as a flash.

Kit sighed at her, loving her even as he sighed. His mother had been right when she had weighed up his future wife at that very first meeting round her sick bed.

'A bonny lass, but too cheeky,' she'd said, and yet, if she had still been alive, surely she would have had to agree that little Maggie Craig had made him a grand wife.

Not a needlewoman by nature or inclination, Maggie had borrowed a barrow from a man across the street, and trundled a second-hand sewing-machine home from the market. From then on she had made all their clothes, even his shirts, and even if they never seemed to fit properly round the neck, who was he to grumble?

She was so restless she had to be doing something, and if it had not been sewing for them and plain sewing for the neighbours, it might have been putting the child out to mind with Clara next door while she went back in the mill.

He had put his foot down about that, right from the beginning.

If only she didn't have such radical ideas. Kit sighed again. He himself was a staunch Conservative, his principles being nurtured by the contempt his mother had passed on to him for the large community of Irish Catholics living in the area round the shop. They, almost to a man, supported the Liberals, whilst Maggie, refusing to conform as usual, supported a party of her own.

The 'Underdogs', Kit called them privately.

At the moment it was the poor bedraggled British Army fighting the Boers, staining, as she put it dramatically, the hills and plains of South Africa red with their flowing blood.

'It is not a matter women should concern themselves with,' Kit had said, shamed into remonstrating one summer evening when they came back from a meeting of the Chapel Elders.

To his horror his wife had stood up and asked in her clear cool voice if it was not a cause for the deepest concern that over sixty per cent of the recruits to the army from the north of England had been turned down because they were not physically fit?

'Sixty per cent!' she declared. 'And what do they mean by physically fit but suffering from malnutrition? You should ask my husband here about the tramps who come into his shop of a night pleading for a penny, whilst there are those who can eat twenty-one courses at one meal. Boasting of it whilst their fellow-men die of hunger in the streets! A fine start to the twentieth century for a country that is supposed to be the finest in the world!'

'Why do you bother yourself about things you can do nothing about?' he asked her, puffing at his pipe, only to find it had gone out.

At once Maggie leaned forward, lighting a taper at the fire and passing it over to him, the wifely gesture giving him the courage to say what he had had a mind to say for a long time.

'Maggie, lass. Why do you have to be at everybody's beck and call in the street? Why is it they come for you when they can't afford the doctor? We've got a child of our own,' he went on, retiring behind a screen of smoke. 'Running about as fit as a fiddle. But for how long? How long when you spent all one night last week sitting up with that little lad in the end house, knowing all the time he was dying of the cough?'

He was trying very hard to make her see, but without the sensitivity to choose the right words.

'Surely you remember what happened with your own mother? She picked up the diphtheria from somebody else's child and went on to die through it. My mother always used to say that charity began at home.'

Too late he knew he had gone too far. He wished with all his heart he could bite back what he had just said, and he knew too that to say he was sorry would only infuriate Maggie more.

Walking with her light step over to the dresser, she took down two pots for their nightly cocoa. Carefully she stirred sugar, cocoa and a drop of milk into each pot, mixing them to a smooth paste. Then she lifted the heavy black kettle from the fire, and filled them up to the brim. He waited, outwardly calm, knowing inwardly the explosion that must surely come.

'No, I don't forget my own mother, Kit Carmichael,' she said, handing over his drink, 'and by all that's holy you don't forget yours either, do you?'

Sitting down opposite to him Maggie curled her hands round the pot. 'Though how can you be expected to forget yours when Rose is turning into the living spit? I'll tell you something I've never said to you before, but sometimes when she looks at me it is as though your mother has come back in her. In fact if I were a fanciful sort of woman I'd say that was exactly what has happened. She's only a bairn, but already she knows how to play me off against you, and you fall for it. Every time. I tell her she can't have something; she runs straight to you and you give her what she wants . . . oh yes, you do.'

'I don't see all that much of her, not with the hours I work, do I, lass?'

Kit's voice was mild. He knew, and secretly rejoiced in

the fact that his little daughter was the image of his mother. Small-faced and gypsy dark, it was as though some mischievous plan had reproduced his mother in exact miniature. Like his mother, Rose was afraid of nothing, would stop at nothing to get her own way, and like his mother, bestowed on him an adoration it would have taken a stronger man to resist.

Maggie was banking up the fire for the night, taking it for granted that was her job, but he could see from her back that she was still angry.

'I wish you wouldn't encourage her to come into your bed, Kit. Now she's in her own little bed she's out and across the top of the stairs into your room before I can stop her.' Maggie pushed her hair away from her fire-flushed face. 'It's not right a bairn sleeping with her father. It's not healthy.'

'I'm just going out to the back,' Kit said, taking the easy way out as usual. 'You go on up. I'll see to the door and the fire-guard.'

Once again, by taking the line of least resistance, he had won. Maggie braided her hair in the front bedroom, still from force of habit tugging at it to make it grow. She noticed that even in her sleep Rose twitched and jerked, as if wondering what mischief she could get up to next. Holding the candle-flame well away, Maggie stared down at her small daughter.

Could people come back from the grave to torment the living? Was the dead Mrs Carmichael trying to punish her for daring to marry her beloved son? Frustrated once in her attempt to kill Maggie, was she now here again, living with them in the house, making trouble between them the way children could alienate husband and wife?

Blowing out the candle Maggie got into bed, heard Kit come upstairs with his light tread, and heard him go into the room that had been her father's. She heard one boot drop to the floor, then the other, heard the springs of the bed creak as he got into bed, and knew that for the first time since their wedding day he was going to sleep without having said goodnight.

A funny old marriage theirs was turning out to be. Wife in one room, and husband in the other. Their child, and what promised to be their *only* child, growing up disliking her own mother. Because it was true . . . God help her, but it was true.

Tears gathered in Maggie's eyes to roll sideways into her hair and on to the pillow as she faced the truth. Always one for facing the truth she faced it now. The dislike between them, mother and child, was mutual. God forgive her, but it was. There were times when she understood how mothers, unable to stand the screaming tantrums, the whining defiance, landed out and half killed their own child.

She wondered how it would have been with the other one, the child who had died before it had had a chance to live: Joe's child. But the thing was settled. No baby and no Joe, and she was wasting her time crying because crying never got nobody nowhere.

12

In 1905, when Rose was a sullen and secretive child just starting school, Joe Barton came back to the town to see his sister Belle.

When she first opened the door to him, she wanted to cry. She was wearing the white cap and apron her mistress liked her to wear, even though the house was only a semi-detached villa at the end of a cul-de-sac. Joe thought she looked even more washed out and servile than she had as a child.

She fidgeted nervously with the corner of her apron as she stood aside to let him in.

'Mrs Armitage has gone out for her tea, so she said we could sit in the parlour when I told her you was coming. Come in and see how nice everything is, but rub your feet on the mat first.'

She led the way down a narrow hall, made even smaller by a round table bearing an assortment of plants, into a room at the front of the house, a room with a bay window shrouded by net curtains.

If she had not said that about him wiping his feet on the mat, she would have broken down and flung her arms round him, but the only time she remembered having physical contact with her brother was when they had slept together. In houses where they had stayed only long enough to get into arrears with the rent before doing a moonlight flit.

'Sit you down then.' She pointed to a chair covered in plum plush velvet. 'It's nice, isn't it?'

Obligingly Joe looked round the over-furnished room, at

the oilcloth patterned with squares filled with baskets of flowers, and at the mantle-cover scalloped and bobbled.

'Aye, it's nice,' he said, then he smiled directly at her, and it was still the same Joe, the same laughing teasing Joe, who had stolen the money just for her, then had to go away rather than face the consequences.

'You got my letter?' she asked, sitting down opposite to him with her hands folded in her lap. 'The minister wrote it for me.' She frowned. 'Well, at least the minister's *wife* wrote it for me.'

'Aye, I got it.'

It was strange, Joe thought, how in spite of the fact that Belle had received practically the same intermittent schooling as himself, she had never managed to pick her letters up.

There was a sadness filling his heart that made him want to clench his fists and beat them on the arms of his plush chair. She was so *old*, this little sister of his. His half-sister from what his mother had once let slip. So prim and proper, with her small feet in their laced-up boots crossed at the ankles. So much a stranger. He smiled at her again.

'Our mam went quick-like,' she said. 'It was the drink. She choked in her sleep.'

Joe stared at the brightly coloured flooring.

'I never wanted to go away, Belle. You know that.'

She shook her head. 'You had to go, Joe, and from how you look you're doing all right. That suit didn't come from no pawn shop.'

'No, it didn't, love.' He smiled at her again, thinking that was all they seemed to be bloody doing, sitting smiling at each other and thinking of things to say.

'I have me own room,' she said, and he saw the pride shining in her pale eyes.

'Want to take me up to see it, love?' His eyes teased. 'I am your brother, you know. It wouldn't be rude.'

Belle stood up, the desire to show off the first room of her own she had ever had too much for her.

173

'Carpet on the stairs,' she pointed out, bending down to feel it as she went before up the narrow stairway. 'There's a W C downstairs, just through the scullery. You don't have to go out to the back.'

She opened a door off the landing into a room sparsely furnished by a bed, a wardrobe, a chest of drawers, and a wash-hand stand with a towel on the rail and a jug and soap dish standing on top. On the wall was a framed text bearing the words: 'Be sober and hope to the end. (Peter 1 Verse 13)', and on the floor a rag rug, pegged by herself, she told him.

'I come up here after I've cleared the tea-things away, then I am free until it's time to go down and make Mr and Mrs Armitage their bedtime cups of Horlicks.'

'And one for you?' Joe asked.

Her eyes opened wide with surprise.

'Of course not, our Joe. Do you know how much Horlicks costs?'

He shook his head at her. 'What you want to do is make enough for two do for three. Mrs Armitage doesn't mark the bloody jar, does she?'

Belle put her finger to her lips, staring at the open door, a door she had left open deliberately, for it would never have done to close it, not with a man in the room, even if he was her brother.

'Ee, I couldn't do a thing like that, Joe. It would be like stealing.'

Joe scratched his head. 'Belle Barton! What about all those times we pinched things off the stalls down the market? You could shove an apple under your shawl quicker than anyone I know. And what about that time when some of the neighbours hived off a sheep from the flock passing the end of our street? Who was it held our back door open? And who was it went round selling cut pieces of lamb till all the street reeked of the smell of roasting meat? You gone holy or something?'

'The Lord Jesus has saved me,' Belle said, folding her top lip tightly over the lower. 'Mr and Mrs Armitage would never have taken me on if I hadn't come from a good Christian family.'

At that Joe threw back his head and laughed out loud.

'A good Christian family? Well, bugger me. That takes the bloody cake that does!'

'You still swear too much, our Joe,' Belle said, more in sorrow than anger.

Just for a minute Joe thought she was having him on, until he remembered that this slight serious little sister of his never had anyone on. He stared round the tiny room, at its stark respectability, at the framed text on the wall, at Belle's house slippers sitting neatly by the side of the bed, and at the Bible he knew she could not read, placed dead centre of the bedside table, its marker spilling out on to the lace-edged cover.

His sister's blue eyes were searching his face, pleading with him not to spoil all this splendour for her, beseeching him not to make fun of her. Willing him, he had to accept, to go away before her precious Mrs Armitage came back.

'You haven't even asked me where I'm stopping,' he asked with mock reproach. 'Or even how long holiday I've got.'

'Where *are* you stopping, Joe?'

She was leading the way downstairs, running her hand lovingly over the highly polished wood of the banister rail. Showing by that give-away gesture that this little house with its modest furnishings had filled a void in her heart that nothing in the whole of her life had managed to fill before.

Suddenly he was reminded of how one afternoon, when she was about eight years old, Belle had helped him to build a puny little fire in a tip used for storing bricks. The fire had been built with sticks, odd bits of wood, old papers, anything that would burn, and Belle had crouched over it pretending to be stirring broth in a pan.

'Your dinner's ready, husband,' she had said, and to humour her he had cracked on to be rolling up his sleeves before washing himself at the slopstone, before sitting down at an imaginary table.

'By the gum, but this tastes good, wife,' he'd said, and her face had gone pink with pleasure.

'It was a nice piece of beef I got cheap from the butcher. Don't forget to mop up the gravy with your bread, there's a good husband.'

Poor little Belle, wearing an old tattered coat, seamed up the front to make a dress, with bare legs permanently navy-blue with chilblain scars. With a nose that always ran a candle, even in summer. No wonder this place was like heaven to her. An' he wasn't going to put no spoke in it for her, not in any way he wasn't.

'I've got to get back, love. Tonight,' he lied. 'Being a business man means you have to be on the spot. I've got four men working for me now. What d'you think about that? This carpet cleaning lark is a cinch, a bloody cinch.'

He glanced down at the hall carpet, and grinned. 'This 'ere carpet of yours could do with a bit of a clean, madam, and no need for it to be taken up and beaten in the garden, madam. Just give me a date and I'll send round one of my men with one of my vacuum cleaners, and we'll have the dirt sucked up and carried away without you even having to get your maid to dust the skirting board. Shall we say next Tuesday, madam?'

Belle's eyes grew round. 'You mean no dust brushed up nor nothing?'

Joe described a shape with his hands. 'About that big and worked with bellows, so all the muck goes into a bag. Into the bag, out to the bin, a pound in Joe Blob's pocket, and there we are!'

'A pound? For cleaning carpets?'

'Five shillings to the operator of course,' Joe said grandly, 'but when you reckon I've got four of them on the go, it adds up . . . aye it adds up.' He tickled Belle underneath her chin. 'Where there's muck there's brass, love, you know that, and some of them ladies down in London like to boast to their friends that they've had their carpets professionally cleaned. I'm in the middle of negotiating a contract for a row of offices in the West End, one of them posh places where they have carpets in the boss's rooms just to show how flourishing their businesses are.' Suddenly serious he jerked his head towards the stairs.

'I've left a bit of something under the cover on your bedside table, love. And you're sure you are proper settled? Certain sure? Because if not you can go up and pack your bag this minute and I'll take you back with me.'

'To London?'

Joe nodded. 'Where the King rides by wearing a top-hat and smoking a dirty great cigar.'

'You've *seen* him, our Joe?'

'Many times,' Joe lied. 'Once he raised his hat to me.'

Belle wrinkled her small nose. 'Oh, our Joe, you haven't changed. But I wouldn't leave this place, not my room. Not the Chapel and everyone what's so kind to me.' She was opening the door on to the quiet cul-de-sac. 'You'll keep on writing to me?'

He nodded, wanting to bend his head and kiss the soft pale cheek, but knowing there were net curtains twitching behind the windows of the neat little houses. It would never do for the Armitage's maid to be seen being kissed by a man. So he raised his hand, then walked away with his jaunty tread down the short path.

It was raining now, the mucky clinging rain sifting its way through smoke-filled air as he walked away from the newly built box-like houses into the streets he knew. Rows of houses, and still more, down to the railway arches, past the canal, down on to its banks where the oily water lapped.

Joe walked on the balls of his feet, walked like a cat. Up and back on to the road again, past the gasworks, into the labyrinth of streets, alleys, the murky courts he had been reared into.

Leaning against a wall, he felt in his pocket and took out

a crumpled packet of cigarettes, flicked one out and felt for a match.

'Blast!' The word came out as a groan. That was all it bloody needed. A fag and nowt to light it with.

Walking on he saw Kit's shop on a corner, with its cardboard cut-out window display of curly-headed girls in red-riding hoods and its little boys in velvet suits blowing bubbles. He went inside.

There were three women in the shop, all with shawls over their heads, and one of them was feeding a baby underneath its concealing folds. They turned around and stared at him, decided they did not know him, and continued talking to each other in loud strident tones.

Just for the hell of it, Joe winked at the youngest of the women, the one suckling the baby, and smiled to himself as she twitched the shawl over the baby's face.

'What can I get for you?'

The man behind the counter was smiling at him, a big fat man with short-cropped curly hair, and an indefinite chin. The front of his hair was combed up into a sort of quiff, and his voice was pitched as high as a woman's.

'These ladies here are not in any hurry,' he went on, still smiling, a tiny hammer in his hand held poised over a tray of glistening brown toffee, patterned with nuts. 'A quarter, did you say, Mrs Parkinson?'

'Tha knows I said two ounces, Mr Carmichael. I'm not made of brass,' the smallest of the three women said. 'By the gum, but tha'd sell a quarter'n of potted meat to one of them vegetarians, tha would.'

'That's a long word for a Thursday morning,' one of her companions said, and Joe smiled to himself.

He was back home all right, even if it was for less than a day. He'd always known that for quick-fire give-as-good-as-you-get, you'd go a long way before you could beat a Lancashire working class woman.

'A box of matches, please,' he said, 'and I'd better light my fag in here, it's coming down like stair-rods.'

'I've seen him afore,' the oldest woman said, when the shop door had closed behind Joe.

'Looks a cheeky type to me,' the girl with the baby said, letting the shawl drop down again because it didn't seem to matter in front of Mr Carmichael.

'Now then, Mrs Parkinson,' Kit said, tapping with the little hammer, then twisting a piece of white paper into a perfectly formed poke as he dropped the pieces of toffee in one by one.

'A nut in every piece, love,' he said. 'And you can fetch it back if there's not.'

Joe walked down the hill, past the house where Kit had lived with his mother, along the main street of shops to the top of Foundry Street.

All right, so he was being a bloody fool. Maggie had not answered his letters, and the last one had been returned with the message that she had gone away.

But whoever lived there might know where she was. They might tell him and he would go and find her. He would demand to know why she hadn't written, because surely, even if she had never wanted to see him again after that last night, she owed him some explanation?

All right, so he had taken his time about writing to her, but he had said he was going to get a job first, and that was what he'd done.

At the bottom house he lifted his hand and rapped smartly with the knocker. He felt the palms of his hands break out into dampness, and his heart was beating with staccato jerks beneath the narrow stripes of his dark grey suit. Waiting only a few seconds, he knocked again, then looked up at the windows. Aye, it looked just the same, but then all these bloody houses looked just the same. Disappointed he turned away.

There was a full hour to go before the hooters went, and apart from a cat slinking across the street, everywhere was deserted. He was standing there, just standing, wondering what to do next when a door across opened, and a youngish woman came out carrying a bucket and a mop.

'Better late than never!' she called out cheerily before getting down on a strip of matting to mop the step. Joe crossed the street.

'Number two, missus? A Miss Craig. I know she doesn't live there any more, but perhaps you . . . do you know where she might be?' He coughed to hide the sudden tremor in his voice.

The woman sat back on her heels and stared up at him. She had lived down Foundry Street for twelve months only, but she knew who he was talking about, and a glimmer of excited suspicion narrowed her eyes.

'Maggie? You're talking about Maggie? Father did away with himself a while back?'

He swallowed hard, feeling the blood rush to his face. He nodded.

The kneeling woman dipped a piece of grey cloth into the bucket, then started to wring it out with hands as red as a lobster's claws. Her mind working overtime, she was trying to remember what she had been told . . . something about a scandal . . . something about Maggie Carmichael having got herself into trouble and not with the man she had married.

'Maggie's still there,' she said at last. 'But she's Mrs Carmichael now.' She let the cloth drop back into the bucket with a resounding plop. 'She's up at the shops as like as not.'

Thanking her with a downward jerk of his dark head, Joe turned on his heel and walked quickly away.

He knew he had been ungracious, even rude, but how was she to know, that sloppy young-old woman mopping her step, that what she had just revealed had been like the shaft of a dagger slicing into his guts? His Maggie married?

He was going to be sick. He could have been sick right there, and it was all his fault, wanting to be somebody, wanting to have something to offer before he came back for her. But she might have answered his letters. She might have told him herself that she had met someone else. She had forgotten him and who could blame her? Who could bloody blame her?

Joe walked with head bent, striding out, past the draper's shop where Maggie was choosing a supply of bobbins of cotton, whilst Rose, unseen by her mother, was emptying a box of pins on to the floor.

So engrossed in his thoughts that he reached the boulevard leading to the station without knowing how he had got there.

'I thought as how Mrs Carmichael was going to faint,' the woman across the street told her husband that evening as he was sitting down to his tea of tripe and onions. 'I told her there had been a fella asking for her, and she went as white as a sheet when I described him. I always said she was a dark horse in spite of her toffee-nosed ways. I wonder if it was him what got her into trouble afore she got married to that nice Mr Carmichael?'

'This is a bit of all right,' her husband said, mopping up the thick grey gravy with a slice of bread. 'Goes right to the spot this does.'

13

Joe Barton paid no more visits to his home town after that rainy afternoon. For a while he left his digs and lived with a widow in Acton, making it quite clear from the start that marriage was not on the cards.

His business flourished, and now he stopped doing any of the cleaning himself, merely visiting housewives in their homes and charming them into agreeing to having the work done by his increasing number of employees.

He wrote fairly regularly to his sister. She was, after all, his only relative, his next of kin, the only link he had with his home town. And when he received a letter one day, written in careful script by the minister's wife, informing him that Belle had married, he was glad for her sake.

Will Hargreaves, the letter said, was a milk roundsman, and he and Belle had managed to get a tiny cottage to rent at the top of Steep Brow, one of a cluster of small tenements, previously lived in by the town's hand-loom weavers.

'There's a loomshop tacked on to the side, and we're turning it into a parlour,' the letter went on, and through the pen of the minister's wife Joe could read the pride in his sister's quiet voice.

She was still working for the Armitages' on a day to day basis, and though she said little of Will, a whole page was devoted excitedly to the rugs she had pegged, and the shiny oilcloth her new husband had tacked to the floor.

Joe immediately sent a cheque of such a high figure that Belle cried for a day after receiving it.

He received in return a brief note of thanks from his new

brother-in-law, writing on Belle's behalf, assuring him with obvious insincerity that there would always be a bed for him, should he chance to be passing through.

'Passing through!' Joe muttered to himself, memorising the address before tearing up the letter. 'That is telling me bloody straight not to make a habit if anything is.'

He worked even harder, banked a good part of his earnings, and told himself at least once a week that his inability to forget Maggie Craig, now Carmichael, was maudlin sentimentality.

He had money, he had power of a sort, and he had women if and when he felt like it. What more could any man want?

Now, as the years passed Maggie was beginning to be worried about the rising anti-German feeling in the country. It was taking the place of bad feelings about the Russians and the French, and Kit told her such topics were none of her business.

'It's not *seemly* to be fashing yourself about such things. Politics are the government's business, not yours, love,' he said.

'But they are my business. And they should be yours!' Maggie cried. 'It's wrong to generalize. There's good and bad in every race, every creed. My father taught me that, and what's more he said we can be *taught* to hate. That's why he was such a good teacher, though I doubt if even he could have taught our Rose much. She doesn't give a damn about her book-learning. I try to help her but she won't let me, an' I could . . . oh I could.'

Kit listened with tolerant affection. He didn't doubt that his Maggie could do anything if she set her mind to it. She never wasted a moment, nor an opportunity. Always think-up schemes to make a bit extra to ensure that Rose was the best dressed kid in the street. Never grumbling about the meagre wage he took home of a Friday. He would watch her sort it out into a box she had made into sections. So much for the rent, so much for the gas and the coal, and never once getting behind with anything. And she was right about Mr Yates at the shop, he had to admit that.

'He's a proper miser,' she said. 'Three shops he has and all he does is count his money in those awful rooms over your shop, sitting there with the damp running down the walls as if he hadn't two pennies to rub together. Why don't you ask him for a rise, Kit? You run that place single-handed now he lets you do all the ordering. It's a wonder he doesn't ask you to bring the stuff back from the warehouse on a barrow. That would save the old skinflint a bob or two on deliveries.'

'He gave me half a crown extra last Christmas,' Kit had reminded her, worried lines creasing his face into a mould of acute anxiety. 'I'm not getting any younger, love. What's to stop him sending me packing and taking on a much younger man? He could get away with paying less than what he gives me, you know.'

Immediately Maggie saw, not only the logic of what he said, but what was more important to her, his real distress.

'You're a soft aporth, Kit Carmichael,' she smiled. 'I only wish our Rose had a bit more softness in her. She's as hard as nails that one.'

For a long time that night Maggie lay awake worrying about Rose in her bed on the other side of the plywood partition now dividing her father's room into two.

It was no good denying it. The years had not mellowed Rose. Far from it. She was old Mrs Carmichael to the life, and she had that way of staring at her mother as if silently promising herself that she would get the better of her one day.

Maggie tossed and turned, wondering . . . was there, *could* there be a hint of the instability that had boiled over into madness in Kit's mother?

'Oh, dear God,' she prayed, turning, as she always did, to prayer when she felt in dire need of comfort. 'Let Rose be happy, because she is not a happy girl, I know that.

She's at some sort of war with herself all the time, an' no matter what I do, or how much I try to get close to her, it's impossible. It's not true, Lord, that love begets love, because I ache to put my arms round her and tell her how much I love her. I want to *ask* her what gets into her, but she would wither me with one of those looks of hers. . . .

'Oh, Rose,' she whispered. 'There's one thing you're not going to get the better of me about. You might not be much of a scholar, but you're never going into the mill like I did. Never!'

Rose went straight into Dobson's mill the week she turned thirteen. There was nothing Maggie could have done about it apart from beating her over the head, and the constant arguments were beginning to wear her down.

She managed to pass the labour exam, and told her mother in no uncertain terms that she wasn't as daft as the scholars who were staying on till they were fourteen.

'I'm fed up with books,' she told her mother. 'I want some money of me own, and I want to learn dancing like me friends do. Besides, I'm not clever and you can't make me no matter how hard you try.'

She walked over to Kit's shaving mirror fastened at an angle over the slopstone in the living-room, and adjusted the stiff ribbon bow at the back of her small head. '*You* went in the mill, Mam, and it didn't do you no harm.'

It was no good trying to correct the way she spoke. Maggie had given up trying to do that long ago. She put her sewing down in her lap and rubbed her fingers over a jerking pain throbbing over one eyebrow.

'I went in the mill, Rose love, because I had no choice. I had your grandpa to see to, and there was three and six-pence to find each week for the rent.' She picked the shirt up again and started to unpick a frayed cuff, pulling at the cotton with her fingernail, unravelling it, then starting to pick again at the other side. 'But you have a better chance to make something of yourself. I am sure I could get you an opening with the milliner in the Hat Market. She goes to Chapel and I could have a word with her.'

The cuff came away from the sleeve, and turning it over she started to tack it back in position. 'You'd have a trade in your fingers,' – she swallowed hard – 'like your father's mother had, and if you get married then you could trim hats at home to bring in a bit extra.'

Rose's scorn brought the swift colour to her mother's cheeks.

'Bring in a bit extra! That's all you think about, our mam. I'm not going in the Hat Market working in the evenings, and I'm not going in no shop neither. I want to have a bit of fun when I finish work, not come home like me dad, flaked out every night.'

Maggie forced herself to keep her voice low. Her face was white now and knowing she was on the verge of losing her temper, excited Rose somehow.

Maggie spoke quietly, fighting for control.

'If I had spoken to your grandpa like that at your age, even though he was a sick man, I'd have been sent straight to bed and made to stay there till I was ready to apologize.'

'There's someone coming in,' Rose said, her voice tinged with relief, knowing she had gone too far with bringing her father into the argument. Thank God for nosey Clara next door. . . .

Clara came straight through, sitting down without being invited to, in Kit's rocking chair.

'He's gone!' she said, pulling a screwed-up handkerchief from her apron pocket and bursting into loud tears. 'He's gone to live with another woman, and he says if I want any money I'll have to have him up for it.' She dabbed at her streaming eyes. 'He said such awful things me mother's taken to her bed. Oh, Maggie, you wouldn't believe some of the things he said. I just could not repeat them, not to a living soul.'

Knowing she was about to do just that, Maggie nodded her head at Rose, but before she could tell her to go up to her room, Rose took swift advantage of the situation.

'Can I go round to Mavis's house, Mam? I'll not stop more than half an hour. Honest.'

She was gone before Maggie could open her mouth to reply, long black hair flying, snatching her coat from behind the door and her tammy from out of the pocket.

Maggie sighed, and turning to Clara, said, 'I'll put the kettle on and then you can tell me all about it over a pot of tea.'

'He called me mother a pissed-out old faggot,' Clara said, setting the rocking chair into frantic motion. 'And what he called me I can't bring meself to repeat. . . .'

Arnie was back within a month, but Clara's mother never spoke to him again. Now widowed mother and daughter slept together in the marital bed whilst Arnie was banished to the back bedroom.

There he could lie and listen to them talking to each other at the tops of their clarion-call voices, referring to himself as ''im in there', and letting him get up to make his own breakfast before he went off to work in the mornings.

Arnie found that in a strange way he was happier than he had been for a long time. There was a kind of peace in knowing exactly where he stood. He could tend his little back-yard garden, and he could sit in his chair by the fire knowing he had won. They had had a taste of missing his money, and once, when the Workhouse had been mentioned, he had seen a flicker of fear in his mother-in-law's eyes. Money was power, Arnie was discovering, and as long as he gave them enough after he had taken out his beer money, they seemed willing to call an uneasy truce.

He was quite insensitive to the spite-filled atmosphere, never having been much of a talker, and if he felt a bit belligerent and did not like what they gave him to eat, he merely pushed his plate aside and said he knew where there was a good meal waiting for him anytime.

Then he would see the swift look of apprehension exchanged between mother and daughter. . . .

Aye, things had changed all right, and they weren't to know he had been chucked out by the woman he'd taken up with when she got fed up with his silences, and his way of staring at nothing for hours on end.

And the next time he got a rise of eightpence a week in his wage he handed it over to Clara with aplomb, just for the sake of seeing the expression on her face.

'Well?' he said, monarch of all he surveyed.

'Ta very much,' said Clara from behind clenched teeth.

When Rose had been working for a year Arnie went on munitions, making big money, as Clara said, and the war in France broke out.

At Chapel the very next Sunday the minister preached a sermon based on what Saint Paul had said:

'He who is not with me, is *against* me!'

'To hell with Saint Paul!' Maggie shouted. 'It made me blood boil when I could see that most of the congregation were siding with the minister. Saint Paul never meant it like that. Taken out of context you can make things mean anything. Does nobody remember the last time? What about all those lads killed in South Africa? What about Benjamin and Jonathan? Do we never learn nothing?'

'This war will be over by Christmas,' Kit soothed. 'That is official. The boys will be back afore we know they've gone, you will see.'

But by the end of that year, the majority of the warehouses in the town were forced to close, and Mr Yates lost two of the shops he had built up over the years. The papers were full of long casualty lists, and Maggie read with horror that one hundred and four thousand men had been killed, gravely wounded, or were missing.

That Christmas Clara, giving her weekly order to Kit, asked for a tin of lobster.

'Sorry, love, but we've no call for that sort of thing in my shop. You will have to go to one of the downtown shops,' Kit told her, and Maggie bent her head over her knitting, working furiously at a khaki scarf in between long sessions at her sewing machine.

'Lobster!' she muttered, then she counted her stitches as if she was telling her beads. 'Let the men come home safe from that terrible war,' she prayed.

The only person who might have prayed that Joe Barton had an easy war was his sister Belle, and she was too busy polishing and sweeping her tiny cottage in the evenings after working at the Armitages' house all day.

Will had left his milk round and gone, like Arnie, into the more lucrative job of working on munitions, even opting for work miles away from home. A wispy and lithe little man, with legs bent like a jockey's, a legacy of rickets from an impoverished childhood, he swore that the army would never catch up with him.

'Strikes and wars will be the downfall of this country, mark my words,' he told Belle, a doting Belle who hung on to his every word in gratitude for him having married her and given her a home of her own.

'Think of them poor sods marching to their deaths. I'm going to die in me own bed, with me hands crossed over me chest, then buried with a nice tongue and ham spread, all civilized like, that's me.'

'Oh, don't talk about dying,' Belle cried, flinging herself into his arms. 'Please, Will. Promise me you'll never die!'

Joe, her brother, marching at that very moment along a treeless road towards the Ypres Salient, thought about the possibility of dying every minute of his waking hours. He was thinking about it now as he plodded one foot gingerly

189

in front of the other, swearing loudly with every step he took.

'You've had your chips if you fall off these sodding duck-boards,' he told a private following behind. 'That mud will suck you down before you can say "Jack the flamin' Ripper."'

'Welcome to this stately home,' he told the private as they climbed down into their dug-out. 'Come on, lad. You'll feel better after a brew-up, you'll see.'

The private stared around him with startled eyes bulging from a dome-shaped forehead. A lad of no more than seventeen who had lied about his age to get into the army, he was doing his first stretch in the forward trenches, and Joe Barton, *Corporal* Joe Barton, looked as if he might be laughing at him.

'What's that shocking smell, Corporal?' he asked, then jumped a foot in the air as a cat-sized rat ran from one corner of the dug-out to the other.

Joe, busy with the task of pouring chlorinated water from an old petrol tin, pretended not to have heard the whispered question.

If the poor little beggar did not know that what he was smelling was dead bodies, men and horses, lying just over the top in no man's land, then he was better left in ignorance for the time being. He would learn soon enough . . .

Joe passed over the tin mug when the tea was ready. It tasted of petrol and was sweetened with tinned milk, but the private drank it down quickly.

'Are there many rats?' he asked, wincing as another scuttled from the shadows. 'That's the second one since we got down here.'

Joe shook his head. 'Rats is nothing to worry about, lad. Don't you bother about them. I've caught more of them than what you've had hot dinners.'

'How?' The pale eyes protruded more than ever. 'I once heard that rats go for you if you get them in a corner.'

Joe grinned. 'We don't make no attempt to corner them,

lad. When we sometimes get a bit of what they like to call meat, we *bait* 'em with it.' He made a throwing motion with his hand. 'We fasten it on to the end of summat – anything does – then we chuck it over the top, and rats, having no brains, sink their teeth in it. Then we pull quick and bonk it one afore it knows what's hit him.'

The private, his eyes looking as though they were about to leave their sockets, stared at his Corporal as if he could not believe the evidence of his toby-jug ears.

'Then we skin them and eat 'em,' Joe teased, relenting when he was aware that the not very bright young soldier was taking his every word literally.

'That were meant to be a joke,' he said.

'All the same I don't think I am going to like it here,' the private said, and thinking he was showing a welcome touch of humour, Joe slapped him on the back, almost causing him to lose his balance.

'I'll watch out for you, lad,' he said. 'It's getting used to it that's the worst, but give yourself a week and you'll feel as if you've been living down here for bloody years.'

The nights were the worst. Accustomed from his furtive, nomadic childhood to walk like a cat, eyes and ears alert for danger, Joe took to soldiering like a duck to water. As a Very light shot into the air he could freeze into the stillness of a marble statue. He could hurl himself forward into the sticky mud, burying his face into the overpowering smell.

Once, to his horror he had found that he had fallen on to the decaying corpse of a soldier, decomposed too far for him to know whether the man had been British or German.

Out in no man's land it could have been either. . . .

And because of his could-not-care-less attitude, Joe's Sergeant, a veteran of the Boer War, found his Corporal what he considered to be a 'natural'. Joe could outswear him, and did so often, as hearing the whine of a heavy shell hurtling death at top speed towards them, Joe's colourful language peppered the air like gun-fire.

When on a night raid the Sergeant was killed with a

bullet smack between his eyes, Joe stepped neatly over the body and carried on moving forward.

The object of the exercise was to demolish a pillbox manned by Germans wielding stuttering machine guns.

'And the main object is to bring one of the blighters back,' his Lieutenant had said.

'As if we was going pheasant shooting,' Joe muttered, moving ever forward into the staccato firing, and believing every tortured moment to be his last.

Not ten yards from the pillbox, he threw himself flat on the ground, and thought wildly of praying. But to whom? To God?

It did not seem possible that with men falling all around him, screaming with pain, bleeding and dying – how could it be possible that God was there?

But if he was going to die, then surely he should be thinking of someone, or something?

Of Belle? Joe tried to bring her pale little face into his mind, seeing her as he had seen her last when she had almost pushed him through the door in case Mrs bloody Armitage came back.

Of Maggie Craig?

Of Maggie who had married someone else, and likely forgotten he ever existed?

'Oh, Maggie! Maggie!' Joe cried her name aloud over and over, because damn it, there had to be *someone* he could call on.

'Bugger and sod everybody!' he shouted as standing up he hurled his bomb in the vague direction of the pillbox.

When his Lieutenant, holding his bayoneted rifle up against the backside of a petrified German, prodded his prisoner back in the direction of the dug-out, Joe was lying once again, face down in the evil-smelling mud.

14

That night Maggie dreamed of Joe. It was as though he was there, in a corner of the room, calling her name. Calling it angrily, not with love. *Cursing* her, Maggie thought, sitting up in bed, shivering, then lighting the candle and reaching for a book.

Across the postage stamp of a landing, Kit slept the sleep of the physically tired, whilst at the other side of the plywood partition Rose coughed and turned, tossed and twitched the blankets over her, then pushed them back as if they were suffocating her with their weight.

Maggie could hear the vague sounds telling her that Rose too was finding it hard to sleep, and she imagined her daughter lying with her black hair spread over the pillow, staring up into the darkness, thinking her private thoughts, dreaming her private dreams, as alienated from her mother as she had been as a child.

The war would soon be over. All the signs were there, and then, please God, there would never be another . . . Maggie laid down her book, blew out the candle, and Joe was there again, back with the darkness, like a ghost refusing to go away.

Maggie got out of bed, then padded silently to the top of the stairs.

'Rose?' she called softly. 'I'm going down to make a pot of tea. Would you like a cup?'

'No, thank you.'

Rose's voice sounded thick as if she had been crying. Maggie hesitated, a hand actually on the door knob, then fearing the inevitable rejection, she carried on downstairs, vaguely worried and disturbed.

If Rose wanted to tell her what was bothering her then she would tell her or not tell her, all in her good time. And besides, Rose never cried. She sulked and winged; she complained and went through black periods of depression, but she never cried.

Maggie sat in her chair by a fire that had almost died, a terrible weight of sadness in her heart, a sadness that she knew was only a small part of her daughter's rejection of her.

And the next day Rose got up heavy-eyed, went to the mill, came home for her dinner as usual, then without speaking to Maggie, went up to her room.

Sitting on her bed she stared at the dividing partition until her eyes glazed over. She knew she should be shaping herself, but she also knew that by running like mad across the back, over the spare ground and the bridge, she could get there just in time.

She sat there for another minute, then, as if a time spring had been released inside her, she flew downstairs, taking her coat from behind the back door, and saying briefly that it was time she was off.

Clara was hanging her washing out on a line stretching from her own yard wall to a post set in the ground.

'Let's hope it keeps fine, Rose,' she shouted, the timbre of her voice only fractionally reduced by the peg held firmly between her teeth. 'I've fetched this lot in twice this morning.'

Looping one end of a flannelette sheet over the line, she pegged it into scallops, giving the fresh wind a chance to billow it out.

'Yes,' Rose said, and ran on.

'Yes' was a useful word to bring out now and again. It did not matter whether she listened to what the other person was saying or not. Yes brooked no argument at the best of times. . . .

Clara watched her go as she hooked a prop into a space between Arnie's long underpants and her mother's button-through flannel nightie. Even Rose's hurrying back looked sly, she decided.

'I would not trust that girl as far as I could throw her,' she told her mother in ringing tones. 'And that's not far with this awful rheumatism in me shoulder.'

'She's a bad lot,' Mrs Hobkirk agreed. 'Going off to the pictures with that Mavis girl out of Henry Street, with muck on their faces. What can you expect?'

'She's learning dancing in the rooms over the Emporium. Half a crown for twelve lessons, paid in advance.'

Clara walked over to the window, feeling cross for a reason she couldn't fathom.

'It's time Rose Carmichael got herself one decent fella and settled down. The war started her off young with boys. She had too much freedom and too much money. There's bad blood there. I've always said so. She's even stopped going to Chapel, and Maggie doesn't go as often as she used . . . Oh, heck, it's started to flamin' rain again.'

After a week of living with a silent Rose who for some reason had stopped going dancing almost every night, Maggie felt the need to go to Chapel.

Yet the minute the choir stood up to sing the anthem she decided that the choirmaster, beating time with his left hand, had a definite look of Joe Barton about him. There was something about the way his hair grew down into a point in the nape of his neck.

'Oh, Lord,' she prayed, using the words she had been taught as a child. 'Oh, Lord, I am sailing on the wide sea. Please guide my little boat for me.'

It was strange though how just these past days Joe had been more in her thoughts than ever. Every other man she saw seemed to remind her of him.

She had seen it in the milkman's grin as he ladled the

milk out of the churns on his cart. When the doctor's man came for his weekly sixpence last Friday she had thought how his smile had the same teasing quality about it.

Maggie opened her hymn book and sighed. She was tired, that was the explanation; she was doing too much sewing, taking too much on, and the mind played strange tricks when you were constantly tired.

The voices of the congregation rose and swelled. No holding back when Methodists sang.

'Once again, 'tis joyous May. Birds are carolling all day. . . .'

But not round here they aren't, Maggie thought, trying to remember the last time she had heard a bird sing.

Then she sat down and closed her eyes as the minister folded his hands over the edge of the pulpit and said: 'Let us pray.'

Obediently Maggie bent her head, willing herself to concentrate, as speaking to God in his simple language, the new minister spoke straight from his heart. No set prayers, dulling the senses with their familiarity. Just a talk to God and his son Jesus, mentioning by name the sick members of the Chapel, thanking for blessings received, and conceding that blessings not received were all part of his perfect plan.

There was a young-old man in the pew to the side of Maggie. When he got up to sing the last hymn she noticed the haggard stoop and the dull vulnerable expression she had seen on the faces of so many men back from the trenches.

The minister himself had lost a fine boy, a young officer who used to stand with his mother in their pew, finding her place in the hymn book and smiling down at her. Maggie turned her head and saw her now, singing as if she meant every word. Blaming God for nothing.

Clara and Arnie were waiting for her outside in the street, and Maggie hoped the surprise at seeing them out together did not show on her face.

'I didn't see you come in,' she said.

Clara nodded seriously. 'No, we sat at the back because Arnie's having trouble with his stomach rumbling.'

Arnie looked affronted, but smiled at Maggie. 'Rose not here tonight then?'

Maggie fell into step beside Clara. 'No, I think she was glad to stop in, she doesn't look all that well. I'm a bit bothered about her.'

Clara, walking next to her husband, was being firmly nudged. He was telling her to keep her mouth shut, she knew, telling her not to interfere in matters that were none of her concern, but she wasn't going to take any notice. Fiercely Clara nudged him back, almost knocking him off the pavement.

She was going to speak her mind, and nobody was going to stop her, so after they turned into the long street of closed shops leading to Foundry Street, she did her sideways sniff before saying:

'Did you know that your Rose went to Doctor Leyland's surgery on Friday morning? Not to your own doctor's surgery up Mercer Street. To Doctor Leyland's where I go?'

'I'll walk on in front,' Arnie said at once, almost breaking into a run.

'He's huffed because I've told you,' Clara said, 'but I think you ought to know.'

'Rose is not a child,' Maggie said slowly. 'She can go to any doctor she chooses without telling me first.' She felt a faint stab of fear. 'She was sick last week, but she soon got over it.'

'Sick first thing in the mornings?' Clara persisted.

Maggie stopped walking so abruptly that a man a few paces behind almost fell over her.

She put a hand to her mouth in a small inadequate gesture of comfort, whilst little things, things she had not considered of importance, flooded her memory.

And because Rose had always been secretive, her behaviour lately had meant no more than possibly the rejection by a friend, one of the many imagined slights Rose took so bitterly.

Then Maggie remembered her suspicion that Rose had been crying to herself in the night.

'Oh, God, dear God!' Her eyes widened with shock. 'I must have been blind. I never thought . . . well, how could I? Oh, Clara, it can't be. She's never kept a boy for long, you know what she's like. Oh, no, we mustn't jump to conclusions. We could be doing her a terrible injustice. She's not that sort of girl. She isn't!'

Both Clara's nostrils twitched in unison.

'You're far too trusting, Maggie. You should have seen her face when she saw me at the surgery. I'd gone for a bottle for Arnie's stomach. Your Rose nearly died when she saw me.'

They started to walk on.

'She'd been in with the doctor a long time,' Clara went on with grim persistence. 'An' when she came out her face was as white as bleached twill. She never even looked at me. Oh, yes, there's summat up all right.'

Maggie walked so quickly that Clara had to take little running steps to keep up with her. In Foundry Street two children played round a lamp-post, swinging from a piece of rope dangling from the short arm at the top as they made fruitless attempts to climb up it.

Maggie turned to Clara. Somehow she had to get rid of her. Knowing Clara she would be likely to follow into the house, not wanting to miss the drama she sensed was about to be played out.

'You did right to tell me. Thank you, Clara,' Maggie said.

But Clara had cottoned on to the fact that she wasn't wanted, and anyway Maggie looked so small, so *defeated*, she almost wished she had kept her big mouth shut.

'Ta-ra, then, love,' she said, and before she had closed her own front door, Arnie was there, his usually passive expression contorted with anger.

198

'You can't let be, can you? That girl would have had to tell her mother all in her own good time, and how do you know you're right anyroad? She could just be having a bilious attack or something like that.'

'You don't go to another doctor when your mother thinks you're at work, and you don't get bilious attacks with carrying on like Rose Carmichael's been carrying on. I wasn't born yesterday, you know.'

Arnie looked at the thin greying hair, the sagging chin and the lines running from nose to chin on his wife's flat face.

'You don't have to tell *me* that,' he said.

Ever since her early morning visit to Clara's doctor, Rose had been numb with a terrible aching despair. It had been a long wait, standing there across the street waiting for the door of the surgery to open. Even when she had been let in, there had been another long wait while the benches filled up with coughing people, clutching empty medicine bottles and trying not to look at each other, but keeping a silent count in order not to miss their turn.

For over two long months now she had kept the awful fear to herself, persuading herself that it was worry, reminding herself that the boy she had done it with had said she would be all right. She wiped a tear away on the fringe of a grey woollen shawl.

He had been so nice, so *different* from all the other boys she had known. So much more the gentleman, and yet . . . she shivered . . . he had managed to persuade her to let him go further than she had ever let any boy go before. Rose faced the truth squarely. It wasn't as if she was a young girl who didn't know what could happen if you egged a boy on. She should have known better than go with him in the park. Mavis had paired off with his friend, but she hadn't done anything so daft; she couldn't get over Rose having done it either.

He hadn't talked much, but as they went through the big ornamental gates he had put his arm round her, and then at the top of the park, past the duck pond, he had led her over the grass and laid his raincoat down on the grass in the shelter of a rhododendron bush.

She was used to boys fumbling with urgent fingers at the buttons on her blouse, used to the power she felt when their trembling legs pressed against her own. It was the one time she felt important somehow. She wasn't pretty, she knew that, too small and too sallow of skin, but at times like that the boys she had been with seemed to think she was a bit of all right.

'You're a bit of a dark horse,' they would say, and she would smile, thinking of nothing at all except the pleasure of moving hands exploring just so far and no further.

Silent tears ran down her face. He was from the park end of the town, she guessed, although he had told her less than nothing about himself. His Lancashire accent was far less pronounced than her own, and the cigarette he smoked was a De Reske and not a Woodbine. She knew and was impressed that he had paid two shillings for the packet of twenty-five, so she asked for a puff just to see if she could tell the difference.

He told her his name was John, but that could have been a lie, just as her telling him she worked in an office had been a lie.

'Which office?' he wanted to know.

'That would be telling,' she said, and he told her she was a little tease, then he kissed her in a searching way, awakening a response that no other boy had ever aroused in her.

It was a response that destroyed his own intention of keeping everything well inside the limits of control. . . .

What happened he had never meant to happen, but this girl was like no other he had kissed. Fierce and dark, with glistening dark eyes, she was clinging to him, and *asking* for it. She should have *stopped* him. All the others had stopped him. It was her fault, her fault entirely.

It had been over so quickly he could not believe that was all it was about. All the jokes he heard at school in the sixth form, the sly winks, the nudges . . . for this?

Leaving Rose at the park gates he ran all the way home, then locked himself in the bathroom to wash all over before taking a book down from his father's study shelves and looking up the symptoms of a certain unmentionable disease.

He was ashamed and terrified, at one and the same time. . . .

If anything happened now to stop him going up to Oxford at the end of the summer, his father would kill him. And his mother . . . oh God, it would break her heart.

Would that girl who had said she worked in an office find out his real name and where he lived? Would her father bring her up to the house and force him to marry her? Would she be waiting for him when he came out of school?

He actually beat his forehead with a clenched fist, beside himself with shivering horror and disgust.

Rose shivered. Even if she went looking for him she could never hope to find him. She remembered that he had been tall, and that, passing a lamp, the light had shone down on to a fair head, but she could not bring his features into even a semblance of recognition. Mavis, who seemed to know about such things, had said he would deny it, even if they found him.

'I'll get you some stuff from a herbalist's shop. Pennyroyal syrup mixed with turpentine. They say it works every time.'

'Have you ever. . . ?'

Mavis tossed her head. ''Course not. I just keep my ears open, that's all.'

Dr Leyland had heard her out in silence, called his wife in from the back of the house, and examined her briefly.

'There's a lot worse things you could be having than a baby, believe me, dear, I know,' he said. He stretched out a hand to the bell on his wide desk. 'Come and see me again in a month, and by that time your young man will have put a ring on your finger, and we'll have a laugh you and me about you thinking this is the end of the world. All right?'

The doctor was a kindly, compassionate man, but his surgery was full of waiting patients, and when it was over he had to go and tell a woman in Marstone Road that the tests sent on from Manchester showed that her husband's illness was incurable.

And this war would not end with the defeat of the Germans. He could prophesy that more than half of the men who were lucky enough to come back from that hell on earth would have the stamp of it on them till the day they died.

Besides, he wasn't getting any younger, and he knew he ought to have talked to that young lass a bit longer. She had a strange look about her.

But there wasn't the time . . . there never was enough time.

So Rose walked away, down the short passage and past the dispensary where she handed over her shilling consultant fee, avoiding Clara's eyes as she passed through the crowded waiting-room.

Back at the mill, she stood at her looms, willing her mind into a blankness . . . as she was trying to will it now.

When Maggie came upstairs wearing her Chapel best hat and coat, she found Rose hunched up and desolate on the edge of her bed.

'Rose?'

The swollen eyelids were raised as Rose registered her mother's flushed cheeks, her unbelief, her pleading look that said she wanted to be told it wasn't true.

Defiance and shame turned her face to the wall, then she jerked a finger.

'She's told you then? I'm surprised she waited till now.'

Maggie put out a hand and trying hard to say the right thing, said the wrong.

'You must tell me, love. Is it right that you're in trouble? We must talk before your father comes in from the shop. He'll be late tonight because he's setting out the window ready for next week.'

'Clara Preston's a vicious old cow.'

The words were almost spat out, reminding Maggie of the old woman in the bed, the bitter woman with a tongue like a whip-lash. She sighed and tried again.

'Rose? Rose, love?'

The softly spoken words, the lack or reproach shocked Rose as badly as if her mother had struck her, and she rolled away to the foot of the bed. When hysteria took over it came as a relief. It cleared at last the dead feeling she had had inside her for the past worrying weeks as she gave way to loud sobs that seemed as if they might shake her body in two.

'Tell me who it was, Rose.'

The next words were screamed at the top of Rose's lungs.

'I don't *know* who it was! It was a boy I met just once, and I don't know where he lives or even what he's called. I saw him *once*. That was all! Now be kind to me! Just try to be kind to me now!'

Maggie stood quite still, listening, but not allowing the shouted words to register.

Rose was a strange girl, but she could never have done that. Not gone with a stranger. That was the sort of thing the night women did.

She was shocked to her soul, yet all she wanted to do was to put her arms round her daughter, but if they had had no real communication before, how could she expect there to be any now? She tried to move and found that she was quite unable to move from the spot where she stood.

She wanted to keep calm, to speak quietly, to go on speaking quietly, but it was as though someone else's voice had taken over.

'You're not like that!' she shouted.

Rose turned a blotched face towards her.

'But I am! You don't know me. You've never known me. Everybody can't be like you, all holy, holy, holy.' She bit hard on her knuckles. 'Always going to Chapel and singin' hymns and prayin'.' Now her voice held the bleakness of a dreadful despair. 'Go away, Mam. Just go away. . . .'

Maggie moved at last. She went to sit on the edge of the bed, careful not to make any attempt to touch the hunched form curled up by the wall.

'Rose,' she whispered. 'Don't shut me out, not now, not at this important time. We have to talk before your father comes home . . . Rose, love. He has to be told, and he'll understand. You know he will. As I'm trying to understand. Just give me a little time.'

Rose turned and the look she gave her mother was so like the look, the never to be forgotten look on old Mrs Carmichael's face that Maggie flinched. Even the voice was the same:

'*Understand?* Me dad understand a thing like that? If he was a proper man he might just *try* to understand, but he isn't, is he? He wouldn't be sleeping on his own in a separate room if he was, would he?'

Maggie tried to control the shaking of her whole body. She had to stay, to listen, to comfort. And yet it was all the same. . . .

But it could not be. It was a trick of the imagination. And could it be that she herself had made Rose as she was, because she could never blot the memory of that night from her mind?

Had the ghost of old Mrs Carmichael merely come

between her and Rose, not been faithfully reproduced in this girl who was her own daughter? Maggie made one of her sudden decisions.

'Rose, listen to me,' she whispered.

And it wasn't easy to tell her child the way it had been with her and Joe. The fumbling words sounded all wrong.

What she wanted to do was to tell, to show Rose, that once, a long time ago, her own mother had been far from holy, holy, holy . . . that she had let a boy make love to her, *wanted* him to make love to her, *needed* him, as perhaps Rose herself had needed comfort.

'I lost the baby in the room across the landing, with no one to tell, and no one to understand. So you see, sweetheart, I *do* understand. I loved this boy, but nobody ever tells us how easy it is to let go, just for a brief moment.' She leaned over to touch Rose gently on her shoulder.

'I love you, Rose. I've wanted to show you before, but there was always . . . always something stopping us getting close.' She closed her eyes. 'I'll face this with you, love, and it won't be easy, make no mistake about that, because folks can be cruel, even those who go to Chapel twice on a Sunday. An' you won't be alone like I was. You'll have me to fight for you, and your father, because he stuck up for me when folks turned on me . . . oh, yes he did.' Her voice softened. 'I think that was what made me decide to marry him in the end. . . . Oh, Rose, little love, don't cry like that. I'm here. I'm right here.'

When Rose came into her mother's arms, it was as though Maggie was holding her child for the very first time.

As though the ghost of Kit's mother had been exorcised, to disappear for ever.

15

When Kit came in that night, it was near to midnight. He was actually stumbling with exhaustion, his face clammy with a thin film of sweat.

'Mr Yates wanted everything down off the shelves and all the stuff in the back room checked, then he asked me to re-dress the window to show off some of the posh foods he's bought in. You'd never think there was a war still on.'

Because Maggie was dreading what she had to tell him, her voice was sharper than she had intended.

'Posh foods? What do you mean by posh foods?'

Kit, bending over with difficulty because of his rapidly increasing waistline, began to unlace his boots.

'Oh, you know, love. Tins of pineapple chunks, and tins of what they call After Dinner Mints. Half a crown a tin they are. He's gone off his chump I reckon. He forgets that most of our customers are like old Mrs Bradshawe coming in begging bacon scraps to stuff a cod's head with.'

'To feed seven of them at that.'

Maggie knelt down and unlaced the second boot. Kit's weight had increased so that his stomach hung like a bladder over the tops of his trousers, and the stiffly starched collars he wore pushed his neck up into a fold as red and loose as a turkey's crop.

'That awful man exploits you!' she burst out, dreading what she had to tell him. 'An' you just let him.'

Rose's cruel words came back to her, making her sharp and irritated, because she knew in her heart there was more than a hint of truth in them.

But Rose had meant what she said in a cruel way, and this man was so good, so good . . . Maggie stood up, ready to do battle on his behalf, still putting off what she had to tell him.

'You ought to try to stand up to him a bit more, Kit. He'll never find anyone like you, and you know it. Where could he find a young man to do the buying as well as the selling, plus keeping an account book, and keeping his shop going when the others have closed?'

Her hands were on her hips now. 'Look what happened early on when so many customers took their coupons to the bigger grocers down town. You hardly lost a single one. They all brought their registrations to you because they remembered how you've helped them and been fair. The old goat knows that, the miserly devil.'

Kit did not bother to respond. For one thing he was too tired and for another he knew his Maggie. She was working herself up because something else had upset her, and she would tell him in her own good time.

All her anger stemmed from concern. She was like his mother in that way, but he wasn't daft enough to tell her. His Maggie had exactly the same mother hen attitude to life – let anyone hurt her family and she would spit in their eye.

And he loved it. Her fighting spirit made him feel safe; it was like warm syrup, soothing and comforting.

He stood up and yawned. 'I'll just go out to the back, love, then I'm off to bed. Rose all right?'

Men *did* cry, Maggie reminded herself as she lay in bed an hour later, as wide awake as if it were the middle of the afternoon. She had felt Joe Barton's cheek wet against her own that night, after he had made love to her, and before he went away.

Kit was an easy crier, she knew that, but his anguish had been so great that he had sobbed in her arms on the sofa downstairs, sobbed like a child with a disappointment so overwhelming he could not bear it.

Now he was asleep. She could hear the rhythmic rise and fall of his snores from the back room, while her own thoughts darted like a fire-fly from one subject to another.

Clara would have plenty to say because she had never liked Rose.

'Bring trouble to your door that one will. There's bad blood somewhere in her and that's not kidding.'

Maggie turned and tossed. Where had they gone wrong with Rose? Was it their fault? Kit's for being too soft by half, and hers for being over-strict?

No, Rose had just seemed as if she wanted to be awkward all round. There were days when if Maggie had said it was a Monday, Rose would have declared it to be a Tuesday.

Maggie pulled the clothes up round her neck. Poor Rose. Believing she was so unlovable she had let a stranger make love to her.

At least she had loved Joe . . . loved him so much that even now the thought of him flooded her body with the ache of remembering.

Maggie sat up suddenly in bed, her long hair falling round her face. . . . She was hearing Joe's voice again, calling out to her in anger. . . .

'Oh, Joe,' she whispered. 'If you need me, tell me where you are. . . .'

Moved from the field hospital in Boulogne, shattered in both mind and body, with a leg wound that refused to heal, Corporal Joe Barton was sent first to a hospital in the south of England, then because his sister Belle was down on his papers as next of kin, to the Royal Infirmary in his home-town.

The week before Christmas in 1918, sleeping fitfully in his narrow bed in the ward filled with wounded soldiers, he dreamed he was standing-to on a trench fire-step.

Dimly he saw the Passchendaele night turn into a pink-tinged dawn. Through bleary eyes he saw the corpse-strewn waste of no man's land. When the order to stand down came he dropped exhausted back into the dug-out.

To Joe the beautiful rosy early morning was nothing more than a hypocritical mockery. It was merely the beginning of yet another day of undiluted horror.

It took him a good three minutes to realize that the dawn he was seeing now was seeping through the tall window behind his bed, and another three minutes to realize that the war in France had been over for more than a month.

Sister Fletcher walked with her springy slip-slap walk down the long ward and stopped by his bed. She was carrying a blanket-wrapped bundle in her arms, and if Joe had not known her as well as he thought he did he might have suspected that there were tears in her voice.

'Mr Barton?' she whispered. 'Are you awake? I wonder if you would do something for me?'

With her free hand she pulled the covers out at one side of his parcel-neat bed.

'Will you take this newborn baby into bed with you and keep it warm? We've just done an emergency in the theatre, and the baby's mother has unfortunately died.'

'Well bugger me!'

Joe pushed himself up on an elbow and blinked, but for once the Sister did not stop to reprimand him for his language. She merely deposited the small bundle beside him, tucked the covers back again, and walked back down the long ward. She lingered for a whispered word with the night nurse, who was cocooned in her own little pool of light at her desk, looked back in Joe's direction, then vanished.

Joe heard her springy footsteps turn into a rapidly receding and totally forbidden run. . . .

The rest of the ward was in complete darkness, but the cold grey light from the window showed him a small round face, no bigger it seemed than a man's fist. It showed him a pout of a pink mouth with the chin sucked in as though the baby knew it was off to the worst of starts, and a surprising shock of jet-black hair growing straight up from a worried, lined and puckered forehead.

'Well bugger me!' Joe said again. 'You poor little sod. You're the baby Nurse Gallagher told me about. The one what the surgeon was going to have to bring on by operating – the one belonging to that lass with no husband.'

Carefully he raised himself a fraction.

'There's not many babies *born* orphans, but I reckon that's what has happened to you, young fella-me-lad.'

He peered intently into the tiny sleeping face. 'That's if you *are* a fella-me-lad. By the left but I've got to watch I don't squash you, little chuck. There, just let me move one arm a bit. There, that better?'

The baby fluttered mauve eyelids, then began making soft little sucking noises, turning its head into the swaddling blanket. Gingerly, scarcely daring to breathe, Joe loosened it with his hand.

'Now, don't go and smother yourself, you little codger,' he said.

He cradled the baby into the curve of his arm, the womanly smile on his thin face at comical variance with the overnight growth of dark stubble on his chin.

'A right bloody turn-up for the book,' he chuckled.

Joe Barton, ex Corporal Joe Barton. Bolshie in outlook, even though back in civilian life, before he joined up, he had been well on the way to being a capitalist. Trusting in nobody and with good reason. . . . Putting out a finger he traced the baby's rounded chin with a feather-light touch, then he grinned to himself as the blob of a nose gave an irritated twitch.

'Sharp little sod, aren't you?' he whispered, so engrossed that he failed to see the way the night nurse approached his bed, then as silently crept away.

He could guess what the rest of the ward would say when waking-up time came at half past five:

'Always suspected old Joe had lost more than his knee-cap and half his brain in France. But we'd never have thowt he was expectin', would we, lads?'

That would be Nobby Clark, shell-shocked on the Somme in March, and still not able to face the outside world. Poor Nobby, still thinking he was in the hospital in Rouen; not able to believe the war was over.

Joe held his breath as the baby sighed, a soft little sigh ending on a whimper.

It was the day the vicar made his weekly round, always stopping by Joe's bed and beaming at him. As if there was summat to beam about, Joe thought bitterly.

'Now then, Mr Barton,' he'd say. 'Sister tells me you've been up on those pins of yours a bit more this week.'

The vicar's cheeks glowed shiny and red, as if he had been at them with a scrubbing brush. They moved up into little round cushions of fat as he smiled.

'Keep it up, man! There'll be no holding you back soon!'

'Holding me back from what?' Joe had asked once. 'From going down to London and trying to do me rounds on crutches? From convalescing with me sister, who doesn't want me anyway? At least her husband doesn't. Holding me back from trying to forget that men I knew well died with their faces shoved in the mud, or their bellies ripped open with pieces of shrapnel? Is that what you mean?'

The vicar's cheeks had glowed redder than ever as he had wished Joe a rapid 'God bless you, my son' before moving quickly on to the next bed.

Joe shifted his position with care. It wasn't fair baiting the little man. He always felt a pang of shame when the vicar had gone on his way down the ward, his Bible tucked neatly underneath his arm.

But what did a man like that know about owt?

Fair enough he must have been too old for active service, but Joe knew he had lived out his war in the northern town, with nothing to upset him but the reading of dispatches. The Rev Shuttleworth had not seen men screaming as their wounds turned gangrenous from the Salient's mud. He had not heard them, some of them, crying for their mothers before they went over the top.

He tightened his arm round the baby, holding it close, willing his own warmth into the tiny body, assuaging the choked-up feeling in his throat by a speech he would have ready for the luckless vicar:

'Right then, sir. What I would like you to tell me is how that oh so merciful God of yours can allow a young lass to peg out, leaving her baby with neither a mother nor a father? Would you not have thought that Him up there would have looked down and decided that she had been bad enough done by by some sod who wouldn't marry her, and seen to it that things would go right for her from now on?'

Joe nodded to himself, satisfied with the neat way he had phrased his speech, then shushed indignantly at the occupant of the next bed, who was snoring rhythmically up and down the scale.

'I haven't minded you keeping me awake all night, old pal,' he muttered, 'but this little whipper-snapper here has to be kept warm and quiet, see? He's going to wonder what sort of a place this is when he wakes up to find there's no titty milk for him.'

Suddenly to his surprise, an amazement tinged with shame at his unexpected weakness, Joe felt a tear ooze out from underneath his eyelids and roll slowly down his cheeks. Putting out his tongue as the tear meandered past the corner of his mouth, he tasted the sad saltiness of it, then he felt the familiar pain run like burning quicksilver down the back of his leg.

For the sake of the baby nestling close to his side, he decided to forgo his usual loud moan, which sometimes resulted in an extra early cup of tea if he could make the moan loud enough to reach the ears of the night nurse sitting writing out her reports at the desk at the far end of the ward.

Instead he thought about the baby's mother, the young black-haired woman lying dead now somewhere down the long echoing Infirmary corridor.

She had been a good looker all right. Sister Fletcher would have skinned him alive if she had known how many times in the past few days he had been on his crutches as far as the side ward where she lay. Oh, she would have been pleased with his progress all right, but shocked out of her starched pinny at the idea of a man patient daring to venture into the women's wing of the Infirmary.

'Nasty mind you've got underneath that apology for a cap, Sister,' he'd told her when she had ticked him off for winking at a buxom ward maid. 'You ought to know better than most that I haven't got the strength at the moment for more than a bloody wink.'

Uttering a sound somewhere between a pshaw and a snort of disgust, Sister Fletcher had flounced around and slapped her flat-footed way back between the rows of beds and out of the ward.

But he had seen the woman through the open door into the small side-ward. He had seen her lying back on high-banked pillows, her long hair lying in two never-ending plaits over the sheet. White as chalk her face with the freckles standing out like spots of undissolved Horlicks on the top of a glass of hot milk. And even in that quick glance he had seen the way the half-moon curve of her surprisingly dark eyelashes lay on her cheeks. He almost risked a whistle, just to cheer her up, because the baby was still inside her then. He had seen the rounded mound pushing the bedclothes up as if somebody had clamped half a barrel on her stomach.

'What is she doing up this end in Women's Surgical if she is in here to have a baby?' Joe had asked little Nurse Gallagher when she came on duty.

'She's going to have her baby by caesarian section,' the nurse had told him, full of importance because she was going to be allowed to watch as part of her training. 'The surgeon, Mr Cardwell, is coming in specially to do it, because there is something wrong with the mother's heart and she can't be allowed to go on and have her baby normally.' Nurse Gallagher's blue button eyes had sparkled with anticipation, then she had gone on to tell Joe that caesar babies were beautiful babies as a rule.

'Their heads aren't pointed like normally born babies, because they haven't had to struggle to be born,' she'd said, then scuttled away before Sister Fletcher caught her gossiping with the patients again.

Joe glanced down at the perfect curve of the rounded head nestling in the crook of his arm. Nurse Gallagher had been quite right. This little head certainly came to no point. Tenderly he traced its shape, feeling the silky hair whisper through his touch.

Poor little Nurse Gallagher, with her pale piggy eyes, and her big red conk of a nose, and her bare arms as mottled as a slab of potted meat.

It would have upset her proper seeing the young woman die on the operating slab, if that was the way it had been. The little Irish girl hadn't been nursing long enough to get used to patients dying. Not young and lovely women like the beauty in the side ward. Joe doubted if Nurse Gallagher would ever consider it all a part of her day's work, as he was sure po-faced Sister Fletcher did.

They could have done with her at the hospital at Boulogne, what with soldiers dying right, left and centre. Or better still, they could have sent her up the line. One look at her horrible miserable face, and even a German minenwerfer would have changed direction – may even have turned back and blown some of its own side up. . . .

'Well, Mr Barton? Tired of holding the baby, are you? I've come to take her away now, thank you very much.'

'What's going to happen to it?'

Joe had never thought Sister Fletcher would answer him, but she did:

'We're keeping her in for a few days, but there's a

grandmother going to take her. She's just arrived with her husband and they want to see their grand-daughter.'

Swiftly she removed the bundle from his grasp.

'Now don't forget it is your morning for helping with the teas; the night staff have been run off their feet what with everything happening unexpectedly.'

And before Joe could say even as much as a 'damn' Sister Fletcher had been and gone, taking the baby with her.

His left arm was still curved round the empty warm space in the bed. It had all been as quick as a trench raid, target reached, mission completed. Yes, sir, please sir, three bags full sir. . . .

But oh, bloody hell, it was terrible this emptiness he felt. He could still smell the new-born smell of the baby, a sweet soft scent, far different from the stink in his nostrils every time they changed the dressing on his leg.

He would never forget that dreadful smell . . . but that was when they had thought his leg would have to come off.

Joe buried his head in the place where the baby had been. By the left, but he had told that still wet round the ears apology of a doctor in France where he'd got off. He had told the bloody lot of them that if they cut off his leg he would do himself in at the first opportunity.

He wasn't going back to Blighty with one trouser leg flapping. He wasn't 'one of our gallant defenders' as a sickening headline in a newspaper had described him and his like. He wasn't cut out to be a cripple, not Joe Barton. Not even Joe Barton, son of a drunken whore, father unknown. Always he had had to fend for himself, just as that poor little sod of a baby would have to.

And that bonny little lass with her gypsy colouring, never knowing that she had a perfect baby with a face as round as a miniature full moon.

It wasn't fair. Nothing in the whole bloody rotten world was fair. . . .

Joe turned his face into his pillow and wept. Quietly at

first, with subdued sobs, then with an abandonment to grief that left him without even the semblance of control. Shaking with unmanly sobs, crying his terrors of what had passed away, crying as he had never cried before, not even as a child.

When the night nurse, going off duty, told Sister Fletcher about it, she nodded with satisfaction, her eyes starting from her head with exhaustion.

'So it worked then,' she said, her plain dedicated face flushing with an emotion which should have made her look beautiful in its compassion, but because of the unfortunate set of her features, made her look merely blotchy and ugly.

'Mr Barton will start to improve from now on. That leg wound of his is only half his trouble. I'm sure you realize that. He just needed to crack, that was all. That swearing and carrying on is all part of his loneliness.' She pinched the bridge of her nose as if she would smooth her exhaustion away. 'Finding out there is always someone worse off than yourself is often the best medicine, human nature being what it is.' She straightened her already straight cap, pushing back a strand of mousy hair.

'Everybody has to crack sometimes, even the toughest nut of all.'

Then, having worked a full night on top of a full day, she went off duty for a few hours, her back ramrod straight, and her feet slapping the polished floor in their quarter to three position.

'She actually looked part way to being human,' the night nurse told her friend as they ate stringy sausages flanked by watery cabbage downstairs in the nurses' dining-room. 'I even dared to ask her what would be happening to the baby, and she said we would be keeping it in for a few days before the grandmother took it home.'

'The mother's mother?'

'There never was a father, if you know what I mean.

Seems the girl, Rose Carmichael, insisted on staying on too long at one of the mills, when she should have been resting with a heart condition brought on by her pregnancy.'

She shovelled her food in from force of habit. 'It won't be easy rearing a baby that size.'

'Especially for a grandma.'

'Oh, she's not in the least *old*. Not white-haired and doddering,' she said, yawning as she stirred sugar into a thick white mug of tea.

It did not occur to Maggie that there was anything extra-ordinary in the fact that she was walking alone the three miles from Foundry Street to the Infirmary, wheeling an empty pram.

Kit had accepted that they would bring up Rose's baby as a matter of course, had taken two hours off from the shop for the funeral, and had agreed with Maggie on the in-scription for the wreath of white and red chrysanthemums:

'The Lord giveth, and the Lord taketh away.'

'Though I'm not too sure I believe that literally,' she said. 'Not if I set me mind to it. Rose died because she was stubborn, right to the end. I don't feel the Lord had much part in anything that happened to Rose. . . .'

She levered the heavy pram down off a kerb, across a street and up on to the opposite pavement, stopping now and again to feel the blanket covers to make sure they were still dry.

They had been airing over the fire-guard and on the string across the fireplace since six o'clock that morning, and still felt warm to her touch.

She adjusted the storm apron, frowning at the frayed elastic holding it in place. The half-crown she had paid for it had been more than enough for a third-hand pram, she decided.

Guiding the pram across the tram-lines, Maggie turned into a side street leading to a short cut underneath a railway arch. A sudden gust of wind lifted the brim of her hat a little, and she stopped to pierce it more firmly to her up-swept hair with a long pearl-ended hat pin. Then, for the second worrying time, she pushed a hand inside the pram to feel the blankets.

'And there's nobody going to feel sorry for you, little love,' she told the empty interior. 'I'll see you go nothing short somehow or other. You're going to have your own little kit of milk every day from Mr Ainsworth's best cow. I've arranged that. There's not going to be any of that skimmed condensed muck for you. You are going to grow up just the same as if everything was as it should be. Your grandma will see to that.'

Her expression was very fierce, the well-defined eyebrows drawn together, and the small chin jutting out, as Maggie continued on her way. It looked like rain and she lifted her face to the sky and dared it to do any such thing.

'You can just wait till I get the baby safely back home,' she told a lowering cloud, then as a tram clattered past, rocking along its rails, she bent her full weight over the pram handle, pushing it up the long steep slope leading to the Infirmary.

The baby was ready, dressed in the long feather-stitched petticoats, one of flannel and two of cotton underneath the pin-tucked nightdress, the hand-knitted jacket made by Maggie during Rose's waiting months.

Everything was too big, she noticed; even the bonnet she had sworn would have been too small for a doll when she stitched it up.

She watched silently as Sister Fletcher wrapped the baby in the grey shawl with darns worked in wool pulled from its fringes, the shawl Rose had been wrapped in as a baby.

Maggie swallowed hard. She had no intention of showing herself up in front of this hatchet-faced nurse, so she blinked and stared at the far wall with its top half painted a sickly green and the bottom a bilious yellow.

'It looks a bit like rain,' she said in a casual-sounding voice.

'Yes it does.'

Sister Fletcher tied the bonnet strings with a ferocious bow, and Maggie winced.

She would throttle the little thing if she wasn't careful, then to take her mind off the lump in her throat she narrowed her eyes and gave the Sister what Kit would have called one of her 'summing-up' looks.

By gum, but she looked a hard one all right. She would not fancy getting the wrong side of *her*, Maggie decided. A bad enemy the Sister would make. She stared at the nurse's ringless left hand. Yes, Sister Fletcher would likely be one of the women who would claim to have lost a sweetheart in France, and God only knew, there would be plenty of them about now. . . .

She held out her arms as the Sister passed the bundle over to her, and marvelled how any woman could look so forbidding when they were handling a baby. Why, even Clara would have smiled if she had looked down at this tiny round-faced scrap with her tuft of black hair showing where the bonnet wasn't pulled down far enough.

Maggie adjusted the frill until it almost covered the baby's eyebrows.

Sister Fletcher was feeling as grim as she looked. Personally she did not give this particular baby much of a chance. She had sent far too many babies out into the world, only to see them return as undernourished infants, bowed with rickets, heads alive with nits, middle-aged before they had even gone off to school.

'She'll have to be fed every two hours I'm afraid, Mrs Carmichael,' she said, 'and that includes during the night for the first few weeks. She's not sucking strongly enough to get all she needs at one feed. You'll find that she gets exhausted then falls asleep.'

The deep resigned sigh showed Maggie that the nurse considered what she was going to say next was possibly a waste of time, but she waited patiently, ready to give as good as she got.

'She will also have to be kept very warm, Mrs Carmichael, and that means keeping her in a heated room all the time. Are you all right for coal, because if not I might be able to put you in touch with an organization. . . .'

Maggie nodded quickly, her dignity at stake.

'The coal shed's that full it's spilling out into the back-yard, thank you very much all the same, Sister. I've been stocking up for weeks.'

She felt the hardening of the lump in her throat. The time for crying was not here. If there was such a time it was when you were alone, shut away behind a closed door so that nobody could see you giving in.

Giving in was a waste of time; she had decided that a long long time ago.

'Thank you for all you and the other nurses have done for my daughter, and for the baby, especially for keeping Rosie here till we got things sorted out an' . . . an' the funeral over with. It's been very good of you, it really has. . . .'

Sister Fletcher waved the thanks away, walking to the door of the little side-ward with her starched apron crack-ling as she went.

'You know your way out, Mrs Carmichael?' she asked over a disappearing shoulder.

Then she took out her jumbled feelings on the first nurse she met, a young probationer who was doing nothing more revolutionary than carrying a bed-pan to the sluice.

Joe Barton, trespassing yet again as he swung his way along the stone-flagged corridor on his crutches, saw the soberly clad back of a small slim woman carrying a baby in her arms.

She did not need to turn round for him to recognize her. He would have recognized that walk anywhere, that straight

220

back, that brown hair slipping its bun and wisping down her neck.

'Maggie!' His heart was beating so fast, beating right up in his throat so that his voice came out as no more than a croak. 'Maggie . . . oh, Maggie!'

The more he tried to hurry after her, the more the crutches got in his way, and when Maggie turned a corner and disappeared from his sight Joe slumped against the wall, drained and exhausted.

He stood there, head bowed, saying her name over and over to himself . . . Maggie Craig . . . *his* Maggie. So that was the grandma little Nurse Gallagher had spoken about. His Maggie, his own love, and they had been within yards of each other, and because of this blasted leg he couldn't even get her to turn round.

Joe raised his head, suddenly filled with an elation he didn't know how to control. Bugger the man she had married, and bugger the fact that she hadn't answered any of his letters. That one glimpse of her had told him something he had known all along. All those terrible months and years in France, she was the only woman he had dreamed of, still was the only woman he dreamed of.

And that baby had been put in his arms because it *belonged* to him. That baby was a part of Maggie, and he had cuddled it and kept it warm right after it was born. No wonder he had felt like he did . . . it was fate, it was a miracle, and the sooner he got out of this damned Infirmary the better. To see Maggie again, that was all that mattered now.

16

Will Hargreaves, Belle's husband and Joe's brother-in-law, viewed Joe's impending release from the Royal Infirmary with the gravest trepidation.

'Don't commit yourself as to how long he can stay, that's all I'm trying to say,' he warned, walking on his bent legs down the stone corridor in time for the Sunday hour of visiting at three o'clock.

'Tell him he can stop for a bit when he comes out next week, but have the sense to emphasize the bit. If you don't, then I will.'

His size seven shoes, tipped with heel protectors, made ringing noises on the floor as he bounced along, narrow shoulders hunched, and small fists buried deep in the pockets of his Sunday jacket.

'We might find ourselves landed with him for good.'

'He *is* my brother,' Belle said weakly, 'and anyway, our Joe will be off back to London as soon as he can. He's much too independent to be beholden to anyone, least of all to you. He's not short of a bob or two remember, and he'll want to get his affairs sorted out once he's found his feet.'

'But he never is going to find his feet, is he? From what that Sister told me he'll always have to walk with a stick.'

'That doesn't make him a *cripple*,' Belle said faintly. Arguments always had that effect on her. She sighed as they turned right into another long bare corridor.

'Please, Will, try and talk to him just a little this time.'

Then Belle walked on, the worriting nature of her thoughts wrinkling her forehead. Because it wasn't merely Joe's leg that was bothering him. It was his *nerves*. Sister had said so.

And Will had no patience at all with nerves. Belle had tried to make him *see*, but it was no use.

'Oh, aye? Your Joe might have been in the trenches, but tell me summat? How could our lads have even begun to fight in France if it hadn't been for folk like me providing them with munitions? Tell me that to be going on with.'

'I wasn't getting at *you*, Will,' Belle said gently, but it was no good.

There was no besting Will. . . .

To get to Joe's bed they had to walk past a bed with a red screen round it. Belle averted her eyes, and closed her ears against the sound of a hollow groan.

'He's just coming round from the chloroform, missus,' a soldier in hospital blue told her, trying to reassure. 'He'll make more noise than that when he finds they've taken another chunk from his leg.'

Belle felt the colour drain from her face, but Will took her by the arm and moved her on quickly. They found Joe sitting on a bed playing cards with a man with large sad eyes set in a long drooping face. He struggled to his feet when he saw them, and put a hand on the man's shoulder.

'Better luck next time, old pal,' he grinned, scooping the kitty of halfpennies from the bedcover.

'Nice of you to come,' he told Belle and Will, then he escorted them over to his own bed and indicated two hard little chairs already hopefully set into position.

'Have a chair. I can come home next Tuesday.'

The word 'home' had been a mistake, and Joe knew it at once by the way Belle flinched, and the way that pint-sized husband of hers shot her a warning glance.

Will at the same time was wondering if he could give Belle a warning kick without letting it show? He and this so-called brother-in-law could never share the same roof and he was astute enough to realize it. It was time Belle knew it too.

Working with gunpowder had not been exactly a bean-feast, but not to be considered of course with charging about in France with a fixed bayonet. Joe was obviously far from well, you only had to see the nerve jumping at the side of his scarred face to see that. And it wouldn't be no bloody picnic having a bloody war hero sitting opposite to him on the other side of his own fireplace, wincing every time he struck a bloody match, and jumping a mile when a lump of coal back-fired. He stared anywhere but at Joe and said a deliberate nothing.

'That's right good news,' Belle said after far too long a delay, and when they had gone, back home to their neat little cottage and their Sunday tea of cold ham and toma-toes, followed by a treat of a tin of pineapple chunks swimming in a sea of Bird's custard, Joe lay back on his bed, remembering the sudden exhilaration he had felt when he had seen Maggie again.

Exhaustion, Maggie knew, was something you learned to live with after a time. Lack of sleep was another.

Not able to take more than a few ounces of cows' milk at a time, the baby woke regularly every two hours, crying with a thin wail, and jerking Maggie out of a twitching sleep on the hard and slippery sofa.

Sometimes she heard it when the baby was fast asleep, she told Clara.

'You look shocking,' Clara said kindly.

So tired was Maggie that she was sure she nodded off for odd minutes, even when she was putting the nappies through the mangle in the yard, or even queueing up in the Fish Market as she was now, leaving Clara to keep an eye on the baby.

The main thing was that Rosie was thriving. She still

cried a lot, still sicked up a goodly part of her bottle, but now she would stare up into Maggie's face with a sort of cross-eyed resignation. And Clara she seemed to adore, a feeling that Maggie knew was mutual.

There was something strangely soothing about the long nights dozing fitfully on the sofa downstairs, the firelight softening the contours of the dark furniture as the fire struck sparks from the burnished steel fender. Maggie drifted in and out of dreams. . . . Once, half awake and half asleep, she imagined that Rose was standing by the dresser smiling at her.

Moving up in the queue Maggie shifted her weight from one foot to the other, and made up her mind not to faint. She was not going to faint in a fish queue, not her. . . .

All the same, it was good to get out into the open again, away from the overpowering smell, out on to the cobblestones of the market-place. She glanced up at the round clock set high in the market house tower, and saw that it was almost time for the baby's next feed.

She would have to hurry. . . .

'It's all right, she hasn't moved a muscle,' Clara said the minute she walked in, then her eye slid down into its corner.

"There's a man been. A tall fella with a walking stick, and no hat on. I told him you'd gone out, and he said he would come again.' She sniffed her disgust at the caller going away without stating his business and saying who he was. 'I can't think who it might be, love. I knew it weren't the Insurance man or the Doctor's man with it not being a Friday, but he asked for you by name so he must have come for summat.'

Maggie was taking the parcels of fish from her basket and handing one to Clara.

'Pay me later,' she said. 'Isn't that your mother knocking on the wall?' She smiled. 'Thank you for letting me get out a bit. I really enjoyed it, there's a lovely fresh wind.'

'It's time you had a bit of life,' Clara said kindly, then

raising her voice and startling Maggie she walked over to the dividing wall and banged on it with a clenched fist.

'I'm coming as fast as I can!'

Her voice dropped two octaves. 'I never thought the day would come when I would admit it, but me mother's really getting on me wick.' She glanced at the baby. 'Oh, I've wakened her up,' she said in a surprised tone. 'She's a light sleeper, isn't she?'

Before she took off her coat, Maggie set the milk to warm, smiling to herself. Yes, she had enjoyed being out on her own in the fresh air even though the wind had been a bit parky. She puffed up the front of her hair with her fingers. And the baby was gaining weight, and the sewing orders were coming in, and even if Kit was laid off from the shop they would manage somehow.

With secret pride Maggie had, for the first time in her life, opened a bank account.

'One of these fine days we'll move,' she'd told Kit. 'We'll have a garden with a swing in it, an' when I hang the washing out it won't bang against a sooty wall. An' Rosie will run to school down a leafy lane. . . .'

She stirred sugar into the milk and began to fill the bottle, then started as the knocker banged three times, making her spill some of the milk over the table.

Telling the baby to be quiet for a minute, Maggie walked through the parlour to the front door.

She could not believe it . . . this man, this thin pale man with the dark hair that flopped down over his forehead had been in her heart and her mind for so long, and yet she could not bring herself to believe that he was standing there.

'Joe! Oh, Joe.' She held out both hands towards him, and he hooked the stick over his arm and took them, and they gazed into each other's eyes, all attempt at pretence forgotten.

'Joe . . . I never thought to see you again. I never . . .'

Joe was the first to recover. 'Well then, Maggie love.

Aren't you going to ask me in?' He glanced up and down the street. 'There's eyes boring in me back. I can feel them. Dozens of them.'

Maggie stood aside, held out a hand to help as she saw the awkward way he negotiated the step, then drew it back when she saw the expression on Joe's face. Then she led the way through the parlour into the living-room, to where Rose's baby slept peacefully, tired after her crying spell, in the clothes basket to the side of the black fireplace.

'My daughter's baby,' Maggie said, overwhelmed now by an unexpected shyness which she tried to hide by bending over and tucking the blankets in more firmly. A hairpin loosened itself and fell with a tinkle to the floor as it bounced off the fender.

'My hair's a mess,' she said stupidly, putting up a hand and trying to secure the straying wisps.

'Maggie, lass. . . .' Joe came up behind her, stooped down to lay a gentle finger on the baby's head, and saw the floor coming up to hit him smack between his eyes.

Taking a deep breath he straightened up, feeling the sweat break out on his forehead as the entire room swam round and round. Groping behind him he felt for the edge of the table.

'I think mebbe I walked a bit too far,' he said, and his voice was a shaky echo, as if it came from a far-off place.

Then somehow, he never knew quite how, he was sitting in a chair, and his head was being held down between his knees, and from the same far-away place a sympathetic voice was saying:

'You'll be all right in a minute . . . oh, Joe, love . . . take a few deep breaths . . . that's right. Now just sit there quietly and I'll make a pot of tea. I've got some tea you'll like. It's special for nowadays.'

Joe fumbled in his pocket for a handkerchief, only to be handed one, neatly folded and ironed into a triangle.

'Now slip your coat off. This room's too hot, but it has to be for the baby. It must be a day for dizzy spells,' Maggie went on, talking quickly and not looking at him, giving him a chance to recover. 'I thought I was going off meself in the fish market earlier on, so I know how you feel.'

He put his head back and found that the room had stopped whirling round, then he watched her as she lifted the black kettle from the fire and poured the boiling water into the tea-pot standing in the hearth.

'Here you are then,' she said a few minutes later as she handed him a cup of tea, sweet and hot. 'Now then, tell me where you've walked from, and where you've been. . . .' She sat down opposite to him, and saw him sitting in Kit's chair, and it was as if there were no years in between; as if nothing of importance had happened since he went away. It was uncanny, but it was true.

'I've walked from Steep Brow,' he told her, answering a question she had already forgotten she had asked. 'It was hard on the knee coming downhill.' He leaned forward, putting the cup of tea on the table. 'Maggie, lass. I know a lot you think I don't. I know about your girl dying, and I know that baby very well.' He nodded towards the basket. 'I saw that baby before you did. I've been in the Infirmary a long time because some compassionate sod of a captain saw it was my home-town, and sent me here to be near my kith and kin.'

He gave a twisted smile. 'And I saw you taking the little nipper out, but I couldn't make you hear when I shouted after you.'

Suddenly he raised his voice, startling Maggie out of her dream-like state.

'An' the first thing I've done is to come and find you, *Mrs Carmichael*. Why did you never answer my letters, Mrs Carmichael?'

Maggie's eyes widened with shock.

'Letters. I got no letters, Joe.'

'One of them came back with NOT KNOWN AT THIS ADDRESS written on it,' he said more quietly. 'So somebody was getting them, weren't they?'

228

Maggie flared up then. 'But you took your time in writing, didn't you, Joe? It was just after you'd gone, for weeks after you'd gone, that I needed a letter bad. I'll tell you how bad, Joe Barton.'

She was hating him and she was loving him. She could not take her eyes from his face, from the fading scar on his cheek, from the nose, more hawk-like than she remembered it, from the gaunt expression he never had before.

He had been through hell, she could see that and she could not bear it. He had suffered and she had not been there to smooth the hurt away. . . .

Maggie, quite without volition, got up from her chair, knelt down by Joe's chair, laid her head on his lap until she felt the touch of his hand on her hair, and cried without restraint. She was crying the years away, but she did not know it; this was happiness if she had recognized it, and Joe's broken words were like healing balm to her ears.

'Don't cry, little love,' he murmured. 'It was my fault, all my fault. I sent for you when I was beginning to be somebody, when I'd started putting a bit by. . . .' His hand, stroking the hair away from her forehead, was suddenly still.

'Oh, Maggie Craig . . . why did you have to go and get married?'

For a moment Maggie too was quite still, then she raised a tear-washed face.

'I'll tell you why I got married, Joe Barton. I married a man who was probably the only man in this town who would have me, knowing that before my own father was cold in his grave I had started to have a baby.' Her gaze was steady. 'Our baby, Joe. An' I lost it upstairs in this house, crying for you. For a letter that never came, and when you did write, Joe, it was too late, and though I never would have thought Kit could do such a thing, I can't find it in my heart to blame him. Not at this moment I can't blame him. One day I might, but now. . . .'

She could hear the ticking of the clock on the mantel-piece. The baby made a snuffling sound, then was quiet again.

'Oh, God!' Joe's voice was ragged, filled with hurt. 'Oh, God . . . what a mess. What a terrible bloody wasted mess.' He gave the arm of the chair a derisory slap with the flat of his hand. 'I never thought . . . I never once thought . . . Maggie. I was nineteen!'

'I know.' Maggie sighed. 'We were both there, Joe, but it's all over a long time ago. I've got my life now, and you've got yours, and maybe it is all God's will.'

Joe jerked her shoulders so that she was staring into his blazing eyes.

'It's not bloody God's will, Maggie, it's not! I doubt if there even is a God, and don't look at me like that. I've had the chance to wonder these past few years out there in France. I'm living with Belle till I'm fit enough to go away again, and she goes on about God's will all the time. What's happened to me and you is me not writing early on. You can't blame God for that. For once I'm sticking up for Him!'

'I'm saying nothing, Joe,' Maggie said wearily, 'but all I know is that if I hadn't had a God to turn to at times I shudder to think what might have happened.' She stood up, small and dignified, smoothing down her unruly hair, and moving so that she stood well away from him.

'It's Wednesday, Joe, and Kit's half-day. I don't want you here when he comes in for his dinner. He'll know who you are straight away, and I can't face that.'

Her face crumpled.

'When they came to tell me that Rose had died, do you know what I did? I went out into the yard and banged my head against the wall till the blood came. Then I came in and started to get Kit's breakfast. So you see I do know how to carry on . . . and, Joe, I'm glad to have seen you again, and I'm so very happy that you came through the war alive, but now you must go.'

Joe got up from the chair with difficulty and came towards Maggie, but she held up a warning hand.

'Now this minute, before Kit. I'm not in no fit state to make polite introductions and neither are you.' The glance she gave the clock on the mantelpiece was full of wild entreaty, and even Joe could see that her control was ready to snap.

'I've never stopped loving you, Maggie Craig,' he said clearly, then turning his back on her he limped towards the door, raised a hand in a mock salute, and was gone.

When Kit came into the house, exactly four minutes after Joe had left it, he went straight to his chair, slumped down into it, wrenched off his tie, and unbuttoning his high starched collar, threw it on to the table as if it had been choking the life out of him.

If Maggie had looked at him properly she would have seen the utter desolation on his round face, the dejection in the droop of his shoulders. But she was rushing around, pulling a white cloth over the red chenille, setting out knives and forks, nervous at the way Kit had just missed seeing Joe, and hearing Joe's last words to her, hearing him say them over and over again.

'I've never stopped loving you, Maggie Craig . . . never . . . never . . . never.'

Bending down to the fire-oven she took out a dish of well-browned hot-pot, and set it on a mat.

'It's ready,' she said, crimson-faced, knowing she would be quite unable to touch a mouthful.

Obediently Kit took his place, then sat with head bowed as Maggie spooned the food on to his plate.

'Aye . . .' he said, then again, 'aye.'

'Kit! What's the matter?'

Maggie saw him for the first time. 'What's wrong?'

Wearily Kit pushed the untouched plate of food away.

'I've been given the sack,' he said in a low voice. Even as

he spoke his hands were outstretched to his wife for comfort, just as he had stretched them out to his mother when things went wrong.

Maggie did not fail him, she never had, but this time her pity was tinged with despair. Standing behind his chair she tangled her fingers in his curly hair whilst he leaned against her, his eyes closed.

Then she was angry, so angry that for a moment no words would come.

'You mean that old skinflint has done what he's been threatening to do for years? Taken on someone younger for lower wages? Kit, he can't have! He wouldn't! Not after you keeping that shop open all hours, working out the rations and doing most of the buying? I won't let him!'

She gave Kit's shoulders an exasperated push.

'I could kill him, that's what I could do. The old goat, the mean, spiteful, miserable old goat.'

Kit shook his head from side to side.

'Nay, love. It's not what you think. He's selling up, lock, stock and barrel, and going to live down south. He's seventy years old, Maggie, and he's made his pile. He says he's earned his place in the sun . . . those were his exact words.'

'And what about *your* place in the sun then?'

Maggie faced him now, hands on hips. 'Does he not think about all the years you've been late home, after slaving behind that counter to help him make his pile? The times before the Act came in and you were working from six in the morning till the last customer came in, and then sometimes for no more than a candle?' Her voice rose. 'And what did you say to him when he told you, Kit? Did you just listen and say nothing at all? Nothing at all?'

Kit spread his hands wide.

'Don't take on so, love. I did let him see that I was cut up about it, of course I did. I even asked him if the new owner might keep me on to manage the shop. I reminded him that I knew where every last matchbox was kept, and that I knew all my customers inside out, and I told him I knew who could be trusted to have a bit of tick. But he said he was sorry.'

'Sorry? I should just think he *was* sorry. An' that's all he was, just sorry?'

'He told me he was selling it to a man who wanted to set his son up in business.' Kit looked away from her. 'He wants me to keep on for a few weeks, to show this lad the ropes . . . just till he gets used to it, you know?'

Maggie felt the injustice of it deep inside her, but what she felt she could not even begin to stomach was Kit's attitude. This time he had gone too far. She felt physically sick.

'And you agreed? You actually agreed to that?'

She wrenched a chair from underneath the table and sat down, not trusting her legs to support her. 'You mean you let Mr Yates persuade you to do *that*? Oh, Kit, where's your pride? Do you know what I would have done? I'd have told your miserly Mr Yates exactly what I thought about him, then I'd have marched outside and thrown a flamin' stone through his flamin' window . . . that's what I'd have done!'

Kit got up, leaving his meal on the table. 'Then I would have got myself arrested, wouldn't I? No, there was nothing I could do, and I'm hurting no one but myself if I refuse to help the new lad coming in. I'll find meself another job somehow. Things are sometimes for the best.'

Maggie stared at him. He was so kind, so good, so weak, so much less than a man that she wanted to cry. No, not cry, but beat her fists against his chest, scream at him and kick him for being as he was, for putting her into this position of being the stronger. For making her responsible for him. She stared at him, her hand over her mouth, seeing the defeated droop of Kit's head, seeing too in her mind's eye, the cheeky, almost arrogant lift of Joe Barton's head as he had left her not half an hour ago.

Joe would have stood his ground. Joe had come through

experiences which Kit could never even have imagined, and he was still a fighter. . . .

Maggie made up her mind the way she always did, quick and swift, before she had time to change it:

'How much is Mr Yates asking for the shop?'

Kit mumbled his reply. 'A hundred pounds. He told me he considered it a fair price, with the two rooms above and the one at the back, even though it is used mainly as a store room. He said that . . .'

But Maggie was not interested in what else Mr Yates had said. She was doing quick sums in her mind, and any minute now she would regret it and it would be too late.

Going over to the dresser drawer, she rummaged beneath a pile of tea towels and took out her bank book. She flicked over the entries, one pound, three pounds, and once when she had sewed for five weeks on the linen of the hotel near the station, an unbelievable six.

She held out the book to Kit.

'A hundred and ten pounds, six shillings and fourpence. Do you think Mr Yates would change his mind for ten pounds, six shillings and fourpence?'

As though he had suffered a sudden stroke, Kit sat without moving a muscle, staring at the bank book.

'Open it, Kit!' Maggie was shouting, forgetting about the still sleeping baby. 'Open it and see for yourself. It's all down there, every single saving. Look at it if you don't believe me!'

He stared at the closely figured pages as if in a trance, running a finger over the column, shaking his head, then when he spoke at last it was to say something that made Maggie want to pick up a knife from the table and stick it in his chest.

Shaking his head in infuriating bewilderment, he said:

'But it would be a dirty trick, lass. What about the man who wants to buy the shop for his son?'

Maggie clenched and unclenched her hands, feeling the nails bite deep into her palms.

'Has anything been signed?' She marvelled at the calmness of her voice.

'No. Mr Yates said it was just a gentlemen's agreement as yet.'

'Then as Mr Yates is no gentleman, there's no problem, is there? That shop is *yours*, Kit. Without this money it is yours the way you've worked it up, and you know it.'

Still he argued. 'Maggie, love. I can't take this. I'd no idea you had saved so much, but I know what you were saving for. You hate the town, you've hated it all these years. Anyway, there's the baby now. It's no fit place for a baby apart from the fact that it would take more than one pair of hands to make that place decent enough to live in. The back is just a store room, and upstairs there is damp running down the walls, and the floorboards are giving. There's mice and cockroaches . . . oh, Maggie, it's a *terrible* place. This house is a little palace compared.'

Maggie's eyes flashed.

'Do you *want* the shop, Kit Carmichael, or don't you? I know what it's like, and I know it's no place for a baby, but Clara will take little Rosie for a while. She'll jump at the chance. So just for once, will you be decisive and tell me what you really want to do?'

He did not need to tell her, one look at his face was enough. Slowly despair was being replaced by hope, and more than hope, a wonder in his wife's capability, a marvelling at the way she could always be relied on to bring order out of chaos. Defending him, shielding him from trouble, the way his mother had always done. . . .

And almost *killed* Maggie at one time, his conscience was reminding him, but Kit had long ago put the memory of that night from his mind. He'd had to in order to replace his mother on her pedestal.

'It's not as nice a district as this,' he said again, his hand over the bank book as if he had already transferred it into his own keeping.

'Do you really think Clara will have the baby to mind?

There's sacking over the windows, love, and plaster peeling from the walls, and I won't be able to help much if I'm in the shop and doing the buying and everything.'

'If I warm your dinner up, do you think you could eat it?' She was too tired to talk about it any more. It was done, and that was that. As he ate she sat straight in a corner of the sofa, watching the years fall away from his face as he waved his fork about to emphasize a point, to illustrate what they would do to make the upper rooms habitable.

Maggie knew that the rest of her life was being mapped out for her, because she knew that the post-war boom would be over almost before it began. There would be unemployment, and when the house was clean there would be days, months and years of standing behind the counter, selling a poke of sugar here, and a bundle of firewood there.

Kit wasn't getting any younger, and there was Rosie to bring up. . . . Maggie sighed. Oh, yes, she could read all the signs. Most of the town's mills needed new methods and new machinery. India's import of cottons had begun to fall off, and she had read that the Japanese weavers were willing to work even longer hours and for far less pay.

Her dream of moving to the country might never materialize, and little Rosie would have to grow up with the street for her playground, and the dirt and the grime as her heritage. . . .

That night Maggie went to Kit and whispered that she would like him to sleep with her.

'I have a great need of you, a greater need than you know,' she said.

He stared, shocked by what he considered to be her un-womanly behaviour, then he turned his head. 'You'd never sleep a wink with my snoring, lass,' he said.

Maggie felt her face sting as if he had slapped her. 'Good night, Kit,' she said quietly.

17

The climb up Steep Brow was easier than walking down. Seeing Maggie again had, Joe felt, done more for him than all the weeks and months he'd spent in hospital.

When Will Hargreaves came home from his milk round Joe was sitting by the fire, whistling and looking pleased with himself. He had gone through a bad few moments when he thought about Maggie going through what she had been through and all his fault, but that was done and past and what mattered now was their future together.

For they were going to have a future together. He had made up his mind about that.

'You happy or something?' Will asked, peeved because Wednesday was baking day at the Armitages' neat little semi-detached, and that meant Belle would not be home till later.

'Mrs Armitage likes her kitchen left clean and the oven done. She's very proud of that oven,' Belle had told him, smiling.

'Silly faggot,' Will had said, hating Wednesdays from then on.

Joe put down the paper he had been skimming through, and grinned, not unaware that his brother-in-law was regarding him with something akin to loathing.

'Not been a bad sort of day, has it?' he remarked for something to say.

'Not for *some* it hasn't,' Will said pointedly.

Joe merely laughed. Then he lit a cigarette and flicked the spent match into the fire, where it struck the bars of the grate then fell into the hearth.

'Pick it up.'

Will's tone was even, but frustration was rising thick in his throat. 'You wouldn't be smoking down here if Belle was at home,' he said, small eyes narrowing with dislike.

Joe did as he was told, still grinning.

'Oh, come on now, Will. You're not past having a crafty fag yourself now and again.' He held out the packet. 'Come on. Have one. We can waft the smell out before she comes home.'

'No, thanks.'

Will felt at that moment as if he could sell his soul for a smoke, but he was in no mood to be patronized by the man sitting opposite to him, the man so obviously chuffed about something.

He unbuttoned his waistcoat one button at a time, slowly and deliberately.

'Feeling up to getting back to London, and all them mucky carpets yet, Joe? You'll not earn much brass sitting on tha backside.'

Joe shook his head. 'All in good time, Will. I know it's not right me being here with you and Belle, but I try to keep out of your way as much as I can.'

'And I more than pay my way,' he added silently to himself.

He clenched his hands, dismayed to find that the palms had grown clammy. The little pulse at the side of his head had begun to throb again. 'It's not easy settling after all this time.'

His brother-in-law unfastened the top button of his trousers, and sighed with relief, as if their tightness had been straining over a billowing paunch.

'So we're back where we started then, are we?'

'What do you mean, back where we started, Will?'

The small eyes narrowed. So he had managed to ruffle the tall self-satisfied bloody hero, had he? Good! It was time Joe Barton realized he couldn't just walk into his house and behave as if he belonged. He belonged nowhere, this arrogant thin-faced so-and-so, with the twitching scar on his face, and his assumption that he had the right to get his big feet under their table.

From what Belle had told him, Joe Barton had cleared off pronto when he had found things getting too hot for him, and if he had found somewhere to go then, he could find somewhere to go now. Him and his big talk of a flat in London and his own firm, what did he know about having to get up at four o'clock of a morning and work for a boss who wouldn't give the skin of his rice pudding to his starving grandma?

Aye, Joe was ruffled all right. He'd wiped that grin off his face, that he had.

'Just how long *are* you reckoning on stopping here?' he asked, then before Joe could answer he got up and went out to the back, leaving him to think that one over.

Slipping his braces down as he went into the yard, Will felt mightily pleased with himself. He'd put his spoke in, and he knew Joe would not repeat what he had said to Belle. Just for a split second he felt a stab of shame when he thought what Belle would say if she knew he had been getting at her precious brother.

'He's all I've got, Will. The only family in the world,' she would say.

Still it had needed saying. Will lifted the latch of the privy, then jumped away as a thin grey cat streaked past him to disappear over the wall into the next yard with the speed of light.

'Thought I saw a rat out there,' he said, when he went back into the house, his humour partly restored, and quite prepared to say no more.

What he wasn't prepared for was the swift reaction to what he considered to be an innocent remark. . . .

Immediately Joe sprang to his feet, the colour draining from his cheeks, leaving him grey and shaking, with his eyes starting from his head.

'A rat? Did you say a *rat*?'

Will studied him intently, realizing he had at last found a way to ruffle his brother-in-law's composure.

'Aye,' he said distinctly. 'We did have some at one time. They come from the tip over the field. Great big rats, as big as cats. What's the matter?' he asked in mock innocence. 'You frightened of them or something?'

Joe felt for the chair and sat down, sweat standing out on his forehead like glistening globules of rain.

It was Ypres again – the first, second, and the third battle, and Passchendaele, and Verdun, and there was a rat nibbling away at the dead hand of a soldier lying across his feet. And he could not move . . . he could not bloody move. . . .

Will pressed home his advantage, a faint niggling guilt at what he was doing spurring him on.

'You're all the same, you lot,' he said. 'Making out that your nerves are shot just to get some sympathy.' He sat down again, dismayed in spite of himself at Joe's pallor, but stung into bravado.

'It weren't no joke for me either, I can tell you, working with TNT. And there weren't no ruddy medals given out either.' He stabbed a finger in Joe's direction. 'I'm not like some who yell out in the night, but I could tell you things, aye that I could. There were times when me chest was so tight I was coughing up yellow phelgm, and me skin was yellower than a ruddy canary's.'

He raised his voice. 'Aye, and there weren't no leaves tickling up French tarts, not even after one of the buildings filled with nitro-glycerine blew up in a ruddy sheet of flame.'

Joe tore at his collar, finding it as hard to breathe as if his lungs were being filled with poison gas. He was no longer in the cosy living-room of Belle's cottage, with the ornaments on the mantelpiece, and the rugs laid out in a neat pattern on the floor. He was picking his terrified way along a duck-board over a stinking mud-flat, his equipment weighing a ton across his sagging shoulders. He was seeing the man in front of him slip from the track and die gasping for breath as the mud filled his mouth and eyes.

He was on his way struggling towards the front line, and the trenches where rats . . . he reached out for Will, lifting him out of his chair, and holding him suspended, his tiny feet swinging clear of the floor.

'Oh, I'm sorry for you, Will Hargreaves,' he said through clenched teeth. 'Heart sorry I am for you that your face turned yellow. Have you ever been so frightened that you shit yourself, Will?'

From his undignified position Will stared straight into Joe's eyes, and the glimmer of tears he saw there restored his bravado.

'It was only a cat, you filthy devil,' he said clearly, and staggered to recover his balance as Joe let him go.

Yet somehow he had won. He was not quite sure how, but he knew that he had won. Now he and Joe Barton could never live under the same roof again, and he was glad. And Belle would be glad, though she would never admit it.

Joe backed towards the curtain at the foot of the stairs, his limp more noticeable than ever. Then he drew the curtain back and stumbled up to his room, his shaking terror and his anger evaporating, leaving him weak and filled with self-loathing.

He ought not to have said that. He could scarcely believe he had said what he had. Sitting down on the edge of his bed, he dropped his head into his hands.

Tomorrow he would go back to London. When his hands had stopped their shame-making trembling he would start packing his few things, then he would be off. Sister Fletcher might have said that he wasn't fit to be on his own yet awhile, but even old po-face didn't know everything.

And he would take Maggie with him. And the baby. She wasn't happy in her marriage, he knew that, even if she hadn't said so. They belonged to him, the both of them, because why else had that baby been put in his bed if it hadn't been a sign?

A sign from the God Maggie believed in. The God he himself wasn't all that sure about.

'It's folks what make happiness, not God,' Joe told himself, levering himself up from the bed and starting to pack.

When Joe went downstairs again Belle had come home, pale and tired from the Armitages'.

He found her in the scullery peeling potatoes ready to drop them into the stew she had prepared the day before.

'Will's told me you're going, Joe,' she said, too tired to pretend that she did not know it was for the best.

'That's right, love, and I appreciate what you've done for me. It's just that, well . . . you know me.'

She nodded. 'It would have been nice if you could have stayed somewhere near. It would have been nice to have a bit of family living near.' She dug at an eye in a mis-shaped potato, taking out her feelings on it so that Joe would not see how upset she was feeling.

'Not enough folks with carpets, nor the money to have them cleaned,' Joe said, then he lowered his voice.

'Besides, love, Will is your family now, and you'll be having babies some day when you get a bit put by.'

Her face flamed and she averted her face as she answered him with quiet resignation.

' I don't think so Joe. They would have come afore now if God had meant me to have any.' She moved to the slopstone. 'You see, I'm not quite like other women in a certain way. The doctor told me it was because I was not fed well enough when I was a child. It's a sort of anaemia, if you know what I mean?'

'Oh, Belle. . . .' Joe picked up the knife and jabbed it into the potato peelings. 'Why must you always be so un-complaining? You make me feel ashamed. Surely something can be done? Maybe if you went to one of them specialists in Manchester? You know, one what deals with women's complaints? I'd give you the money, love.'

Her cheeks glowed red again.

'It wouldn't do no good, our Joe, and anyway Will doesn't want no children,' she said simply, and bowed her head, resigned quite passively to the inevitable.

'Then I'll be off in the morning,' Joe said, and they stared at each other, each wishing there was more they could say, but knowing equally that there was nothing.

18

In the long wakeful stretch of the night, propped with a pillow against the bed-end, Joe smoked one cigarette after another, remembering the way Maggie had looked when she had opened the door to him.

There was something about her, something he couldn't put a finger on. She had seemed as untouched as when he had laughed with her as a young girl, as vulnerable and trusting as a young lass in love for the first time.

He narrowed his eyes against the upward curling smoke as he recalled, for some reason, the lonely housebound women he had often met on his rounds before the war. Hungry-eyed and nearly asking for it, and though God forbid his Maggie was not like that, there was something not quite right. She had been terrified of him touching her, and the conclusion he was coming to was that it had not been him she was frightened of, but herself. . . .

Joe drew too deeply on his cigarette and started to cough.

And it wasn't easy walking all that way downhill, carrying a case and managing with his stick, but he stopped now and again pretending to be looking in a shop window, or waiting for a tram. By the time he reached Foundry Street he was hot and sweating, and his knee was aching with the familiar throbbing grind.

He did not attract all that much attention in his badly fitting suit, but one woman, standing on her doorstep gossiping with a neighbour, said:

'That man is back from France. You can tell by his face, even without seeing his stick. It's awful to see them so pulled down. What they must have been through is hard to realize.'

Her neighbour nodded. 'Aye, it was a terrible war, but it's over now, and there will never be another, that's one blessing.'

'You look ill,' Maggie said when she opened the door to him, just as if she had known he would be coming; as if they had arranged it all the day before.

'You don't look all that well yourself, love,' Joe told her, and she led the way through into the living-room, pushed the kettle over the flames, and set the tea-pot down to warm in the hearth.

'I didn't get much sleep,' Maggie said, being careful not to look at him, not wanting him to see the joy just having him there shining from her eyes. 'Sit down, then, Joe.'

He put his case down by the dresser, and lowered himself stiffly into the rocking chair. 'And you sit down, lass. There's something I have to tell you, and I want you to take it all in, every word.'

Maggie did as she was told, then folded her hands in her lap and waited, her head dropping so low that all he could see was the top of her piled hair.

'I had a bit of a dust-up with Will,' Joe said. 'I only just stopped myself from belting him one. So I can't stay there any longer. I'd outlived my welcome there, anyroad.'

Just for a moment the memory of what Will had said about the rat in the yard caused a spasm of pain to cross his face. Maggie glanced up briefly and saw it, and her own heart contracted in sympathy.

'Joe Barton,' she said, trying to make her voice light. 'You seem to make a habit of setting yourself against somebody, and running away. *And* calling here to say goodbye first.'

As she spoke it came to her that she never seemed to have a normal conversation with this man. When they had

245

been young it had all been teasing and laughter, and now, after all these years apart, they still talked with an intimacy as if the years between had never existed, as if all the trivia of politeness and small talk had been dispensed with, leaving them free to say exactly what came to mind.

She got up and got down the cups from the shelf. She got out the big glass sugar-bowl and clattered teaspoons into saucers, keeping her back carefully turned to him.

'So I won't be seeing you again, then?'

He came and putting his hands on her shoulders turned her to face him, standing so close she could see the puckered line of the scar, and the way his dark eyes were flecked with green.

'I've told you to *listen* to me, lass,' he said, and all at once she was aware of the excitement in him, the barely controlled violence.

'Don't touch me, Joe,' she said, and even as she said it she was aching for him to pull her close, to hold her face between his hands, and to kiss her with the mouth that was not fleshy as Kit's was fleshy, but firm and strong.

'Stop messing about with those bloody cups. I don't want a cup of tea. I'm not here to be soothed with tea,' he said.

Turning round he picked up the poker and pulled the stand away from the flames. 'Tea's not what I've come for, and you know it.'

He came close to her again, and putting his arms around her, held her close. She could feel the heat from his face, and she knew that she was powerless to push him away.

'Joe,' she whispered. 'I'm not that young girl you came to say goodbye to long ago. It's not the same, an' it's not going to be the same. Go and catch your train, and be happy, and, Joe . . . you'll take care of yourself? You're not fit to be on your own, not yet.'

He gave her a little shake.

'I've been taking care of myself all me life, love. All my life. You know that.'

'Yes, I know that,' she whispered.

And then he kissed her. Gently at first, with his mouth softly covering her own, searching with sweetness, tracing her face with his lips, murmuring her name.

'Maggie! Oh, lass, you're so beautiful. So bloody marvellous and beautiful. You know that I love you . . . you must know that I've always loved you.'

He kissed her with passion, tangling his fingers in her hair, then letting her go so violently that she groped behind her for the arm of the chair.

Sitting down, she buried her face in her hands, but grasping her by the upper arms, Joe pulled her to her feet again.

'An' don't go and tell me I shouldn't have done that, because you wanted it as much as I did,' he said brutally. 'Tell me, Maggie, because it matters. It has a lot to do with what I've come to say. Has your husband never kissed you like that? Ever?'

For a long moment she was silent, then she shouted:

'No, no, no!'

And she was crying, openly in front of him, crying her shame away, feeling the hot tears run down her face. Sobbing her rejection of the night before away even as she despised herself for her disloyalty.

She raised her face.

'Joe. Don't ask me to talk about it. Not about Kit. He is the kindest, the most considerate man in the whole world. He hasn't done the brave things you've done, Joe, but in his own way he's been brave.' Her breath caught on a sob. 'I'm the wrong one, not Kit . . . He can't help being . . . being different. It's just that he's not made that way, that's all. He can't help not having *feelings*, Joe.' She was talking wildly, agitated and uncontrolled, and giving herself away with every word she spoke.

'And now you must go. Take your case and go. Please.'

Joe cupped her face in his hands, and Maggie even in her distress thought they were the kindest eyes she had ever seen. There was a tender sympathy there, an understanding, and a love that made her close her own eyes against it.

Joe spoke quickly and with urgency. . . .

'Now listen hard, Maggie love. If I could, and if there was time, I would get down on me knees to the bonniest, the bravest woman I've ever known. But I'm down on my knees in me heart, lass. An' that's the way it's going to be from now on.'

He let go of her, and limping back to the chair sat down and felt in his pocket for a cigarette. She saw that his hand trembled as he held the lighted match, and knew she would have to hear him out.

It was no good though. There was no 'from now on' for either of them, but she had the sensitivity to realize that what Joe was about to say had been well rehearsed in his mind. And when he began to speak she knew she was right.

'In two hours from now there's a train to Preston. That train goes to Crewe, Maggie love, and from there on to London. It's a long journey, lass, but it won't seem long, because you are going with me.'

Maggie shook her head violently, but Joe put up his hand for silence.

'You and the baby. *Our* baby, because that's what she is. It all fits like a pattern. You losing ours, then me coming back here and Rosie being put in my arms just after she'd been born. Me coming to find you. Will forcing me to act quickly. I thought it all out in the night and there's no other explanation than that it's a sign. Maybe from that God you're always on about.'

He nodded towards the basket by the fire. 'You can wrap her up well, and there are . . . there's a place at Crewe where you can get warm milk for her bottle.'

He had gone very pale, but Maggie let him carry on.

'We'll get her there all right. She won't come to no harm, an' we'll go to an hotel till I can get my place fixed up nice. Then it will be you and me and her, just like it was meant to be. You'll never want for nothing, Maggie, not for the rest of your days.' He stared down at the cigarette smouldering away in his hand, as if wondering what it could be.

'So just you go upstairs and get a few things together, not much because tomorrow you can go out to a fancy London shop and buy yourself and Rosie anything you need . . . no, not anything you *need*, anything you want.'

He grinned. 'And I won't take no for an answer, Maggie lass. You gave yourself away when I kissed you. You feel just the same way as me, and don't go saying it would be a sin, for staying apart would be a greater sin. Love, the kind of love we feel, doesn't come all that often, and what I saw in France taught me one thing:

'You have to take what you want from this life, 'cos nobody is going to hand happiness to you on a plate. Nobody.'

His face darkened. 'And it's our turn, Maggie. It's *our* bloody turn.'

There! He had said what he had come to say, but he had never dreamt it would take so much out of him. Drained and spent, he put his head back, closing his eyes, so that Maggie saw his face as she imagined it would look when he was dead. White and still, with the only thread of colour the pink scar tissue running down one cheek.

It was very quiet in the little room, quiet with the hush that came at that time in the morning. When Clara began raking the ashes from her fire-back at the other side of the wall, Maggie jumped as if someone had suddenly prodded her in the back.

'But I can't come with you, Joe,' she said. 'I can't leave Kit. He needs me. You don't know just how much he needs me.'

'And don't *I* bloody need you?'

Joe opened his eyes and stared straight at her. 'I need you in a way he has never needed you. You said so yourself, Maggie. Oh, Maggie love, you are still a young woman. You can't live out the rest of your life in this house, in this town. There's another side to life down there.'

He leaned forward, his thin face serious and intent.

'Do you want to grow like the rest of them? Like my

249

sister Belle? She was a washed-out child and now she's a washed-out wife. Maggie? Do you really want to turn into a worn-out drab, waiting on a man what needs a mother more than he does a wife?'

Joe threw the half-smoked cigarette into the fire.

'Oh aye, I know his sort. There were some like your husband in the army. Soft mammy's boys who should never have been breached. Show them a woman, a real woman, and they'd have run a mile. You can't stay here with a man like that, little love. You need someone to care for *you*. Not t'other way round.'

Maggie shook her head sadly.

'Now it is your turn to listen, Joe Barton. Even if I wanted to leave Kit . . .' She lifted her chin. 'And I can't and I won't. It could never be as you say. For one thing, I burnt my boats yesterday after you had gone.'

She glanced over to the dresser drawer where the bank book no longer rested beneath the pile of tea-towels.

'Kit came home and told me his boss had sold the shop to somebody else so that he could retire on the proceeds and the pile he's made over the years. Kit had worked that shop up from nothing, doing all the buying and the figure-work, besides working all the hours God sends for no extra. Yet that mean old goat of a boss gave Kit the sack. Just like that.'

Maggie nodded towards the drawer again. 'I'd been saving up, bit by bit, not much, but it was all money I had earned with sewing, every penny of it. I gave it all to Kit and told him to go and buy that shop for himself. I said I would ask Clara to have Rosie to mind till we got things straight. I told her about it early on this morning, and she's over the moon about it. She reckons she never wanted babies, but to see her with Rosie is a revelation.'

She nodded. 'So I am committed, Joe. That shop is in an awful district – nearly as bad as Montague Court – but there are two rooms above, and I'm sure I can make something of them. It's a *challenge*, Joe. I can decorate those rooms myself, and in between I can help Kit in the shop.'

Twice again she nodded her head. 'So that is what I am going to do, and even if I was the sort who could just walk out on her husband I can't now. Because it is too late.'

'Come here.'

Joe spoke quietly, but the command rang out like the crack of a whip.

'Come here, Maggie. Over to me, and kneel down by this chair, then look me in the eyes and tell me you don't love me. Never mind what you have just been saying – them's only excuses. Just come and tell me that one thing.'

Slowly Maggie obeyed. She got up from her chair, walked across the front of the fireplace, then knelt down by Joe's side on the pegged rug.

There were tears glistening in her eyes, but she wasn't going to let them fall. Crying was a waste of time. Nobody knew that better than she did, but she had to try to make Joe understand. This time he would go away for ever, so what she had to say was important, because she wanted him to remember her words.

'Joe . . . oh, Joe. I can't tell you that I don't love you, because it would not be true. I don't think I have ever stopped loving you and wanting you. Even on my wedding night I stood at the window upstairs and looked up the street, wishing with all my heart that you would come round the corner. I saw a shadow an' I thought it was you. I *made* it into you before it disappeared for ever.'

She blinked the gathering tears away.

'You are my only true love, Joe. I think, like my mother, I was only meant to love one man, and that one is you. But, Joe . . . dear Joe. Nobody has things just the way they want them. Nobody. Life is a compromise for everybody in some way or other. Even Kit has to make do with me when probably he would be happier with someone who didn't blow their top as often.'

She dashed a tear away from the corner of her eye.

'Kit will come home tonight, and the shop will be ours. I know what I have facing me. I know that all right. I have

251

years of serving in the shop, fighting to bring up little Rosie decent, looking after Kit when he is too old to work such long hours, and yes, you were right. I will probably grow old before my time. . . .'

Now the tears were rolling down her face. 'My father used to long for what he called a "glimpse of green", and there's none of that where I'm going to live, Joe, I can tell you that.'

'Where is the shop?'

Joe's voice was cold and he was looking at her as if not a word of what she had been saying had penetrated.

Maggie told him the name of the street where Kit's shop stood on the corner, then she drew back on her heels startled as he banged angrily on the arm of the chair with his fist.

'And you talk about bringing a child up round there? I know you, Maggie. I know you of old. What will you do when Rosie wants to go out and play in the gutter with the rest of the kids in that neighbourhood? Will you lock her up in her room and hope she ends up talking as nicely as you? Will you wash her hair every night to keep the nits out of it?'

Joe thumped the chair arm twice more. 'What sort of a man is this Kit who would *allow* Rosie to be brought up round there? And where do you come into it? Strikes me he's a selfish bastard as well as a . . .'

Maggie put up a hand to cover Joe's mouth, and he took it, and turning it palm upwards, bent his head and kissed the blue veins on her wrist. Immediately she tried to pull away, but he held fast.

'Look, lass. I'm going now. I am going down to the station on me own, because I know you have a lot of thinking to do, then at twelve o'clock I am going to send a taxi-cab for you and Rosie. If it comes back without you then I'll know. But talking's not my way, and we've said all we need. . . .'

He jerked her to him and kissed her hard, so hard that

she felt the pressure of his teeth. So long that when at last he lifted his head she opened her eyes and saw the ceiling dip and sway towards her.

'It's me or him, Maggie. A straight choice. One or the other. You'll not be fulfilling your part of the bargain you made when you got wed, but then he's not fulfilled his either, has he? If I go alone this time it will be for ever. I will never come back to this town again. Ever. . . .'

Maggie felt him move away from the chair. She heard him unhook his stick from the dresser, and she heard the front door slam behind him.

Too shattered, too filled with emotion to get to her feet, she stretched out her arms across the seat of the chair and gave way to wild and anguished weeping.

It was a cold, bitterly cold day, with the sky hanging low with the threat of snow. Joe walked slowly, past the statue of Queen Victoria on the Boulevard, past the tramcars with their overhead cables, and across the wide stretch of road to the station forecourt.

He spoke briefly to a cab driver who nodded and wrote down his instructions, then in the entrance hall he walked over to a window and booked two tickets for London.

Then he sat down on his case to wait. . . .

He was quite calm, as calm as he had always been when waiting to go over the top in the trenches. He was so pale that one or two people, rushing for their trains, glanced quickly at him then looked as quickly away.

There were so many men like Joe Barton in those early months after the war had ended, hanging about at stations, wearing suits that did not fit right, looking as if they were waiting for nothing, with nowhere to go.

War did that, they told themselves, and there was nothing anyone could do except feel pity, and a sort of shamed gladness that it was all over without having affected them directly.

And Joe, sitting as still as Queen Victoria's statue, saw none of them. Every muscle in his body, every nerve inside him tuned into waiting for what might be.

What *had* to be, he told himself, praying to a God whose existence he had never even acknowledged.

There were only five minutes to go when he saw the taxi-cab turn in a wide circle and chug into position at the front of the station.

When Maggie got out wearing her long dark coat and a small velvet hat pulled well down over her forehead, he saw that she was carrying a brown paper parcel, and nothing else.

'The baby? Where's Rosie?'

Joe hurried her towards the ticket collector's box, then up the slope to the platform, so overwhelmed at seeing her that he could talk only in jerky syllables.

Maggie shook her head, not looking at him.

'I couldn't bring Rosie. She is too little. Joe, you know that.' She glanced up at him. 'You knew that if I came it would not be with Rosie.'

She was as deathly pale as he was himself, and when he tried to take the parcel from her, looping the stick over his arm as he tried to manage without it, she clung to it.

Walking by his side, and looking straight ahead, she said:

'I've left her with Clara. But only for a few days, Joe. An' I want you to know, before we get on the train, that I am coming back. I am definitely coming back. I cannot leave Kit. You have to know that.'

As they reached the top of the second slope up to the platform, the train was in, bursting with great clouds of steam which rose and dissolved against the filth of the high glass roof.

The guard, his whistle already in his mouth, had his green flag at the ready, as he stood by his van, watch in hand.

'We are going to miss it,' Maggie said, but Joe stopped dead, staring at her in blank amazement.

'You mean to tell me you are just coming away with me for a holiday? A ruddy flaming holiday?'

The whistle blew. Joe wrenched open a door, almost pushed Maggie inside, then with a strength he had not known he possessed, dragged himself in after her, throwing the case in first.

A porter, running alongside the train, slammed the swinging door, his mottled elderly face scarlet with anger.

'Tha silly buggers!' he shouted. 'What's t' trying to do? Commit bloody suicide?'

The compartment was empty, and as the train drew slowly out of the station, they sat opposite to each other. Joe with his case on the seat beside him, and Maggie with the neat brown parcel tied with string held carefully on her knee.

'Well,' she said. 'I never thought I'd manage it, but I have, and we're off, aren't we? Aren't we then?'

Joe stared at her. He had imagined that the first thing he would do would be to take her in his arms and kiss her, and never stop kissing her till they got to Preston.

But this wasn't the Maggie he had left sobbing on the floor only two hours before.

This was a Maggie he had never seen before. This was a woman with fierce determination in her expression, a woman who knew what she was doing and exactly why. A far far cry from the joyous vulnerable girl he remembered best.

'I wrote a letter for Kit to find when he comes home tonight. I propped it in front of the clock like they do in all the best stories,' she said.

Her head was up and her voice rang clear over the sound of the train wheels.

'I had a long think after you had gone, Joe. I had a long look at myself, and at what was in store. I weighed up the consequences, and I came to the conclusion that a few days out of my life was not going to change things too drastically. If Kit were stronger – if I thought he would come after me and try to find me and knock you about – then I might have thought different. But in this case his weakness has turned out ironically to be my strength.'

She unbuttoned her carefully darned gloves and frowned at the stitches along one finger.

'I told Clara some cock and bull story about a sick relative down in London, and though she knew I have no relatives, sick or otherwise, she was too busy settling little Rosie into her house to be over-inquisitive. . . . And in the letter I told Kit the truth.'

Joe's mouth dropped open.

'You told him you were coming away with me? And you think he will have you back?'

The head in the small velvet hat nodded.

'He will have me back, and worse than that he'll forgive me, Joe.'

'And what about me? Where do I come into these calculations? Might I ask that? Have you got me weighed up an' all?'

Maggie put the parcel down beside her, then came to sit beside him. There were tears sparkling on the ends of her long eyelashes, betraying her calmness.

'Joe, dear Joe. All I knew was that nothing, no power on earth, could have kept me off this train. You see I tried to see how it would be with you gone. For ever this time, just as you said, and I couldn't face it. I couldn't let you go. Oh, Joe, if I have to spend the rest of my life paying for what I am doing, I don't care. Not at this moment I don't. The future was so bleak, and I love you so much, so very very much. . . .'

Then she was in his arms, and he kissed her, and then they were silent. As the train rocked and swayed, and the fields, hoary with frost, flashed by the windows, Maggie snuggled closer and began cautiously to dare to accept the faint beginnings of happiness. Of a joy she would only have dreamed about had she stayed.

There was a dreadful aching weight of guilt on her, but

as she told herself with her usual practical northern common sense, if she really was sincere in her guilt, then she could get off at the next station and go back.

And she was not going back. For just a little while she was going to be the woman she might have been if she had married Joe Barton and not Kit Carmichael. And she was going to give as well as take. She was going to take that dreadful suffering look off Joe's face, and make him smile at her the way he used to do before their long separation and the war.

When they changed trains and were standing on the platform, it came to her that she was wicked. Really wicked, so that, according to her Chapel upbringing, all she could expect was a burning in hell's fires. Maggie had never believed that merely to confess to some misdeed put it right with God, the way Catholics did.

For a minute she shivered, only to feel Joe's hand firm on her arm.

'Will you never stop surprising me?' he grinned.

Once more they changed trains, and by the time the main line train pulled into Euston station, Maggie was asleep with her head on Joe's shoulder.

It was only as they got down from the taxi-cab and Joe propelled her through the revolving doors of the big hotel in Paddington that she really became aware of her surroundings.

'I must have been tired,' she whispered, and Joe smiled down at her telling her to stop where she was for a minute.

The foyer was wide, and so were the flight of steps straight ahead. There were potted plants everywhere, and it was all so huge and impressive that Maggie felt she wanted to turn and revolve herself back through the doors again.

Telling her again to stop where she was for a minute, Joe went over to the curved reception desk, then came back to her smiling.

'They've had a cancellation, so we can have one of their

best rooms,' he told her. Then they followed an ancient hall porter along a wide corridor to the right.

Surely the corridor was as wide as Foundry Street? There were lights set high in the red-flocked papered walls, and a marble surround either side of the crimson carpet.

She hid a smile at the grand way Joe tipped the porter, then as he left them alone, she stared around her in amazement.

'You could fit the whole of our upstairs into this room,' she cried. 'Oh, Joe, just feel these curtains, and this bedspread! Lined both of them. Oh, I'm not used to materials like this. Beats cotton fent, doesn't it?' As she stroked the spread she was doing rapid calculations in her mind.

'It must have cost a fortune, an' it's not skimped, neither.'

She opened the wardrobe door and it swung back, revealing a cavernous interior. 'Oh, Joe, my two clean blouses are going to look a bit lost in there, aren't they?'

'See through here,' he said, opening a door, and Maggie stood on the threshold of a high-ceilinged enormous bathroom, and clasped her hands together, like a child who has suddenly seen riches beyond her wildest dreams.

'A proper bathroom! An' taps! Hot and cold! Just look at that marble surround, and feel these towels!'

She picked up a white and fluffy bath towel and held its softness to her face. 'This beats bringing the bath in from the yard on a Friday, and filling it with jugs and heating the water up with pans and the kettle off the fire. Oh, Joe. Can I have a bath right now? Right this minute?'

He smiled on her with love. Now he had got his Maggie back. This was how he had always remembered her. Laughing, joyous, cheeks flushed, hair wisping down from its slipping bun as she darted from one thing to another, exclaiming, incredulous, eyes sparkling.

'Just a minute,' he said, pulling her to him, and tilting her face with his finger so that he could look deep into her eyes.

Then suddenly he threw back his head and laughed out loud.

'Well, bugger me! You've got odd eyes, Maggie, lass. There's one brown and one with green in it. You should be in a circus alongside the bearded lady, or in a tent on the fair, did you know that?'

'The odd-eyed woman from the north,' she agreed, and then they held on to each other, rocking and laughing, then as quickly serious and intent as he bent his dark head and kissed her mouth.

And later, when they had bathed, and sworn that neither of them was hungry, they made passionate love, with Maggie's white cotton nightdress tossed to the floor in a heap of white.

Maggie buried her hot face in Joe's shoulder and sighed.

'Why is sinning so lovely?' she wanted to know.

And uncomfortably but cosily, they slept in each other's arms all night and woke up so hungry that they were first in the dining-room.

'You are so beautiful it hurts my eyes just to look at you, lass,' Joe said.

'If I am then it's you what's done it,' Maggie replied, and they ate bacon and eggs, sausage and tomatoes, and when Maggie wondered aloud how such food could be Joe wrinkled his nose at her.

'Money buys anything, lass. I learnt that a long time ago. You can be happy without much brass, oh aye, but with it you can be doubly so. Especially when you have known the other way. That is one advantage of coming up the hard way, you never take nothing for granted.'

They got their coats, and he took her outside into the cold frosty morning, and as they walked along Maggie had to keep stopping to stare at the tall buildings, and to watch the traffic streaming by.

'Why does everything move so fast? Even the people? Where are they all going to, Joe?'

He touched the tip of her nose. 'I know where we are

going, love. Into that shop over there to buy you a dress. A brown dress trimmed with green to match your eyes. Both of them.'

'No!' Maggie's face changed its expression to one of dismay. 'I can't go home with a dress bought by you, Joe. You must see that. I don't think even Kit would stand for that.'

But they were already in the shop with its lavish Food Hall on the ground floor, and Maggie forgot her dismay as she left Joe's side to move rapidly from one counter to another, eyes sparkling as she pointed out one display, then rushing over to the next.

'Look at that tea, Joe! Oh, my goodness, half a pound of that and you would have to starve for the rest of the week. And that coffee! Oh, it can't cost that much. It can't possibly!'

There were biscuits in shiny brightly coloured tins, succulent whole hams laid out on marble slabs. Oranges in flat boxes, with every other one wrapped in silver paper, and chocolates in boxes as big as trays, with pictures on the front of the Tower and Buckingham Palace.

'That's what we are going to do tomorrow,' Joe told her. 'This leg of mine won't stand up to much walking yet, so we are going to hire a taxi-cab and get the driver to take us round to see the lot. The Palace, and the Tower, and Oxford Street, Trafalgar Square, Piccadilly Circus . . . everything!'

Then because she was adamant about the dress he took her into the fur department and bought her a muff. It was soft brown fur, and lined with silk with a pocket inside, and she couldn't get over it.

Privately Joe thought she was splitting hairs about her acceptance of the muff and her refusal of a dress, but he said a diplomatic nothing, not wanting to spoil her pleasure.

Maggie kissed him thank you, right in front of the smiling saleswoman, and when they came out into the street again, he bought a bunch of early primroses from a flower girl, and Maggie pinned them in front of the muff, and insisted on wearing it there and then.

They slept the afternoon away, and when Joe tried to make love to her and failed, Maggie held him close and told him that it did not matter.

'Loving is sometimes just a holding,' she whispered. 'Like this. It doesn't have to be no more. Just a touching and a holding.'

And when he slept she thought of Kit and the way he always shied away from any physical contact with her.

As though he doesn't like the feel of me. As though my skin is repulsive to him, she thought, sadly.

Then, remembering how the night before, Joe had kissed her all over, lingering at the hollow of her throat, moving his mouth downwards over the slight swell of her stomach, she blushed.

Then the pale winter sunshine, filtering through the tall windows lay like a blessing on their closed eyelids.

There was so much to say to each other, so much catching up to do. Foundry Street was another world away; it was another life, and though there were heart-stopping minutes when she wondered how Clara was coping with Rosie, and when she saw Kit's face as he read her letter, she pushed the thoughts away with a ruthless determination.

'This is to last me for the rest of my life,' she told Joe, and when he asked her if she would like to go and see where he had lived before he went to France, she shook her head.

'That would make it too real, love. This . . . all this is a dream, and though I know I have to wake up, I'm not ready yet. Not yet. Waking from it is going to last me a long long time.'

They walked hand in hand in Hyde Park, and he showed her where the toffs rode, and where, in summer, lovers sat on the grass.

'It's all so *light*,' she told him. 'It is as though the sky is higher than it is at home. I thought the Corporation Park was lovely, but this is so fresh and clean, and yet there are

motor buses and charabancs not far away. Open charabancs, even at this time of the year.'

'Aye, winter doesn't seem to *dwell* so much down here,'
Joe agreed, then she ticked him off for talking like a south-
erner, and teased him for turning into a toffee-nosed snob.

'I am never going back, all the same,' he said seriously,
and they sat for a while on a bench for him to rest his leg,
whilst London sparrows pecked hopefully round their feet,
and two men in top hats walked by, twirling silver-topped
canes.

That night their love-making was ecstatic. They were
becoming more used to the needs and desires of their bodies,
and Joe was filled with surprised delight at the way Maggie
responded, and sometimes even took the initiative. So
natural was her giving, so completely without shame that
he realized this was the way God had intended her to be,
as she expressed a love that had been kept in check for all
the barren years of her marriage.

When, around midnight, she said she could just do with
a cup of tea, he immediately rang for the chamber-maid.

'Joe!' Maggie reached for her nightdress. 'You are
terrible. What will she think, us wanting a pot of tea at this
time?'

'Just put it down there, and thank you. My wife will
pour,' he said grandly when the tray arrived.

The pride in his voice, and the possessiveness turned
Maggie's heart over, and her hand as she picked up the
pretty flowered tea-pot, was far from steady.

'One more day,' she said. 'It's got to be faced, Joe. I
have to go back, you know that.'

He was so thin, sitting up in bed, holding the gold-fluted
cup in his hands, so vulnerable, so much younger looking
than his years now that his face was gentled by love, that
she felt the tears spring to her eyes.

'I can't leave Kit,' she said quietly.

'No,' Joe agreed equally quietly. 'You can't leave Kit
because he needs you. You've told me that over and over.'

He looked at her with anguished eyes. 'He needs you to mother him and to slave for him in that bloody awful little shop. Kit Carmichael needs you to keep him going, and to be his strength and his bloody rod and his bloody staff. But what about me? What about me, Maggie? Don't I count for nothing? Aren't my needs as great as his?'

Maggie put her cup down, and going over to the dressing-table, sat down and stared at herself in the walnut-framed mirror.

She had shed ten years over the last few days. Her hair was softer and curling more. Her skin had a luminous quality about it, and her eyes were bright, with the whites shining clean. Joe's love had transformed her; she was fulfilled and replete with the kind of love that rarely happened between a man and a woman, the kind that had happened for her and Joe.

'I married *Kit*,' she repeated. 'And even if he did destroy your letters, I was married to him when they first came. He stuck by me, Joe. In the Chapel, in front of everybody, he came and stood by my side when they turned on me. I cannot forget that.'

She turned round to face him.

'Kit could be a drinker; he could beat me. He could be mean and selfish and cruel, but he is none of these things. He nursed me, Joe. When I would almost certainly have died, he sat up with me day and night, and sponged the fever from me and saved my life. I wouldn't be here with you now but for Kit.'

Her head drooped.

'And he married me, knowing I had lost a baby to some-one else. . . .'

She got back into bed and tried to pull Joe down beside her, but he resisted.

'Aye, you've told me the credit side. Now tell me the other.'

He took his cigarettes from the bedside table and lit one before he went on:

263

'Tell me now about how he has never been a proper husband to you, Maggie. Tell me how he worships you with his body, because that is what it says in the marriage service.'

His voice rose. 'With my body I thee worship . . . How often has he fulfilled that side of the bargain? And while we are at it, how ever did you come to have Rose? Was it another immaculate conception or something?'

For a moment Maggie felt the awkward fumbling flabbiness that had been Kit. She shuddered.

'There's more to life than that, Joe. More to a marriage. That is only a small part of it.'

'But it's not!' Joe exploded, stubbing out the cigarette and reaching for her. 'It's a *need*, Maggie my own love. It is this and this and this . . .'

And this time his loving was brutal and selfish so that she cried out, but when he slept at last it was to sink into one of his fighting screaming nightmares.

He was drowning in a sea of mud. He was crossing no man's land, his bayonet at the ready. There were shells bursting all around him, and the staccato putter of machine gun fire was in his ears. The air was silvery green with the glow from Very lights, and his sergeant had dropped dead at his feet with a bullet through his head.

Maggie held him, whispered to him, smoothed the hair back from his sweat-soaked forehead. Then when he slept again she crept from the bed and went through into the vast marble bathroom with its gleaming taps.

She sat there on the edge of the white bath and faced up to her own particular hell.

Never in a million years could she leave this man. He needed her just as Kit needed her, and oh God, there was no way she could split herself in two.

She shivered as the cold marbled floor struck icy cold into her legs and feet, and she rubbed at the tops of her arms as though the chill had reached up to there.

She could go back to Lancashire, and she could bring Rosie back with her. She could live with Joe, and Rosie would be brought up as a Londoner. Joe would make more money, she knew that. Joe was on the up and up, she could sense that when he talked about what he had planned to do.

There would be no more sewing at turning sheets and replacing frayed cuffs on shirts, no more counting every penny. They would walk in the London parks, and Rosie would learn to talk differently, and Joe would be the father she would never have known.

They would be happy. Without certain knowledge of that, Maggie knew this would be so. Joe Barton was her man. If things had been different he would have been the only man in her life. Like her mother with her father, they would live out their lives together, not without tiffs sometimes, because loving somebody did not mean, in Maggie's code, that you always had to agree with them.

But Kit was there. Gentle, kind, affectionate Kit, who without her would be a nothing . . . a great soft nothing.

Slowly Maggie walked back into the bedroom. She got into bed and Joe's arms immediately closed round her, straining her close to him, even in sleep.

She felt the strength of his arms, and knew that where Kit would give up without her by his side, Joe Barton would not.

Oh, Joe loved her, she knew that. He loved her desperately, and he would grieve for a while; he would be angry and lost for a while, but he would survive.

And survival seemed to be what it was all about.

Joe bought a shawl for Rosie the next day. It was a whisper of a shawl, worked in cobweb scallops, and Maggie knew that the baby's tiny fingers would soon be caught up in it, but she said nothing.

She was living on borrowed time now, every hour and every minute ticking away, and that night, their last night together, Joe took her to a music hall.

'You won't need your muff, lass,' he told her, but she could not bear to part with it. She sat with it on her lap in the hot smoky atmosphere of the little theatre, stealing glances at Joe now and again as if she would remember every line of his thin face.

The music was loud, and a big woman with tightly curled hair sang at the top of a powerful voice, while the audience stamped and cheered her on.

A tall man in a red lined cloak made a woman disappear into thin air, and when she appeared from the wings everyone stood up and yelled aloud their delight.

They drank stout, and when it was all over they decided it wasn't much of a walk back to the hotel.

'It's a bonny night,' Joe said, and Maggie took his arm as they strolled back along the wide pavements.

'Just look at those stars,' she said.

'Aye, it's a bonny night,' Joe said again.

It seemed there was nothing left to say, or at least nothing they dared to say, and Joe ordered whisky to be sent to their room, and for the first time in her life Maggie tasted the fiery liquid, feeling it run smoothly down her throat and warm the place where her heart seemed to have frozen itself solid.

'You are really going back then?' Joe said when he had drained his glass twice. His voice was slightly slurred and his eyelids drooped, concealing the expression in his dark eyes.

'Methodists don't drink,' Maggie said, holding out her glass for more. 'Drink is the scourge of mankind.'

'And the source of all evil,' agreed Joe, holding his own glass high.

When they got ready for bed Maggie laughed at Joe in his long underpants, army issue. She had seen them before, but now with the drink warm inside her everything seemed silly and funny.

Joe laughed at her when she tripped over the hem of her long white nightdress.

'Whoops a daisy!'

'No, whoops a Maggie!'

They made love to mingled laughter, and then fell

asleep with the suddenness of a stone flung down the well of Maggie's childhood.

Breakfast was a solemn occasion, with Maggie settling for toast and tea, and Joe pushing his poached haddock to the side of his plate and leaving it there.

Back in their room Maggie unfolded the brown paper she had laid neatly in a drawer, and wrapping her few belongings in it, tied it with the same piece of string.

'My mother used to have a box with all different lengths of string stored away, some too short to be used for anything at all,' she told Joe, trying not to look at the empty coat hangers swinging in the dark recesses of the huge wardrobe.

He looked at her without a smile.

'Oh, aye?'

And the last thing she did was to go into the bathroom and look around. She ran a hand over the marble surround of the wash-stand, and she turned on the hot tap and let the water trickle over her fingers.

She looked up at the dark green patterned wallpaper stretching away to the high ceiling, and she picked up one of the big white towels and reminded herself that somebody else would be washing them. They wouldn't fill a living-room with steam as they dried over a clothes horse round the fire.

'I am not going to kiss you goodbye,' Joe told her, taking his stick and his case and somehow managing to open the door for her.

Maggie tried to keep her mind on the towels.

'That's all right,' she said.

Joe paid the bill, then out in the wide sweep of the fore-court he hailed a taxi-cab, and helped Maggie inside.

'It would have to be raining,' he said.

He sat back, his head sunk deep on his chest, and his hands resting on the curved handle of the hospital issue walking stick. Then at the station he booked a single ticket for Maggie, and walked her towards the barrier.

'If you want me, I have written Belle's address down here,' he told her, giving her a slip of paper which she concealed in the fur muff. 'I won't be settled in a place for a while. I have a lot of things to see to first.'

Maggie nodded. Politeness, it seemed, was all that was left, all they had to cling to.

'Thank you, Joe. Thank you for giving me the best, the very best time of my life,' she whispered. Then her face crumpled. 'Oh, Joe, what can I say?'

'Nowt!' he said sharply, lapsing into dialect as he always did when troubled. 'There's nowt at all to say now, is there, lass?'

'God bless you, Joe,' Maggie whispered before she turned and walked away, handing her ticket to the man at the gate, having it punched, putting it away safely in the pocket her muff, then walking away down the long slope to the train.

She dare not turn round. If she turned round and saw him standing there, the dark hair falling forward over his forehead . . . if she saw him she would have to run back.

And there could be no running back. . . .

When the guard blew his whistle and waved his green flag, the train moved forward slowly, out of the station, past the tall grey lodging houses shrouded in a mist of fine rain.

Putting her head back Maggie closed her eyes.

She had done what she had done, and when Kit came home that night she would be there, waiting for him, no doubt with his tea warming in the fire-oven, and little Rosie asleep in her basket.

Kit would cry, oh he would most certainly cry, and she would comfort him, and talk to him, and he would try to understand.

God forgive him, but he would already be trying to understand.

Then when a few weeks had gone by he would tell her he had forgiven her, and she would accept his forgiveness, and in his simple loving way he would never know the truth.

The truth being that she would have preferred him to rant and rave at her, to call her all the names she deserved, and even land out at her and clout her one.

But Kit was Kit, just as Joe was Joe.

The two men, so different . . . the only men she had ever known,

'Oh, Joe . . .' she whispered as the train gathered speed.

'Oh, Joe, my love, my dear, dear love.'

'Mammy, that lady's crying,' a small boy sitting on the opposite seat said in a loud voice. 'Why is she crying?'

His mother put a finger to her lips and shook her head.

'It's rude to stare,' she told him.

Other Arrow Books of interest:

A LEAF IN THE WIND

Marie Joseph

She was hardship's child – born to struggle and to serve.

He was fortune's favourite – born to flourish and be served.

They lived worlds apart. Jenny was the girl from the cat-meat shop, born into squalor and defeat. Paul Tunstall was a soldier and a gentleman, arrogant and charming, with his silver-light eyes and boyish smile. And yet from the moment they met there was a spark between them – and their separate lives of pain and loneliness seemed to beckon to each other.

But should she succumb to that plea in his eyes, to that longing in herself? Should she cross the line of class, the boundaries of propriety? Dare Jenny risk all to lose herself to love?

MARIE JOSEPH

Marie Joseph is one of Britain's top-selling authors and her books are available from Arrow. You can buy them from your local bookshop or newsagent, or you can order them direct through the post. Just tick the titles you require and complete the form below.

☐	EMMA SPARROW	£1.75
☐	FOOTSTEPS IN THE PARK	£1.50
☐	GEMINI GIRLS	£1.60
☐	A LEAF IN THE WIND	£1.95
☐	LISA LOGAN	£1.95
☐	THE LISTENING SILENCE	£1.75
☐	MAGGIE CRAIG	£1.95
☐	POLLY PILGRIM	£1.75

Non-fiction

☐	ONE STEP AT A TIME	£1.75

Postage _____

Total _____

☐ Please tick this box if you would like to receive a free sheet of biographical information about Marie Joseph.

ARROW BOOKS, BOOKSERVICE BY POST, PO BOX 29, DOUGLAS, ISLE OF MAN, BRITISH ISLES.

Please enclose a cheque or postal order made out to Arrow Books Limited for the amount due including 15p per book for postage and packing for orders within the UK and for overseas.

Please print clearly

NAME...

ADDRESS..

....

Whilst every effort is made to keep prices down and to keep popular books in print, Arrow Books cannot guarantee that prices will be the same as those advertised here or that the books will be available.